Books by Stuart Cotterill:
    The Legacy of Ma Jun – Book One of the Dragon Scripts

MAJUN'S LOST TREASURE

MAJUN'S LOST TREASURE

Book Two of the Dragon Scripts

By Stuart Cotterill

ISBN: 0692474560
ISBN 13: 9780692474563

Acknowledgement

I AM MOST GRATEFUL TO the China I love for inspiring me to write these novels. Its culture and people have meant so much to me these past years since living and working there.

As always, I thank my friends in Beijing and Inner Mongolia; they continue to motivate me and are always in my thoughts as the stories unfold.

Thanks, also, to my editor, Susan Snowden, who encourages me, and whose guidance was invaluable as I wrote this second book, and to Susan Hanning for her reading the finished article..

I especially appreciate my wife and daughter's unwavering support on my journey into this new endeavor.

Finally, to the readers of *The Legacy of Ma Jun* who pressed for Book II in the series, I thank you above all.

Prologue

Beijing, China

Professor George Mathers, an American, and his Chinese wife, Xiao Ping, were skeptical that their fellow Professor Cai Levee knew where to find a second coffin. They were anxious to finally publish their story, but it was taking quite an effort to get the authorities to approve the release of their findings. George Mathers thought it remarkable that the Chinese would let them print anything, but maybe they were now being more open to the world -- or wanted it to seem that way.

Elements of their story may well have been written off as sheer fantasy by some of their critics; the existence of scales from ancient dragons and the unusual writings on them was surely a hoax. Especially since neither the Chinese nor Americans were willing to talk publicly about scales or reveal where they actually were. George decided they had nothing to lose by taking another trip down to Zhangjiajie after all the team had been through together. He was still skeptical about finding a second coffin with more scales and another treasure to support them.

George was irritated that his wife ignored his doubts that a second coffin existed, but at least they would see Sam and Ivy again and the resting temple on the mountain, now that it was renovated. Cai Levee, their colleague and friend from the Tsinghua University, had made reservations for them to fly from Beijing on China Southern

Airlines to Zhangjiajie. They would arrive late in the afternoon and head off to Sam and Ivy's hiker's lodge where they had stayed when the first coffin was discovered.

"Are we really staying there again?" Cai asked.

"Yes, we are, and they're giving us the old jeep again."

"That thing, George? You people drive me crazy sometimes!" George smiled as Cai shook his head; he and his wife knew Cai Levee was well paid by Chinese standards and whenever he traveled preferred to stay in the best hotels.

"Come on, Cai, you'll enjoy it. Getting soft in our old age are we?"

"Not at all. But that place again? The rooms are drafty, the jeep is a clunker, and all those hikers will want to know what we're up to. Can't we stay in town?"

"Xiao Ping has booked rooms for us. We're staying there, with or without you! It's closer to the mountain and we both like the hosts. It's up to you if you want to stay somewhere else."

Cai complained over the days until they left. George could tell he was sulking over staying at the lodge, continuing to refuse to give them any clue as to where he thought the second coffin was. He would just smirk at them as he had done for days and say, "I am my father's son, I am my father's son. That's what Ma Jun said and that's all you need to know!'

They were the last words of old Ma Jun to Xiao Ping, thinking she was his wife, dying in her arms not far from the mountain. It was the legacy of the generations of Ma Jun that led them to discover the dragon scripts. George gave up asking Cai more about the second coffin; if the visit turned out to be a vacation trip he would soon get back to finishing the story of the dragon scripts as planned.

CHAPTER ONE

The day George and Xiao Ping left for Zhangjiajie the pollution level in Beijing was low, thanks to a breezy day and night before. From their apartment you could see as far as the western hills, the dawn rising behind the outline of the mountains announcing a clear blue-sky day ahead. The journey to the airport by taxi took some time. Another accident on the highway brought into question the driving skills of some locals, who seemed oblivious to the rules of the road. Such events had long ago convinced George a car was pointless for living in Beijing.

Cai Levee always arrived at the airport at the last possible moment and ended up fighting to get through security to the gate in time. It was a game he liked to play. George and his wife waited at the gate with no sign of Cai until the last call for boarding came, trying to decide whether to get on the plane or stay. Since the tickets were nonrefundable they boarded the flight. Xiao Ping complained about Cai's unreliability again. As the stewardess was trying to close the outer door, Cai came in breathing heavily, but grinning from ear to ear, "That was good. Bit of a run through security, but I'm here!"

"One of these days you'll miss the damn flight, Cai. Next time at least call us, will you?" George said shaking his head.

"I'm here, aren't I? Relax, older brother, who wants to hang around an airport anyway?"

They soon found out Cai had been brought by university car, not surprising since he was fast becoming a highly regarded professor at China's leading university. On the way to the airport his taxi's tire blew out; he'd seen George speeding by and tried to catch his attention but couldn't.

Within minutes of the plane's takeoff for Zhangjiajie in Hunan Province, both Xiao Ping and Cai Levee were sleeping. George envied the Chinese for their ability to sleep anywhere, even in meetings during the day. As for George he never could sleep on planes; today he spent most of his time on the flight wondering what clue Cai had in his head that might open a new chapter in their story. If they could really locate the second coffin that would be great, but he still thought it highly unlikely. After the first coffin and its treasures were found on the mountain there must surely have been officials looking in all the other caves in the area. As far as he knew they had found nothing either.

George's colleagues slept through the meal but woke up just before the announcement that they were twenty minutes from landing. The plane arrived on time and the three quickly passed through baggage collection to the pickup area, where Ivy from the hiker lodge was waiting for them.

"George! Xiao Ping! Welcome back. It's so good to have you staying with us again. You too, Mr. Cai."

Xiao Ping hugged Ivy and thanked her for picking them up; it seemed to be a busy time for the lodge as five other guests piled into the van with them. Aside from warmly greeting George's group, two hikers who joined them were old friends and regular visitors. George thought the other three were climbers judging by their physical appearance and dress. Xiao Ping winked at George and pointed to one of them surreptitiously, jabbing him harshly in the stomach as if to tell him he needed to get in shape too. Cai saw what was going on and chuckled as he pointed to his own stomach, pulling up his sweater to reveal a tight t-shirt underneath and a midriff in better shape than George's. The drive to the lodge was pleasant enough with the two hikers trying to get to know the others.

At the lodge nothing had changed since George's last visit, although the place was getting more customers these days. The Mathers were given the same room they had the last time, but Cai elected to have a room well away from theirs, muttering something about not needing two love birds disturbing his sleep. Ivy advised them the old jeep was ready to rent again; she and Sam had cleaned it, gassed it up, and trusted George remembered the starting sequence that Sam had taught him. They all had a good laugh remembering the antics of the last trip and the all-important three bangs on the dashboard to get it to start. They now knew it had been a joke by Sam and Ivy, but in the end it really was the only way George could get the "damned thing" to start.

George looked at Cai one more time before they headed to their rooms. "So, Cai, are you going to finally tell us why we're back here again? And please stop smirking like some eunuch at the palace being asked about his sex life."

"George, everything is in order and working fine, thank you, in that area. Tomorrow all will be revealed. I told you that Xiao Ping had the answer all along from Ma Jun."

"We know, we know. His dying words, right? I am my father's son, I am my father's son, blah, blah!" George was ready to give up.

"Exactly. Now you two sleep well and don't wear yourselves out; I hope tomorrow we'll find our coffin!" Xiao Ping quickly interrupted. "You hope? Cai, you only hope? After all this you better be right. If not and George doesn't, it'll be me who turns you into a eunuch."

Cai chuckled and headed off to his own room. George thought he seemed a little less confident this time about the location of the second coffin.

—⊶⊷—

They were up early the following morning and headed out. The Jeep fired up after George banged on the dashboard as prescribed. They drove out of the main village area along a narrow road toward Tianmen Mountain, passing a hardware store, noodle restaurant, nail salon, and tire store. A small bar's outside snooker tables were covered in road dirt and so badly worn that playing on them seemed impossible. They parked while Cai disappeared into the hardware store for a long time before sticking his head out and yelling for George to give him a hand. He had found what he wanted in five minutes but apparently spent fifteen minutes more negotiating over the price for every item. To George, the prices were so low he wouldn't have wasted his time arguing, but he knew that for the Chinese this was a game as much as a principle. No deal was complete without healthy bargaining. Afterwards the buyer always tells his friends what a great deal he got and the seller tells his fellow shopkeepers how much he made off of some fool from Beijing.

The pair headed out the door with shovels, pick axes, hammers, two large hand chisels, and a bag filled with miscellaneous items that appeared to have no purpose. After loading the jeep, Cai and Xiao Ping headed off to the noodle shop, flask and food storage cans in hand, to see what they could buy. Finally they headed off to the mountain and the scene of their earlier visits.

—⊶⊷—

The old jeep pulled into the parking lot. As before, the area was as deserted as ever. They wondered if the old monk they met on earlier visits

4

would suddenly come around the corner chanting his sutras. In a way they were hoping he would, just for old time's sake.

They started up the mountain carrying only their food to see how everything looked before lugging the heavier supplies up. George took one backpack with thermos flasks and three meal cans that fit together snugly to form one meal package. They took the familiar trail to the resting temple and located the turnoff where they found the original coffin.

They climbed the mountain pathway, reliving the events of the past, until they found the side path off the main trail leading to the cave where the first of what was supposed to be two coffins was originally discovered. Xiao Ping noticed right away that the path marker had been permanently removed. Someone had obviously attempted to plant some shrubs along the side trail to make it less obvious that it ever existed. This appeared to have been done to keep prying eyes away, but since they had spent so much time there in the past it was easy for George and Xiao Ping to find. Before going on, though, they decided to take a look at the resting temple again.

"Wow! Look at it now!" said Xiao Ping when she saw it. "That's amazing. They did a beautiful job. I can't believe it's the same place. Look over there in the corner. Old Ma Jun's murals are still there. And here, look here, there's the symbol of the horse still in the floor. They never moved it!"

Xiao Ping continued to explore the restored temple while George shook Cai's arm. "Look, Cai, are you going to finally tell us where you think the damn second coffin is or not?"

"Of course not! You two just don't get it, do you? - Everything old Ma told Xiao Ping when he was dying has proved out so far, hasn't it?"

"Yes, to a point, but one coffin not two."

"Listen to me, George - The story says that Ma's ancestors originally buried the treasure in two coffins, right? You found the sale agreement for two new coffins to replace the old ones, right? You found two old broken coffins in the cave, right? There has to be a second one there!"

"But we found only one, Cai! All of this was just to confuse everyone. The one coffin with some treasure and the scripts is all there is, period! It's an incredible find in itself but the real treasure is the story of the first dragons on those scales. Look at what it took to decipher those ancient writings. And think of what we've found. Maybe they really are the scales of a dragon that no one believes existed. I'm not even talking about all we went through with the military getting their hands on them. We're lucky we're not all in prison, even killed over them! Look at what they tried to do to them, Cai. Those things are indestructible!"

"No, George, no. There's more, I tell you. Even the scripts on the hundreds of scales we've translated show there is more, and a real treasure must be with them too. Of that I'm sure. It's here and I'm going to prove it."

"You're dreaming. I only agreed to come for Xiao Ping's sake. Can we at least get on with this?" George was growing more frustrated by the minute; he looked over to his wife for some kind of support, but she was plainly annoyed with his continued pessimism.

"Please calm down, both of you. We're here now. Let Cai do what he has in mind and see what we find. I came here because I believe there's a second coffin too. Where it is, I have no idea, but if Cai finds it, great. If not I'll make his life a misery for months to come!"

After Xiao Ping finished speaking the tension eased and they went further inside the temple where the renovations had been very tastefully done. The original Ma Jun paintings were there still, but were now encased in glass to protect them. This really was a peaceful environment to rest in, and they took advantage of it for ten or fifteen minutes to further calm down before following Cai - to wherever he was headed.

They went back down the trail and again turned off the side pathway, retracing their steps from their earlier visits. The authorities' efforts to conceal the pathway from prying eyes lasted about fifty meters, and then the path was back to the way George remembered it, although there were a few new openings in the mountainside along the way. To George these were diggings by someone looking for the second coffin. While they looked in each one as best they could, Cai merely did so out of curiosity and no more. When they arrived at the first cave, where George and Xiao Ping originally found two empty coffins, they all went inside. It remained as it was when they had left it, but without the coffins Ma Jun had set there and that the military found at the time of George and the others arrest.

George hugged Xiao Ping as memories flooded back to him. How their years of working in China researching its myths and fables had led them to the village near Zhangjiajie and the discovery of old Ma Jun. Of the memories too of that fateful week when Ma Jun's family legend was revealed to Xiao Ping in his delirium before death. How Ma had been the last of the Ma generations guarding a treasure of writings and relics that turned out to be connected with a fantastic story of the earliest dragons in China. They had turned out to be the oldest writings discovered in China, old beyond belief of the experts that looked at them. George wondered how many times they must have been moved for safety due to major historical events. Ma Jun had related to Xiao Ping his stories of the Taiping Rebellion and the more recent times of the Cultural Revolution. How many other events might have impacted the scripts history under the generations of Ma's guardianship?

After a few more minutes discussing the past events they continued on until they reached the area that a rockslide had covered up. They were surprised to see the pathway cleared and another cave opened up where the slide had blocked the path.

"Look around; it's likely the military was instructed to have it cleared and checked for the second coffin, or maybe the local authorities decided to do it. What if they found something and never told any-one?" George asked.

"No, I don't thinks so," Cai said. "We'd have heard about it. I'm sure they would have called in Diao Lijun at the Palace Museum again." At least shown him any new markings they found." Cai thought for a few moments before adding, "Any treasure that accompanied those scales would have been taken by the military for their own use unless some of the underlings arranged for it to disappear and then claimed they found nothing."

Xiao Ping interrupted the conversation saying it was a bit late to think about that; they should press on. Once they finished looking around, they headed along the path, now much easier to traverse without having to climb over any rockslide. They looked for the second cave where the original coffin had been hidden by Ma Jun and his father from the Red Guards during the Cultural Revolution. They passed two more freshly dug openings before they reached the original cave, which this time was the only one re-sealed except for a small opening at the top.

Cai stood before the cave and looked back at both of them. "This is where the other coffin is hidden, my friends! No question about it. Tomorrow we'll find it." He waved caustic comments aside with such confidence that even George began to feel that perhaps he was right. But, when George asked him to explain why he was so sure, he again smiled, saying "Tomorrow, tomorrow!"

Xiao Ping suggested they get started that afternoon, but George said that by the time they went back for the tools and came back up the hill it would be dark again. Cai preferred to start the next day too and suggested buying a couple of camping lights so they'd be more prepared. George couldn't argue at that point so they left hoping that tomorrow would be the day they'd all been waiting for.

CHAPTER TWO

George and his wife were up at daybreak and met Cai for breakfast. They talked with Sam and Ivy at length. From what they could gather quite a few people had been to the lodge after their last visit. Both government and military folks had asked about a Professor Mathers and his Chinese wife. Apparently the room the pair had stayed in was searched and Ivy was questioned about where she'd taken them. There had been repeated questions too about another weekend when another American, Scott Ramey, had visited for the reopening of the resting temple with Diao Lijun from Beijing. Sam was told that if any of them ever came back again he was to call certain numbers and advise the authorities right away.

"Will you be reporting us being here now?" George asked, alarmed but surprised at Sam's casual mention of it.

Sam just smiled with somewhat of a rebellious air about him, "Do you prefer it if I don't yet? What are you two up to anyway? Is it illegal? If it is, I'm afraid you can't stay here. Then again you three seem honest to me."

Cai and Xiao Ping looked at George with a puzzled. "Sam, we're just looking for something that other people may want to find. It's of historical interest, nothing sinister, but could be valuable. I suspect these visitors were trying to find out whether it exists or not."

George could see Sam thinking for a few moments before Ivy looked at him, shaking her head. "I'm sorry but I better call them. I could wait until after your visit and then say you left quickly. I don't like those people. They're not nice people. I know there will be trouble for us and our business, though, if they were to find out you visited us and we did not report it."

George could see Cai was taken back by the revelation that they were still being monitored. Cai thought Sam should wait until tomorrow evening, then call to report they were there. If asked, Sam could simply say his visitors claimed to be writing a book about the discovery they made some time ago and were only visiting to refresh their materials. George agreed this was reasonable and to some degree true. Sam somewhat hesitantly agreed and left.

The others looked at George with raised eyebrows. He said his response to Sam came out without him thinking and he felt sure they could trust Sam to hold off calling until the next evening. Even that raised alarm bells among them. They had assumed this whole affair had gone quiet, that no one was following their progress or interested anymore.

Cai was concerned, "Is our visit going to stir up another hornet's nest whether we find anything or not? Maybe we should have said nothing about it to Sam!"

"If I hadn't said anything to Sam it's likely he would have already called. Best that we do what we've come here to do. If we find anything we can contact Diao Lijun. After all, we're only interested in the scales, not the treasure if it exists."

Cai nodded, but George could see from the way he and Xiao Ping looked at each other that while the scales were his prime interest from an academic standpoint, the treasure was something they were focused on. Xiao Ping was concerned that if Sam called the authorities the next evening they might not have enough time to do what needed to be done. She recommended trying to persuade Sam to wait another day and to tell him that if they found anything they would be calling the authorities anyway.

George felt they were headed down a slippery slope of white lies that would lead to more trouble, but he reluctantly agreed. Xiao Ping left and went to talk privately to Sam. When she returned she said Sam had not registered them yet and agreed to hold off. He would cover for them for a couple of days before making the call. Now that it seemed they could land in trouble again, the atmosphere surrounding their little trip became more serious. George was the only one who began to feel they should advise the authorities before going any further.

———— ∞∞∞ ————

They left the lodge that morning and drove to the mountain in silence, each deep in thought. George wished they had announced their plans to the authorities and the university, not the least Diao Lijun, and laid out what Cai suspected about the second coffin. While not the easiest way to handle the situation, it would have been safer, especially knowing the people they had been dealing with. George made up his mind then and there that the first thing they would do, if anything were found, was to contact Diao right away. They would simply tell him they had this wild idea, which it was, and had found the rest of the scales and whatever treasure was with them.

Arriving in the abandoned parking lot at the lower level of Tianmen Mountain they looked around to see if anyone else was in the area; it was as quiet as usual. They unloaded the supplies Cai had purchased; along with two battery-powered night-lights, which would be useful if they were still there past dusk. Xiao Ping carried the largest backpack, while George and Cai walked up with the heavy tools. They hoped they would not run into the monk from the monastery on the mountaintop, or any of his colleagues and have to explain what they were up to

Finally they reached the turnoff for the path to the caves. Xiao Ping and Cai were in good physical shape and, while breathing a little heavier, seemed unaffected by the rigors of the climb. George, on the other hand, was panting and sweating profusely. Xiao Ping commented that he really needed to get in better shape, but George reminded her he was no youngster anymore, that fifteen or more years over she and Cai made a big difference.

Once they reached the cave, George and Cai set to clearing rocks away from the cave's entrance. It didn't take long. It had been done with haste and no real care, certainly not as much as Ma Jun must have taken originally or when George and Xiao Ping last sealed it. Having a few tools with them made the job even easier and soon they had easy access to the cave except the light was somewhat dim, so Xiao Ping brought in the two lights Cai had bought, along with her camera. Looking around the cave they could see that the large bat population had been working overtime depositing their feces on the cave floor. The imprint and outline of the coffin they originally found was unmistakable; the bat droppings were thinner there, even though there had been some digging around the rest of the cave by others. At that point Cai grabbed an axe, pushed a shovel in George's hand, and told him it was time to go to work. George understood Cai was convinced the other coffin was still buried in the cave, but where? He wondered if they would have to dig up the whole cave again.

At that point, Cai leaned on his axe and began to retrace the entire story yet again. He talked through it step by step until he got to the comment that Ma Jun had been so intent on repeating before he died to Xiao Ping that he was his father's son.

"Twice he stressed that, thinking Xiao Ping was his wife. Understandable really after seeing her photo. Anyway, to my mind this is the key to the mystery. When the father and son buried the coffins in the temple originally what did they do? For safety they buried them one on top of the other. I'm convinced that Ma Jun again buried them on top of each other here too. If anyone found the first one they would assume there was only one. Just as everyone has."

George shook his head in disbelief, "You're kidding, Cai? That's it? Your grand theory after all this time is based on a couple of loose phrases? You put us through all the anticipation just for this? Look around you; they've obviously dug here too. They'd have found another coffin if it was here!"

"Maybe, maybe not. I still believe his reference to being his father's son refers to Ma Jun doing just what his father did. He set out decoys for the safekeeping of the coffins, twice over, moving the coffins to another cave and burying one under the other."

Xiao Ping spoke up. "But, Cai, when Ma Jun told me his story he thought he was talking to his wife. Why wouldn't he tell me the truth about where he had hidden them?"

"I agree with Xiao Ping," George said. "I think your argument is flakey, Cai. I'm certain that General Zhu and his henchman, Yi, searched the cave thoroughly."

"Look, I frankly don't know why he didn't tell his wife where the coffins were, but to me, looking around the floor now shows a half-hearted attempt to find another coffin. There's a thick layer of droppings from the bats! Clearly no one has dug with any amount of vigor since we were here."

George looked around again. "But surely they would have used some metal detector or ground monitoring device to see if anything was buried here."

"That could have happened, but we would have heard about it through Diao. I'm sure of that!" They decided to let Cai have his day as he swung the axe into the cave floor where the coffin outline stood out.

There was no hollow thud as Cai drove the axe into the ground and tried to break the surface so that George could get a shovel in to start digging. For ten minutes Cai's axe just bounced off the hard rock floor. It was beginning to look like they'd come a long way again for nothing. While Cai took a rest, Xiao Ping took a hand chisel and a large hammer and tried to get some kind of a hole started. All she managed to do was blunt the chisel. When her energy began to flag, George got down on his knees and cleaned up the area in the shape of the coffin. As he looked at all the marks on the cave floor and turned the light on them he began to change his mind.

He took the pick from Cai's hands and walked over to another area and struck the floor; the rock broke much easier. He went over to another area and did the same thing again.

"George, you're wasting your time, they've been all over this floor, just like you said," Cai muttered,

"Can't you see this? I'm no geologist but I know enough to see that the rock under the coffin is different from the rest of the material in this cave. That's why it's hard to break through. I reckon this is not the real cave floor. It's got to be a large slab. Unless we find the edges to pry it up, we'll be beating on this all day for nothing."

George's hunch that there might be something there seemed to lift up Xiao Ping and Cai's spirits.

It took another hour using two hand chisels and heavy hammers to create the outline of a misshapen rock they might be able to pry up, depending on how thick and heavy it was. Once they had created an outline and started digging around it their excitement grew. It was definitely a separate slab of rock and not part of the original cave floor. Their presence and noise disturbed the bats until finally a whole legion of them to decided to depart for some other cave. Although the Chinese revere bats for their good fortune, neither Xiao Ping nor Cai was comfortable with the noise they made, or the touch of bats to their necks and faces as so many streamed around them and out of the cave.

Using the chisels and two pry bars, George and Cai tried for some time to lever up the slab they had uncovered. It stubbornly clung to the floor where it rested, resisting every effort to get it to move at all. They cleared more of the floor around the slab to see if they could find other points of the slab to get their pry bars under for better leverage. After several attempts and getting Xiao Ping to apply a little extra force, they finally were relieved to experience a slight movement in the slab. It was nothing to get excited about, but enough to indicate that eventually this thing would give up its secret.

They repositioned to the other side and gradually, by wiggling the slab from opposite ends, the slab started to move. Eventually they were able to raise and turn the slab on its side and away from the coffin shaped outline.

The ground below the slab was also different from the surrounding cave floor material; when Cai hit this newly exposed surface with his pick the noise made it evident that something was indeed below the material. They began to dig out the compacted rocks with as much care as possible so as not to damage whatever might be hidden underneath. As the material cleared, their excitement grew. After what seemed a very long time they were finally able to carefully extract another coffin and slide it to one side. One of them alone could not lift it; it took all three to get the coffin out and move it to one side. They wondered how Ma Jun and his aged father had handled this alone. Yet another mystery.

Cai did a little dance around the cave with Xiao Ping, both laughing as they sang over and over, "I am my father's son, I am my father's son!" George had to admit Cai was right all along. But now, even before trying to open the coffin, he wondered what would happen in the future with the authorities, especially Commander Yi and General Zhu. He shuddered at the thought.

CHAPTER THREE

Commander Yi's department in Beijing had expanded over the years. He was still under General Zhu's leadership; Zhu was one of military intelligence's leading players. Yi stayed close to him. Zhu was in line for promotion and often said he appreciated Yi's loyalty and dedication. Yi knew Zhu was making a determined effort to bring him along as his successor, a tough taskmaster who was careful to both mentor and keep him in line when needed.

The dragon scale affair had faded from the department's priority list. The scientists that worked on them had given up efforts to understand them or discover how to duplicate their amazing properties and capabilities. Yi had wanted to continue to follow the case but Zhu always told him to forget the whole affair and focus on more pressing matters.

Yi, however, was sufficiently strong-willed to have taken some matters into his own hands. He did not keep Zhu fully apprised of all that he put in place at the time of the discovery of the scales in the caves. Yi had never believed the story of only one coffin being found and was suspicious that the other coffin had been moved and hidden elsewhere. He had his people continue to monitor the efforts of this Professor Mathers and his team, even though Zhu had instructed him otherwise. He also maintained a watch on Diao Lijun, the director of the Palace Museum and antiquities who the authorities had put in charge of the scale research project. That the military's own labs had never been able to destroy any of these so-called "dragon scales" was as much a mystery to Yi as anyone else, but he too saw the military uses of the materials if their properties could be harnessed.

The months went by with no unusual activity being reported to Yi. Agents assigned to follow Professor Mather's work at the university labs began to wonder what the point of it all was. They became lax in their attentiveness to what was going on, but only to a point.

Although exhausted by the time the coffin was finally removed, George and Xiao Ping were excited about what might be inside. It was much heavier than the first one they'd found. Since Cai had been the one to guess this second coffin really existed, and where it was, George gave him the honor of opening it. The lid was eventually pried off, and inside was the same ancient wrapping material as in the first, but this coffin was crammed full.

Cai pulled the lights closer to the coffin, donned a pair of white gloves he had brought along, before slowly easing back the covering. There were two rough sections of materials inside. One consisted of scales again, but they seemed more jumbled than they had in the first coffin, as if things had been repeatedly taken out and put back in. The other contents were wrapped separately, but not in the same material. Although it was old, it was clear that it dated back maybe to the Middle Ages and must have been added at some stage. As Cai peeled back the wrapping they could see it was some kind of robe, incredibly ornate with elaborate thread work and obviously done by highly skilled crafts-men. The outline of a dragon was beautifully embroidered on the cloth in bright gold thread. Their excitement levels rose.

Xiao Ping was recording every step of the process with her camera as Cai revealed the coffin's contents. George paused as she lowered her camera; they were all in awe when the elaborate covering was removed; there lay a treasure trove of items. There were articles of jade, as well as various stunning items of jewelry: an array of gold, silver and bronze pieces, and gems of many kinds. At that point they all stared in amazement, not just at the additional scales George had hoped to find, but the priceless items that spilled out around them. What to do with the find suddenly took on greater importance.

They were now faced with a greater dilemma than on their first discovery. It felt like déjà vu to George. He said they had no choice this time but to call the authorities; the find was just too important and valuable. Xiao Ping agreed but Cai was reluctant to rush to this conclusion. If the same people became involved, what would happen to these items? How many would survive to see the light of day? The stories of years of losses from the Forbidden City through pilfering and items being sold by the eunuchs during Qing Dynasty rule, even by the last emperor, were well known. Cai said the level of corruption that lingered in China still posed potential problems with safeguarding the treasure.

They argued for some time but finally agreed to call Diao Lijun, seek his advice, and then make their final decision. They would have to be quick, however, now that the cave was unsealed and the coffin opened. George vacillated back and forth with the others about whether to re-seal the coffin and cave, come back the next day, or divide the contents and take the items with them.

None of them seemed keen to stay in the cave overnight and in the end they decided to take the contents with them. Xiao Ping had photographed many items though the lighting too poor to produce the highest quality images. They would do that back in the hotel and send them off to Diao. George had little time to look at the dragon scales, but estimated there were somewhere around four hundred of them, half of what they had discovered before.

They would create a photographic record of the items for Diao Lijun to see and have a record should anything "walk" away in the future. If Diao felt the need to announce their find in the cave they would simply take them all back and start the announcement from there. They divided the coffin's contents between the three large backpacks they had brought with them, George and Cai taking the heavier loads. They would leave all the tools and retrieve them the next day depending on how their call went.

The group struggled back down the mountain trails with backpacks crammed full. George's knees began to ache beneath the heavy load. It was not so bad going downhill, but he wondered how the next day would be if they needed to bring the contents back up.

On the journey back to the lodge George worried about the problems they may have created for themselves. If they had only been talking about more dragon scales, the potential troubles for them were likely minor, but the treasure was an entirely different matter. Who knew what difficulties they would cause? In the hotel Xiao Ping and Cai set about cataloging the treasures, working as quickly as they could. It took the whole night to do the job properly. There were two hundred forty - two items including some thirty pieces of finely carved jadeite and twenty pieces of uncut jade. Cai bet these were the highest quality of jade and alone worth more than their weight in gold. Among the precious stones and metal pieces were a number of items that Cai felt were adornments emperors or kings would have used in ceremonial rites.

Even the wrapping had turned out to be some form of emperor or king's robe, in itself a remarkable discovery. Once fully unfolded it was both beautiful and impressive, dragons formed the central design and covered the outer surface as well as the inside. Dragons on the outside of the robe surrounded one main figure on the back of the robe, it was raised above all the others and had both gold pieces and thread used to give the outline it's depth and form, a find in itself.

As Cai and Xiao Ping continued to catalog items they prepared multiple e-mails for Diao, since one file would be too large to send. George took it upon himself to call Diao to discuss the situation directly; he needed to prepare him, as the e-mails would likely take all night to complete. It took some time to track down Diao as he was out with a group of visitors from Africa, brought to visit the Palace Museum by members of the Foreign Trade Ministry.

George's call surprised Diao Lijun who was alarmed to hear that George was in Zhangjiajie. George explained quickly what had happened, how Cai had this idea that the other coffin was still there. He told Diao how he and Xiao Ping expected the trip was going to be a wild goose chase and not worth telling Diao about, but they really had found the other coffin, buried right below where the first one was found! He explained to Diao the dilemma this posed with the authorities. After the last run-in with the government, the military, and other outside powers, George did not need a repeat scenario.

George could tell Diao was extremely excited about what he had described, but even he sounded more cautious than ever. He advised George they needed to contact Zhu's people, saying there was no other way without the potential for serious problems for all of them, personally and professionally.

" Look, George, the best thing is for you to send me the photos as planned overnight. I'll review them to get a better sense of what you've found and how to better explain all this to Zhu. If he agrees, there are other people I want to talk to. I'll get back to you in the morning with the results of those discussions. Maybe sometime after ten. How does that sound?"

George agreed, and it became clear within a few minutes of the first e-mails going out that Diao was staying up to receive them. He was euphoric on his first call back to them; he was amazed by only the first few pieces.

"My god, George! By the heavenly kingdom of the emperors, this is not just the find of the century in China. If the additional pieces are of the same quality and as precious, this will be the find of a lifetime. I can't wait to see and hold them myself. This is truly unbelievable!"

George was surprised by Diao's reaction and the ideas he was throwing out for the future, already formulating ideas as to what the items might be and wanting them to be a part of the Palace collection. Strangely, the dragon scales that had been the real object of George's search took a backseat in the conversations, even though George pointed out how some of these new scales had markings similar to those found in ancient mapping documents.

At 8 a.m. the next day, Diao placed the call to Zhu but was told he was traveling and would not be back for a week. When told it was extremely important they advised Zhu had indicated that all calls were to be transferred to Yi for action and follow-up. Yi was in communication daily with Zhu, who was away on an extremely sensitive mission. Diao had no option but to transfer to Yi on the matter, but had to wait for him to get back from a meeting.

Yi at first sounded angry and concerned to hear what had transpired with Mathers and the others heading back to the caves and finding what no one, including Yi's original team, had been able to find. He softened, however, when Diao explained how Mathers had determined they needed to be forthright in respect to an incredible find of treasure. They were contacting Zhu to report their findings because of the additional scales found and requesting confirmation of how the Chinese authorities would like them to pursue everything moving forward. Yi advised Diao that this clearly was above him and obviously not just a scale issue; it rested with Zhu and specific departments in the government. This was, however, of enough importance for Yi to contact Zhu directly and obtain instructions from him as to how to proceed. Yi said it would be at least an hour before he could get back to Diao. In the meantime he asked Diao to at least e-mail him a couple of photos of the items, for discussion purposes, but to say nothing about this to anyone for now.

About an hour later Yi called back. "Diao, Yi here. I've spoken to the general who has also spoken to the minister. There are two basic areas that they require the Mather team to follow through on. The first is in respect to the scales. The team should continue their work on translating the new scales. The military are not interested in further samples for testing; they've exhausted all avenues in this regard. Once they complete the cataloging work on the scales they are to turn them over again. They are to be stored with the first ones they discovered and retained for future display, or to be used as required. The second area of the so-called treasure is a different matter and the Mather team will not be required to handle them." Diao was taken back by Yi's brushing aside of any future involvement in the treasure by Mathers.

"I'm sorry, Commander, but I must say these people deserve to be involved in all aspects of this discovery. I will have some very unhappy colleagues on my hands if that is our leaders final decision."

"There is no discussion on this, Diao Lijun, but I do have good news for you: the treasure is to be turned over to your care for study and retention at the Palace Museum. At some future date when the origins and history have been developed they will be announced to the world and can be displayed in the museum or wherever the leadership recommends. That instruction is final. You and I need to discuss this further in secret. I have been assigned to work with you on all matters associated with this matter and we may only talk to whomever is authorized by the state."

"But what about Mathers and his colleagues? Surely they will talk."

"Under no circumstances will they discuss anything except the scales under the original agreement; that's still entirely subject to our review and approval. As regards the treasure, they have never seen it. Is that understood?"

"I can't see them staying quiet about this, Yi."

"Remind them of their meeting with Zhu in Wuhan at our safe house. Ask them if they want to find themselves in some burned-out wreck of a car."

"I can't tell them that, surely."

"You can tell them what you want, Diao. You are in this too, you know. You are being watched carefully. Those are your instructions. How you handle them is your problem. Understood? Do I tell Zhu you are not in agreement with our leaders' directions?"

"Of course not, Yi. I will always follow their instructions. You know my reputation." Diao could feel the call was ending as Yi's tone softened. "I'm sorry, Diao, if this appears severe but Zhu understands the situation you are in. Everything will work out for you this way. We can talk in greater detail when we get together in private. I think you will be quite interested in what we have in mind."

Diao was unsettled by the conversation but the comment had also been made that if indeed the treasure was as valuable and priceless as Diao indicated, then a special section would have to be constructed in the museum to house the artifacts and keep them secure. To this effect the articles would be taken to the Palace Museum under secure guard, assigned to Diao Lijun; only the people he needed for authentication would be allowed to work on the project. Around-the-clock security would be provided, assuming the treasure was as extensive as indicated. Diao and Yi had agreed that Yi would arrange for transport the items from Zhangjiajie to Beijing. Diao would meet the team at the lodge to help in their transfer to the airport by military security. Upon arrival in Beijing the scales would be released to Mathers' team for review, and the precious objects transferred under Diao's supervision to the vaults in the Palace Museum. Yi would assist with security checks at the museum area to ensure there was adequate protection of the treasure.

Diao phoned George and outlined the results of his call with Yi, he advised George to have everyone ready by 10 a.m. the next day when he would arrive. Special containers would be brought to their rooms for packing. Diao told George the team should handle the packaging, as

Zhu and Yi did not want members of the general security team exposed to the objects at this early stage.

──── ❧ ────

When George related his discussions with Diao the team was disappointed by the news of the artifacts being moved into Diao's control right away. George was excited, nonetheless, to be looking at this new trove of scales, even though the treasure was something to behold. Xiao Ping and Cai were furious about being swept aside from researching the precious objects. They were still photographing more of the remaining articles to e-mail to Diao. It had taken far longer than expected. Now the question was, had they done the right thing? George was sure they had. What he did not know at the time was that Cai Levee, as unpredictable as he could sometimes be, had quietly removed ten of the smaller items before Xiao Ping got to fully document them. He had set them to one side; there were so many items that neither George not Xiao Ping noticed the shortage.

R The next day after 10:30 a.m. Diao Lijun arrived at the hotel in a large black passenger van with seating for twelve. He came into the lodge to meet them while the rest of his group stayed in the van. George could see four individuals clothed in paramilitary type uniforms sitting in the van with three others in plain clothes. The three were clearly military personnel judging by their haircuts and physical appearance. George greeted Diao in the lobby and took him upstairs to the room. Diao told George about his escorts and how he had not wanted to alarm anyone in the lodge with military people entering. He looked weary having been up most of the night. He had not managed much sleep either on the military transport during the couple of hours flight to Zhangjiajie. The van was assigned by Yi to pick them up, and then transport them along with their finds back to the military section of the airport.

In the hotel room, Xiao Ping and Cai were waiting for them; although pleased to see Diao, both were angry at being sidelined from the treasure find. Diao tried to assure everyone he would keep them fully up to speed with his work. He said he was trying to persuade the authorities to include them in the authentication work, as well as recognize their involvement in the discovery once the items were finally on display. Not wanting to delay a moment longer, Diao anxiously asked to see the items that he had only seen via e-mail. Cai carefully pulled back the twin bed covers where all the objects were laid out. George smiled as Diao started to tremble and needed to steady himself, reaching out for the bedroom chair to sit down. He just sat there staring at the items, muttering to himself in Chinese under his breath. They were all a little concerned as Diao's face reddened, until he emerged from this strange trance to say that he was awestruck.

"For all the precious items I've supervised in the Palace Museum, or even those that were taken by Chang Kai-Shek and the Guomindang when they fled to Taiwan during the communist takeover, I've never seen anything so exciting or valuable in my entire career. This is incredible. I just do not know what to say!"

He gently picked up some items for closer inspection, putting on a pair of white gloves he always carried in his pocket. His expressions of awe continued as he rotated some of the pieces, held them to the light, and inspected them with a magnifying glass. He kept muttering superlatives as he gently put one piece down and picked up another. Sometime later George finally showed him some of the dragon scales. Diao was pleased they had more scales to develop the translations made to date, but after seeing the treasures he seemed to have little interest in them.

"I must stress our leaders' gratitude to you all," Diao said, "I know you're not happy but it is still a great honor to be provided these scales to continue your work. Especially since funding will now continue to be provided to you in recognition for your find. The government wants to keep the find secret at this time, however."

"I bet they do!" muttered Cai.

"No, no, it's not like that. They also asked me to pass to you that there will be no repercussions from going out on your own to find them, despite failing to advise the authorities ahead of time. Likewise, there will be no recrimination for your friends the lodge owners. They should have called the authorities when you were back in the area. Yi gave very strict orders in that regard. All this is being disregarded and there will be no records of their failure on file."

George was relieved that Sam and Ivy would not be in trouble, but worried about what problems he, Xiao Ping and Cai now faced. Diao asked if they had run into the monk on the trails during this visit and George confirmed they had not. They had been surprised and disappointed not to meet him again, but told Diao the renovation work on the resting temple had been well done and was complete.

Soon, Diao indicated the need for them to get moving. He called down to the van and asked them to deliver three trunks to the hotel room, then to wait for everyone back in the van. The plain-clothed guards duly delivered the trunks to the door and were not allowed in at that point; after they left, the trunks were brought in. The trunks held a supply of packing materials that Diao had organized from the museum. The scales were packed in one trunk relatively quickly. If the military could not destroy or even mark them before, there was not much likelihood of any damage to them, no matter how badly they were packed. They still handled them, however, with the same care and respect as in the past. Once they were locked in the trunk, the keys were given to George. Packing the other two trunks took far more time; Diao's experience in this regard was clear in the wrapping of each item and professional manner in which they were placed in the trunks.

Upon completion, both trunks were locked and ready for transport. Diao retained all the keys for those trunks, then asked everyone if they were ready to leave. George advised him they had a little personal packing to complete, that Diao ought to head downstairs for coffee and give them twenty minute to finish. They could then carry the trunks down and check out. Diao agreed, but said he would talk to Sam and cover all the costs of their stay there, as well as making sure Sam and Ivy got a little extra for the good service they provided and rental for the jeep. He told George another of Yi's team was already at the cave area cleaning out the tools left behind and sealing it up. They planned to photo the area once more and check everything before bringing back the empty coffin.

Diao told them about the plans he already had in mind for the treasures, that part of the exhibit, when the articles were on display, would be to show the coffins and a mockup of the cave with the tools used in the discovery. The cave itself would be sealed properly to ensure it remained undisturbed for the future, unless it became a tourism spot for the resting temple and the Ma Jun legend once that was finally revealed too.

CHAPTER FOUR

About twenty minutes later the door opened and three plain-clothed guards walked in with Diao, who seemed quite embarrassed and nervous, "I'm truly sorry about this everyone, but Yi and Zhu have asked these people to inspect your rooms and luggage for security purposes."

"Still don't trust us, huh? George asked.

"No, no. I mean yes. We do of course. They just don't want any suspicion later."

George glanced toward Cai, who quickly stepped forward, waving his arms to welcome any inspection the guards wanted to make. "Go ahead, no problem, I'll take everyone downstairs for coffee. When they're finished with our personal bags they can take us to the airport for the journey back. Just don't mess them up!" There was no body search. Before boarding the plane they would pass through the latest security apparatus and if anyone had something hidden or secreted on their bodies it would be found.

Diao apologized yet again as they left the room. Cai winked at George and Xiao Ping but said nothing further as they headed downstairs to the dining room and coffee area. Cai went over to Sam and ordered three coffees, chatting quietly to him for a while. He put Sam at ease about what was going on, explaining that there would be no problems for him with not phoning the authorities. He later told George that Sam said Diao had covered all their expenses. He also gave Sam a handsome payment for the use of the Jeep and gave a handsome additional payment for any trouble he and his team might have caused the lodge or their guests. Sam had asked Cai what it was all about, why these people were here, and what trouble they were in. Cai had assured him it was really nothing to be concerned about; he told him they were all working together on a special archeological project, which seemed to satisfy Sam's curiosity. No one said much as they drank their coffees. The guards were in the van waiting for everyone to come out. Diao finally came over again and assured them all was in good order. Nothing had been found in the search, but he was going to give Sam more money for cleaning the rooms which were in a state of disarray. George watched Sam and Diao negotiating back and forth in true Chinese fashion, Sam declining to accept further payment, Diao insisting several more times before both parties had displayed the correct level of humility in giving and accepting the additional monies.

The guards brought the bags and trunks down from the rooms for the journey to the military airfield in Zhangjiajie. George and the others said their farewells to Sam and Ivy, pledging they would return some day in the future.

The journey into Zhangjiajie was quiet; no one wanted to talk with Yi's men around them, other than mundane comments about the area and local sights. The van was waved through the military side of the airport security, past some older buildings with darkened windows. There were guards at every door, and rooftops bristled with antenna and satellite dishes. On the runway an unmarked military transport aircraft sat waiting with its cargo doors open. All the bags and trunks were packed safely onboard as George's team and the three guards from Beijing boarded the flight for immediate takeoff

---

Two hours later they landed at a remote airfield outside Beijing where Commander Yi and a contingent were waiting. George had visions of being whisked off again to some secret location for questioning. The first time that happened to them was when they discovered the scales; it had been harrowing for him, especially when his wife was isolated from him. He was always uneasy around Yi. It was clear to him that only Zhu's methods had prevented this Yi from using violence or even torturing them at the time. He was a big man for a Chinese, as was Zhu. George saw Yi as a reasonably intelligent man but sinister, stone-faced on the outside but hiding a brutal side itching to act.

He thought his leader, General Zhu was different; he was far brighter, had a fatherly manner. He was definitely ethical, unlike Yi, but perhaps even tougher at his core. George had seen Yi deferring to his leader but no doubt eager to be running the operation. The way Zhu had sought out the truth behind their first discovery still sent shivers down George's spine when he thought about it.

They were taken this time to a conference room in a nearby building and asked to recount what happened during their visit to Zhangjiajie. The plans for the artifacts were re-stated; the scales would go with George's team back to the university building, and some of Yi's team would accompany Diao to the museum with the precious objects. Work had already begun to secure a private area at the Palace Museum for the retention and study of the articles. Although there was one remark indicating Zhu was disappointed about not being pre-warned regarding the action taken by George and the others, he felt the matter was handled satisfactorily. About the only response George could add was that he originally felt the visit would be a wild goose chase and they had not wanted to make a big issue over it.

With the airport meeting wrapped up, Yi and Diao prepared to take the treasure portion with a contingent of men by armored vehicle to the Palace Museum. Three additional men had already been assigned to work at the museum with Diao. Yi's expression hardened when he reiterated to everyone the government's requirement for secrecy in this matter. There would be no tolerance of any deviation, and the consequences would be severe. The scales were placed in an unmarked van. A smaller team was assigned to take George's group to the university so they could begin their appraisal of the rest of the scales. They still had all the equipment from their past efforts. They'd learned so much translating the first batch that George expected they could complete the project much faster than before.

———— ⟨⟩ ————

The scales were deposited at the university lab room before they all headed home to clean up and rest before beginning the first phase of activity. George knew the others were unhappy about losing their involvement with the treasure; at least with Diao still being involved they would not be cut out completely. There was grumbling from both Xiao Ping and Cai Levee, but George was relieved that he wouldn't be pulled out of bed again and dragged off to some remote location for questioning.

———— ⟨⟩ ————

Yi's team escorted Diao with the precious items into a safe area of the Palace Museum. They made sure everything was isolated and under lock and key before leaving him and his assistants to begin a full inventory and investigation of all the pieces. Diao mentioned later to George that they left an additional guard in the building to protect the items full-time and presumably to watch over him and his assistants. The guard dressed casually and carried a museum employee badge to remain inconspicuous, but Diao noted the man was associated with Yi and totally loyal to him. Diao told George that he was more fortunate since the authorities had given up on all the security arrangements they'd insisted on for the first scales.

— ∞∞∞ —

Gradually George and his team settled in to the next phase of work, and their excitement over the additional scales began to come back. A few days later Cai came into the lab in the morning with a large box and a broad smile. He settled in the seat he always used and called George and Xiao Ping over to look. The box had been well wrapped; it was addressed to Cai Levee at his rooms at the university. The labels indicated they were university reference books. The sender's label was clearly no book publisher. It had been addressed through EMS special delivery service; the sender was Sam at the hiker's lodge. Cai opened the box gently to reveal ten carefully packaged specimens taken from the treasure found in Zhangjiajie.

"Shit, Cai! What the hell have you done now? Are you completely crazy?" George could barely contain himself; Xiao Ping seemed concerned but more interested in what was there. She told George to calm down and looked at Cai for a while before saying anything.

"How did you do it, Cai? What are we going to do with these things?"

"I'm sorry, everyone. Really. I was afraid this would happen, that we'd somehow be cut out of this. But I couldn't stop myself; there was so much there. I boxed them up the night before Diao arrived and asked Sam to send these 'books' to save me having to carry them back. I told him they were given to me by associates from the University in Zhangjiajie."

George was concerned that Sam might have questioned that later, when he saw the trunks brought down and taken away. Cai assured George it would be okay, pointing out that Sam was a good friend, had always been discreet, and never asked many questions - especially when the authorities he didn't like were involved.

"What are we going to tell Diao?" Xiao Ping asked,

"We can't tell him just yet, although I feel a little guilty in that regard. What I know for sure is that we'll never sell them or take them out of the country. So many items of our cultural heritage have been sold, plundered or stolen out of China. I'll make sure that never happens to these."

After a heated discussion they all agreed that for now Cai would put the pieces out of sight while they worked on the scales. George trusted Cai to take care of it. He told Cai to store them away from the university and his home. Cai said he already had the location in mind and how he would secure them. George reluctantly left, telling Cai that somehow the pieces would have to be re-discovered for the authorities, and in the not too distant future.

CHAPTER FIVE

Diao Lijun began cataloging the treasure items and preparing presentations for the museum board on a special display. Zhu and Yi would also have to be informed about all such actions as they had been officially assigned as protectors of the find until a public announcement was made. Diao assumed the authorities would treat the scales and precious items as separate finds, given their skepticism regarding the translation of the first series of scales and the dragon stories they contained.

The artifacts, however, would leave no one in any doubt of their authenticity. Their sheer splendor would guarantee a huge success once on display at the museum; it would surpass anything showcased anywhere in the world. His initial review, once all the pieces were laid out, showed a clear division of some twelve periods of time. The design, materials, and style indicated they could have been from specific eras; however, which era was baffling at first. Identifying the materials the articles were made from was not difficult. They were made from every precious metal or gem known, with variance depending on what must have been desirable at the time or deemed to be the most valuable.

Diao kept Yi apprised of the reviews as they developed and occasionally stopped by the university to keep George and the others up to date. He knew how interested they were in the find. Diao discussed the progress with Yi, who would pass on the information for onward reporting to Zhu and the ministry. Diao was told that under no circumstances were these items to be discussed or the display of them with anyone else at the museum for the time being. If he was asked he was to deny their existence. Yi also told him the thinking at the highest level was that the display should not house the originals due to their value. Thefts from the museum had taken place over the years.

Yi recommended that the genuine pieces be stored in the central banking vaults rather than the museum, and Diao thought that was a good idea. He was concerned, however, that if copies were commissioned, word of the find would leak out quickly within the antiquities community. Yi suggested using a number of different entities, assuring him the government was in a position to assure full protection against any illegal copies being made. The government was also ready to pay handsomely for first class duplicates. They were not interested in having simple fakes produced.

Yi said the government would like the display to be unveiled at the next celebration of the founding of the People's Republic of China on October first, the anniversary of Mao's 1949 declaration to the world. This would, however, mean starting the duplication process even as the items were cataloged. Diao promised to think about it and come up with some proposals in this regard.

Yi added that the authorities were very pleased with the find, particularly with Diao Lijun's team and the way they were handling this. The potential duplication of key pieces was to be kept confidential from all non-contracted parties in the early stages. As far as the authorities were concerned that included Mathers' team.

So much secrecy was troubling to Diao, but Yi assured him that he would soon understand the importance of it; the leaders wanted to stun the world when the timing was right.

George's team's first step with the scales was to again photograph each one and digitally map them, setting up the identification system as they had done with the original discovery. Once Xiao Ping completed that task with help from the others, they moved on. The work was slow-going of course since they were without their former colleagues Charles, Arthur, and Zhao Feng to help. George did contact Charles and Arthur to see if they might be free to give a hand again, but said nothing of the treasure or how they had found the new group of scales.

Although they were excited for George and happy to hear about the turn of events, they weren't in a position to leave what they were doing. George and Cai were able to plug the new data into the original computer programs formerly used by Arthur that generated a 3D image of the tail of a dragon. They were pleased to have been able to do it with a little help by phone from Arthur, but the program failed to function until Xiao Ping pointed out that the two batches of scales were slightly different in color.

They separated out the scales that were the same size and color as the tail scales and ran those alone with the originals. These turned out to be some of the missing scales from the first group. The remaining scales, however, would not fit the tail section at all, and that frustrated the three of them. Daily they reprogrammed the system to see how they could add to the existing views, talking to Arthur by phone and regretting that he'd left the team.

After eliminating the ones they thought could have been part of the first batch, the program started to make progress. Within the week a shape appeared before them. They were all excited and thought they knew what it was, but decided to bring Professor Ding in for authentication. A fellow professor, Ding specialized in anthropology and had been the first to guess that the previous scales were from a prehistoric creature that he theorized was capable of flight. George should have asked Diao or Yi first for approval to involve Ding, but in his excitement forgot to do so. He assumed that since Ding had been aware of the original review, he was "in the circle" so to speak.

Before showing him the image George explained that they had finally found more scales but declined to tell him how. He did assure him that there were no more in existence, as far as they knew.

As they initiated the computer program Ding grew more excited as an image developed. Objects dispersed across the screen, scales exploded back and forth before forming their final shape. When the image settled after about fifteen minutes Ding gave out a loud whistle, grabbed a chair, and sat in front of the screen, taking his glasses on and off several times before expressing his amazement. As ever, Ding was puffing his chest out as he shouted at Cai and George, "Yes, I was right before, this is indeed a prehistoric creature. Just as I forecast all along. A creature able to fly. What's more amazing is these scales are from the head, and, yes, it is horse-like. If I didn't know better I would say we have in our possession the protective scales from the head of a large dragon! But no, that can't be. That's for children and legends. It's some kind of flying creature. Of that I'm sure, but it cannot be a dragon. It must be an unknown species, It does resemble a Pterodactyl."

"Do you mean a pterodactyl, Professor?" George asked.

"Same family, Mr. George, same family. I must admit the head looks more like the Komodo dragon though. Fascinating, fascinating. Oh yes indeed, this will cause a stir in my world! Oh my, if this really is our China dragon, what a discovery indeed!"

Sitting back he could only mutter that if it was real and the legends of the Chinese forefathers were indeed based on fact, then in some age a kind of dragon may have indeed walked the earth. He could offer no other expert opinion and assured them he would stake his reputation on his assessment.

They told Ding that none of them was at liberty to discuss any findings outside of the room. They begged Ding to keep this information under wraps until permission from the authorities was obtained. Cai told him they were in the process of translating unique writings on the scales and once the work was complete he would let him know what they revealed. He told Ding that when they came around to publish findings to the academic world, a statement would be included to say, "First authenticated by Professor Ding of Tsinghua University." Ding promised to maintain their confidence; he said he did not need trouble with the authorities as he had painful memories from before still haunted him.

Professor Ding left the lab in high spirits, but not before predicting that there would be endless discussions over whether the scales were real or fake.

"We don't want a controversy like the Shroud of Turing argument," George commented.

———— ✺ ————

The team set about trying to see if they could discover the order of writings on the new scales to aid in translating this second part of the story. What was most exciting was that several of the scales had little writing on them, but were clearly maps of some kind. More about them would no doubt be revealed in the writings once they advanced to the translation stage. Luckily now they had the keys to this work, and were confident that the translations would be completed in a few weeks as opposed to many months.

Diao came by to fill them in on the progress of the items at the museum but was also excited by what the new scales might reveal. His only disappointment was that the authorities were focused solely on the treasure in their possession. They still viewed any of the work on the scales as fantasies created years ago, by what means no one could explain. Nor could anyone determine why the scales were as indestructible as they were. The authorities had simply stopped any further research on them and were content to leave George and the team to work on them. In the meantime, Diao advised that work on the other treasure was confirming his initial estimates that the pieces in the treasure collection covered twelve periods of history. Diao believed one of the periods dated from the Xia Dynasty, which supposedly dated around 2500 B.C. and to date was only known through legends and very limited archeological evidence.

"Maybe you all know this has in the past been referred to as the Bronze Age but the precious items from that time feature precious stones of incredible beauty and size. The other periods feature greater use of gold and silver along with diamonds, emeralds and pearls, as well as unique jade pieces. The styles are quite different from era to era, but the quality of each item is superlative."

"What kind of a collection do you think this is, Diao?" George asked.

"We're not sure yet, but what I can say is that for as long as I've worked with antiquities at the Palace Museum, and been involved with the later Chinese dynasties, the items are definitely imperial relics of some kind."

Diao described his plan to develop a unique exhibit using copies of the relics in the Palace Museum, mentioning his concerns that once his work was completed the authorities might decide to switch the location to the National Museum off Tiananmen Square.

George knew it well and had visited it on numerous occasions over the years. The huge museum was built in 1912; it had been fully renovated in 2010, with a new exhibit covering the revolutionary period following the collapse of the Qing Dynasty. Diao was obviously desperate to keep the treasure under his management in the Palace Museum.

Yi continued to be the prime interface for Diao and the team at the museum, telling everyone that General Zhu was busy with state projects. In his latest meeting with Diao on the progress made, Diao tried to educate him on the subtleties surrounding the objects and why they had determined there were twelve basic periods of history. Currently activities were under way to determine the approximate age of the relics to further refine how they would be displayed. The evidence that one of the periods seemed to align with the Xia Dynasty of legend was exciting, but again circumstantial. Who ruled during the earlier periods remained open to conjecture. All of that was of little interest to Yi, but he knew Zhu would be far more knowledgeable in that regard. "All very interesting, Diao, but what's the market value of this collection?"

"It might surprise you, Commander. Each piece would fetch millions of U.S dollars at auction, certain ones tens of millions or more. It's better to think in terms of billions and not millions!"

"That's incredible. With that in mind, our plan for creating copies for display is critical. General Zhu will need a write-up of your estimate so that he can obtain approval to expand the budget."

"I thought we should discuss it with others in our field first. Surely more additional experts need to be involved in this."

"I can only go by Zhu's instructions on this. I assume that because we were in on this before they are keeping us involved for now. Certainly if these are as valuable as you claim the leaders will want absolute security and secrecy on this. The general must already know something from the earlier reports. He's instructed me to plan more security coverage for the items at all steps in the process with additional personnel and support equipment."

Diao requested a couple of days to put a formal report together for Zhu. Yi advised him to direct the correspondence through him as Zhu was tied up. Diao shared the names of five companies capable of copying the items at the quality level that was needed; he had gathered examples of contracts the museum used before for this type of work. He added additional sections on confidentiality, as well as an approval process to ensure the copies would be as near perfect as they could be.

Yi committed to have the authorities' lawyers review the proposed agreements. They would refine any clauses that needed reworking and complete a security review of each company.

"How long do you think it will take to complete the exhibition copies?"

"Theoretically several pieces could be completed before October of next year for the display since its only April now; I'm not sure yet. In addition, we would need advance approval of the display and its final location some months ahead of the October date in order to get everything ready."

"That's easily done." Yi joked. "After all, we built the Great Hall of the People in Tiananmen Square in less than a year."

Yi told Diao his work was being fully recognized at the highest levels, and that he and Zhu would support his proposal to keep the exhibit in the Palace Museum.

———— ∞∞ ————

When Yi next met with Diao he confirmed that the authorities had completed their review of the companies to handle the duplication. Four were deemed acceptable but one was questionable. The contracts proposed by Diao had been thoroughly vetted and there were a number of revisions, most of which were minor. The contracts were to be between the contractor and a special committee established to handle the transactions and keep them confidential. The contracting party was named "The China Relic Preservation Group." All contracts were to be signed by Diao Lijun as a director, but Yi and General Zhu would countersign as a part of the monitoring process.

The authorities had approved better payment terms than Diao recommended, as well as incentive payments for early completion. These payments, however, could be withdrawn if the finished articles did not meet agreed-upon quality levels. The early advance of cash was the idea of the security team so that artisans were not struggling in any way financially and tempted to take anything - or make unauthorized copies for their own use at a later date.

Yi advised Diao to go ahead and negotiate the contracts through the four selected companies, and advise the contracted parties not to be surprised if a special security team visited them before they began, or during their work. Each of the companies was to sign confidentiality agreements and could not be made aware of any others involved. They were forbidden to talk to any of their colleagues or friends; doing so would mean immediate cancellation of payment and a significant penalty. The authorities wanted to assure maximum global news impact when the find was finally announced.

———— ⚬⊱⊰⚬ ————

Diao decided to divide the articles up based on each company's specialty and work they had done before. They would not receive work from one era or dynasty but a cross section. Due to the sensitive nature of the task ahead, Diao personally met with the owner of each company to sound them out carefully about taking on these contracts. They were lucrative contracts and the owners were intrigued about the relics they would work with and where they came from, Diao simply told them they had been drawn from collections all over China for a special exhibit. The duplicates would be placed on display for security reasons.

Once the contracts were signed, Yi insisted on holding private meetings with each of the company owners. Within twenty-four hours of those meetings the initial upfront funding was transferred to each entity. Diao and his assistants were then cleared to begin the dissemination of relics to them, closely monitored by Yi's security personnel.

The owners said little of their individual meetings with Yi, but Diao thought they seemed a bit unnerved by the experience. He was not surprised; Yi was a large man with an intimidating air and a dour personality. He made most people around him nervous. At the time Diao put the owners concerns down to the unusual nature of the contracts and the requirements for secrecy.

CHAPTER SIX

Work on translating the scales continued. The maps discovered in the second find were in pictogram format; George and Cai could see where mountains, rivers, plains, and what appeared to be volcanoes were located. They assumed that once the translation of these was combined with the others, the purpose of the map would become apparent. Whether it was just an overview of a kingdom or identifying the location of something was still in question.

Another challenge was the time period that the maps referred to and what part of a kingdom they may have represented. There was a further difficulty with mapping the scales; laid out at whatever random placement a different map appeared every time. George hoped there was going to be some information in the translation that could confirm the correct map layout.

The team were still bitter about being removed from the research on the treasure, driving Xiao Ping and Cai Levee to become secretive about what they were uncovering, not just to Diao but especially to Yi. Cai was especially upset. "They've cut us out of it, George. We can do that to them too, you know!"

"That's not wise, Cai. This thing could be even bigger than before. If it's true of course."

"It's true! Xiao Ping and I are sure of it. The new scripts make the current find sound a minor discovery. Those rulers paid an incredible amount for protection - or assistance, as they called it - from the

Dragons over the centuries. Those so-called 'keepers of the dragons' have guarded the treasure for centuries."

"I know all of that. I've read it too," George said. "If you believe that brief mention in the script that is."

Xiao Ping grew animated. "Well, I believe it! I'm intrigued by the early references to the keepers of the dragons. What if generations of the Ma family were the real descendants of some of these people? These maps could lead us to an even greater find! Of that I'm sure. These authorities, whoever they are, who don't want us involved can go to hell."

At Diao's next meeting with Yi, he was introduced to the new Minister of Culture who had just been appointed. His name was Wang Fan, originally from Xiamen in South China. He had excellent Communist Party credentials, connections, and organizational skills, but Diao could see quickly that his background was anything but cultural. Whatever the Party was rewarding Wang Fan for in this appointment was not clear, but it was something one did not question. It was a new position, likely spurred on by the country's efforts to emphasize more than ever its cultural influence around the world.

"Comrade Diao, Zhu regrets he cannot join us due to the current workload with the Party leaders. He and my colleagues agree that you and Commander Yi however are doing a fine job on this particular project, and I'm pleased as the new minister to get to know you and your team. I understand the importance of this project. The need for secrecy must be frustrating but for the authorities it is deemed crucial."

Wang Fan then asked if Diao needed anything more at this time in support or funding. There were some equipment upgrades needed, but other than that they were being well supported. Wang Fan advised Yi to make sure anything Diao needed was procured and supplied to his team as soon as possible.

Wang asked Yi about the security status. Yi confirmed that all was under control but he needed additional security personnel to oversee the duplication process that was under way. He had placed only one individual full-time with Diao and his assistants.

After almost three months, progress on the scripts had been made at the university. Most exciting was confirmation that the map, wherever and whatever it was describing, was associated with a story, about a region of kingdoms that pre-dated China's consolidation under Emperor Qin in 221 B.C. The map depicted landmarks around active volcanic regions. Cai was convinced that by talking to geologists about past volcanic areas of activity and river basins they could begin to assemble the map scales into the correct sequence. He was planning to talk to Professor Hu JinJing at the university. She was a close friend, renowned throughout China and well connected to other geologists in the provinces.

Cai told George he was sure she could help but it might take some time. He would prepare separate sketches on the computer, and remove certain highlights on the map that seemed to point to a location where the dragons existed. If she saw the scales and map outlines, Cai suspected her curiosity would get the better of her and that she would become inquisitive as to the origin and meanings of the maps.

He said she had majored in this subject many years ago and dedicated her career to studying volcanoes, although in recent years she'd focused on the study of earthquakes, especially after the tragedies in Sichuan in 2008. George told him to go ahead but to be very careful with her; they agreed to say nothing to Diao about approaching her.

The first pieces of the treasure collection were secretly delivered to the selected companies within a few weeks of the contracts being signed.

The first pieces had been fully chronicled and their composition identified. Age estimates were not released at this stage, despite inquiries
from the companies, who had seen nothing like them before and were
keen to put them into a specific dynastic period. A high content of
precious metals and gems was pervasive throughout all the items and
added to the mystique surrounding them. The contractors, after holding the initial pieces in their own hands, quickly understood they were
dealing with unique and valuable relics. Their concern about having Yi's
security personnel around them quickly evaporated. They recognized
that if they lost any piece they would face serious repercussions, just as
Yi had warned them.

Two of the firms added to their own security to further protect
themselves.

Diao arranged for the four groups to meet separately with the new
minister, Wang Fan, so that each could became part of the overall exhibit project team. Diao and his team were actively involved in the duplication efforts. The items needed to be of a superlative copy level, and
they had to be completed sooner rather than later. There was obvious
pressure to meet the target date but the copies had to be outstanding
in their own right.

Another month went by before Cai told George he'd received a call
from Hu JinJing suggesting a meeting. Cai had asked JinJing if they
could meet for dinner and include both George and his wife. She had
no objection after Cai advised her they were all working on the same
project. They booked a separate room at the Da Dong Duck Restaurant
along the third ring road, agreeing to meet the following Friday evening. Cai felt they all needed an evening out where they could let their
hair down a little but rest up on Saturday morning should they overin-
dulge. George wasn't happy to hear JinJing had a reputation as a baijiu
drinker. He wondered how Xiao Ping would get along with her, the

two sharing a prowess for drinking the clear white liquid he disliked so much.

That night they had a great meal at the duck restaurant. Hu JinJing was really entertaining and, true to her reputation, insisted on a number of heavy toasts that left even Xiao Ping in a somewhat fragile state. After the final dish of the evening arrived, Cai insisted that JinJing bring everyone up to speed on where she was with her study of the map information he'd provided to her.

"Why, Cai, such an easy project to work on. I thought you were going to give me something really difficult to do!"

"It took you long enough!"

"Guilty as charged. But I only picked it up the other night. Sorry…."

George was quite taken back by her comments and flinched as Xiao Ping glanced sideways at him. Clearly she did not care much for JinJing; her expression communicated to him that she felt JinJing too full of herself. George was happy, though, to hear she had the answer to how the maps were put together and what parts of China they covered. JinJing had impressed him that evening with her knowledge despite the drinking; he thought perhaps Xiao Ping was just jealous that he and Cai had sat there quite captivated by her. She was, after all, a beautiful Asian woman and very smart too. George imagined that JinJing's presence made quite a few men melt.

They learned more in the next couple of hours about volcanoes in China and their history than most people would ever want to know, although she made the discussion entertaining and interesting. After a half hour, George could see Xiao Ping begrudgingly accept that JinJing truly knew her subject as she became thoroughly engrossed in the presentation too. Finally, JinJing took papers out of her briefcase assembled from the separate pages Cai had prepared. She spread them out on the cleared table, moving them around to the order she indicated was definitely the layout of the map.

"Look here, this map obviously covers the northeast of China. This section here, that's the border today with North Korea." She pointed to the crude outline of a large volcano. "And this, my friends, this volcano and these other smaller volcanic areas make it only one place your map can be!" She paused, smiling at Cai.

"So where exactly, JinJing?"

"Changbaishan, you idiot, Changbaishan."

She said this was still the most active volcano in China, and further explained how one of the largest eruptions in the world over the past ten thousand years occurred there in 960 A.D. the Baitoushan eruption. It was estimated to have been three times the size of the Krakatau eruption in 1883. Small eruptions had continued since the fifteenth century, but the last eruption had occurred in 1903. Despite the relative calm since, she said the volcano was still considered by Chinese scientists to be potentially the most dangerous volcano.

"There's a large lake in the mouth of the volcano, eight hundred fifty meters deep. A disturbance would threaten some hundred thousand Koreans that live close by or on the mountain. Within China, Changbaishan is not well known, due to its remote location, but we continue to monitor activity within the mountain. Details of the first major eruption are limited except in legends, as are references to other activity in bygone years."

With that central theme covered, JinJing laid out all the areas covered by the map, again strangely anchored in all cases by the volcano locations. What was most peculiar in her view was that this map could not have been put together at ground level; it had to be drawn up at some elevation.

"Where did you copy these map details from anyway?" she asked, "Whatever map you got this from was developed before any known cartographic mapping that I'm aware of. I'd like to see it; it would be worth a lot academically as well as being very valuable."

George could see Cai wrestling with how to respond and jumped in, "The truth is it was taken from an antique map; the collector asked us to determine where it might be located. The authenticity is still in question, but we don't have the original copy to be able to comment too much." George told her they were impressed with her interpretation of the map, that China had been one of three potential locations for the undated map. George promised JinJing he would pass along her name to the owner and emphasize how interested she would be to work with him on detailing the map further.

"Look, everyone, it's time to relax," Cai interrupted. "What about a karaoke club for a night of singing? Who's game?" JinJing accepted right away, as did Xiao Ping. George with his poor singing voice and drinking ability tried to decline, but found it too hard to say no. The evening ended up like many others, with George struggling to sing anything in tune but, as always in China, being complimented on his singing ability. He always found that amusing, knowing full well he sounded awful.

Cai finally decided about 2 a.m. that it was time to call it a night and picked up the entire check. George was happy not to have to go through the ritual of offering to pay and arguing over it with Cai for five minutes. Cai and JinJing finally headed off. Xiao Ping raised an eyebrow, but George thought no more of it than the host escorting his guest home to make sure she was safe.

The next day Cai laid out the scales in line with the map JinJing had drawn up for him. He identified all the areas and landmarks except for four or five that involved another call to JinJing. Coupled with the translation the pieces now made more sense. Everyone looked at the results that Cai had projected on the lab wall. They stood there for what seemed a long time before George broke the silence, declaring that perhaps they really did have a treasure map staring them in the face.

"I'm wondering if the stories in the scripts can lead us to some kind of regal tomb that dates before Emperor Qin, perhaps some kind of burial chamber. Hell, if that were true it would reveal even more secrets of a forgotten time in the history of China. Imagine what that would do for all of our past work!"

They all looked at each other with the same question written across their faces, "What now?"

———⊗⊗⊗———

George and his colleagues understood that the Scripts told the story of the end of the last dragons in China and that the hope of the Dragon Keepers was that some would return to continue protecting the kingdom. Cai said, "This refers to the last leader of the dragon population being entombed with the main wealth of the kingdom. Says it was collected over many centuries of rule. I checked and there are more details in that regard in the stories from the scripts. The map was intended to lead future keepers, when and if new dragons returned, to the place where their leader was buried. That's where the penance given to all the predecessors is stored."

They began to discuss more seriously the possibility of searching for its location in hopes of uncovering further evidence of the dragon history. "If Hu JinJing is right and the location is somewhere in the northeast, then that poses more problems. None of us has any experience working there. It's awfully remote!" said George. The proximity to North Korea was of particular concern to him as an American, should they wander across the border in their search.

———⊗⊗⊗———

One morning while George was walking by the entrance to the university, a motorcyclist sped towards him. Stopping briefly the rider handed him a letter and sped off. George thought the masked rider was female because of her general physique hidden under a leather motorcycle jacket and pants. He instantly thought back to the woman who had delivered the pizza box with the discs and coding keys that helped them break the original script codes before.

When he arrived in the lab area later, only Cai Levee was there. When Xiao Ping finally arrived, she told George she'd stopped by a friend's office to catch up on things. George told them what happened that morning and began to carefully open the envelope. The envelope was marked Personal and Confidential' to Professor George Mathers in a plain brown envelope, Inside there was only one sheet of paper inside, obviously typed on an old-fashioned machine rather than a computer. It said, "Events are changing. Diao is at risk. Trust only Zhu.

There was nothing more in the letter, other than two words at the bottom right corner, "Black Knight."

They sat staring at each other wondering what this could mean and who the Black Knight might be. George phoned Diao right away, not sure what to say but to ask him to visit as soon as he could. What concerned George was that Diao had been acting a little strange the last few weeks, acting more nervous than usual. Whenever George asked what was wrong Diao had assured him all was fine.

"Was Diao there?" Xiao Ping asked.

"No, there's no reply from his mobile or the office phone, but the receptionist said Diao and his assistants are away. They'll be returning tomorrow."

Cai didn't appear concerned at first. Finally he looked at George and Xiao Ping. "You know, it's a bit strange. None of us has seen Zhu for months. Maybe we should try to reach him instead. I certainly wouldn't say anything to Yi, especially if this warning is for real."

George nodded. "You're right, Cai, it's weird, but getting to Zhu is a problem. We don't have his direct number. If we take this letter seriously, then trying to contact him via Yi isn't a good idea." As they discussed how to contact Zhu, they realized that in all the months gone by no one had heard anything at all direct from him. All contact had been through Yi alone. It hadn't occurred to George before; now with the letter in hand it seemed suspicious. "Think about it," he said. "The only recent contact from Zhu was when Wang Fan, the new minister, delivered us a so-called message direct from Zhu." George wondered aloud if he was being overly paranoid.

"I'll try to contact Zhu somehow and arrange a private meeting," Xiao Ping said. She felt she had a way to track him down, declining to say more.

Cai, whose concern was on the rise, warned George not to use their office or mobile phones to call; he would buy disposable phones and change phones cards periodically if subsequent calls were needed. George cautioned Cai and Xiao Ping that they needed to stay calm, that perhaps a chat tomorrow with Diao would put their suspicions to rest. They both just raised their eyebrows as if to say, "You must be joking again of course!"

"And who could the Black Knight be? Cai added.

CHAPTER SEVEN

The next morning, they came into the lab early, continuing to work on the script translations and refinement of the maps. They were putting more current location definition to the pictograms, even though some features of the map described in the scripts had vanished over time. George called Diao again with no reply and checked in with the museum. The receptionist confirmed they were driving back from the Datong Yungang Grottoes in Shanxi Province where they were checking on some Buddhist statues and artifacts. If the traffic near the Badaling district by the Great Wall did not hold them up they would be back by 3 p.m. She promised to pass along George's message as soon as she saw Diao.

The following morning George called Diao's phones again to no avail. Cai brought up the issue of the note they had received and his concerns for Diao's safety. They tried to check if Diao was with Yi for some reason but were told by the adjutant that Yi was not in either. George decided if they could not get in touch with Yi, then they should contact Zhu. Xiao Ping had not been able to find him yet, but told them she needed to leave right away

———∞∞∞———

An emergency intelligence meeting was in progress in Zhongnanhai next to the Forbidden City. The parking lot was jammed with government cars. It was evening and since all of the cars were black the whole area had a sinister air. Most of the vehicles were popular Audi A6 models, although there were a number of Chinese-built cars and SUVs. A number of police motorcycles were parked near the entrance. A side room was filled with drivers smoking and playing cards as they waited for their leaders to finish.

A uniformed policeman strode through the lines of cars clearly looking for a specific vehicle. He was somewhat smaller in build than the others, but no one paid any attention to him. None of the vehicles parked in the area was locked. Security personnel had to have full and ready access to all vehicles in any situation, and drivers were under orders to leave ignition keys in place in case of an emergency. No confidential papers or other belongings could be left in the vehicles.

When the rider found the vehicle he was looking for he quickly opened the back and placed an envelope on the floor. Leaving the area in seconds, he returned to one of the police bikes, climbed on, and with its light flashing left through the gate.

After the meeting concluded, tasks were designated to the various heads and leaders. Zhu left with others; some would be heading to work, some for home. Zhu was one of the luckier ones in that he would at least get some sleep that night despite problems brewing again in western China; a terrorist alert had prompted the urgent meeting. Zhu's driver was already in the car with the engine running, waiting for the cars ahead of him to move toward the exit. Not much was said between the two as Zhu settled in to his seat to get a little sleep. He soon felt something under his shoe and noticed an envelope. Picking it up cautiously he asked the driver if he had left something in the rear of the car. The driver said he had not.

The envelope did not look official, Zhu's name was scrawled across the front; beneath his name were the words "Personal and Confidential." Inside he found a second one marked the same way. Inside this one was a brief note expressing concern about Diao. In light of recent events, he was asked to meet Professor Mathers privately as soon as possible. The letter contained an unlisted number for him to call.

It was early in the morning when Zhu called George Mathers. They talked for some time; he was surprised to hear that George received a similar warning note telling George to trust only Zhu. George asked how things were going, as they had not seen him for a good many months. Zhu admitted being very busy but told George he had kept up to speed on the new trove of scales they had discovered. He was looking forward to hearing more details on how they were adding to the stories from the first batch.

He was surprised when George asked him what he thought was going to happen to the other treasures they had found and the planned exhibition next year. He also questioned Zhu about Diao, wondering if he was all right. Zhu felt something was amiss but was not sure what. "Look, Professor, can we meet tomorrow evening? I have to fly somewhere for further follow-up with Yi and his team, but I do want to meet with you as soon as possible."

"Of course, General, let me know where and when."

"Good, it's settled; please wait for my call." He hoped that together they could understand more of what was behind the warnings they had received. He gave George his private number to contact him in the future.

Zhu spent a full day in meetings with other security personnel away from the capital. He had arranged to meet Yi and his key team leaders at nine that morning for a full update on the intelligence data received on terrorist activities and the warnings of potential attacks. Most of Yi's team arrived promptly; everyone knew Zhu was a stickler for timeliness. Yi and one of his assistants were not there but had sent their apologies. The note said they were in the city of Datong interviewing three individuals who had recently arrived there and were reported by neighbors regarding suspicious activity. Zhu was not happy with Yi's absence, which meant he was left with underlings to update him on their operations.

He called Yi directly on his cell phone in front of his officers, something that would send another message to Yi of how displeased he was. He was quite angry, and demanded that Yi meet him in Beijing at five thirty that same day. Yi told him it would be difficult, but when Zhu offered to pick him up by helicopter he declined the offer, indicating he could get what he needed done and be on his way early enough.

Zhu continued with the meetings, disappointed to hear from both his team and the local groups how limited information was at this stage. At the conclusion of the meeting he had a number of calls to make before heading back for the meeting with Yi in his office. He also needed to confirm arrangements for meeting later that same evening with George Mathers and asked his personal adjutant to track down Diao Lijun; he needed to talk to him urgently too.

George did not receive a call from Zhu until eight that evening asking him if he minded being picked up to travel to an undisclosed location; he said it was up to George if he wanted Xiao Ping and Cai Levee to come along too. George thanked him for offering to pick him up, but hoped this was not going to be a repeat of the first time they met when they were all bundled off to some mysterious site. Zhu laughed and reassured him that this time was different, but he still needed to keep the location a secret.

As George expected, Xiao Ping and Cai wanted to come along; they were still in the lab and had been coming up with some pretty wild ideas as to what might be going on. Both were especially concerned about the lack of contact from Diao.

Zhu wanting to see them late that evening indicated to George there might be more to it than just Diao's whereabouts. A van arrived to pick them up about a half hour later with two of Zhu's men in plain clothes presenting their ID cards. They explained how sorry they were to have to blindfold them again. They said they just needed to keep the building's location secret. The blindfolds were given to them to put on themselves; there was no hint of problems, easing Xiao Ping's concerns. The radio was turned on throughout the journey, supposedly for their comfort, but George suspected it was to mask outside sounds that might indicate where they were headed. They arrived within thirty minutes. George could sense that the van was in an underground parking area.

He felt that this was a different location than before. A number of sharp turns indicated that the underground parking area and the facility were deeper underground than the last one they had been dragged off to in Wuhan. Surprisingly, when they left the van and entered the elevator, they went down even farther instead of up. As soon as they exited the elevator the guards politely told George they could now remove their blindfolds. The three walked nervously down a long corridor decorated in such a manner that it could not be a military facility. They were led toward a conference room and as the guards opened the door General Zhu immediately rose to greet them.

His welcome was surprisingly warm, and he again apologized for the way he had brought them there. The political situation at the moment meant that he was unable to visit their lab at the university, and he told George he wanted to keep the meeting as private as possible. He began by asking about the note they had received. "I'm flattered it says you should trust only me, but have you any idea who authored the note?"

"Actually," George jokingly told him, "It had occurred to me that perhaps you were the Black Knight!"

"No, no really, I am not the source." He again asked everyone in the room to maintain the strictest confidence about what he was going to discuss. "If you cannot handle that then you are all at liberty to leave the building. Please think about it before answering." He left George to talk with the others and departed the room to arrange tea for everyone.

George knew this was a government building judging by the furnishings and decorations for officials at the highest level. Cai warned George that the meeting was clearly important to merit them being brought into a place like that.

"How do you two want me to respond to Zhu?" George asked.

Cai answered, "It's up to you, George, we're with you either way, but it's important to find out what's going on. If we stay out of it we may never know."

George nodded in agreement as Zhu returned with a female attendant who laid out tea for them. They sat through quite an elaborate tea ceremony before receiving their drinks. She was very pretty, and though efficient and courteous, was clearly not a member of the military. As she left, Zhu smiled at Cai, who was obviously admiring her looks.

"Gentlemen, and lady of course, I must explain that we are here under the protection of a certain high-level minister who needs to remain anonymous for the moment."

"We guessed as much, General. Whatever happens we're here to listen and help in any way we can. The note and Diao's disappearance are unsettling. We want to know what's going on."

Zhu began by outlining what he personally knew about the situation to date, recounting how Commander Yi explained to him that George's group had uncovered a second coffin and that arrangements had been made to work privately at the museum and at the university lab to translate the second group of dragon scales and their texts.

"Yi also told me of Diao's plan, with the approval of our leaders, to unveil a display next October at the Palace Museum, or the National Museum in Tiananmen Square commemorating the anniversary of the

People's Republic. This would include a display of the scales along with an emperor or ruler's robe you found in the second coffin. Nothing was going to be said about the special properties of the scales, but copies are being commissioned to go in the display."

As Zhu recounted this, George glanced at the others with raised eyes. It was becoming obvious what they were about to hear.

"Our recent conversation on the phone alarmed me when you mentioned a treasure. My assumption was the scales and robe were the treasure items, but my concerns rose when you mentioned Minister Wang Fan visiting Diao often to discuss the progress. Wang Fan is indeed the new minister of culture, but as so often happens in such appointments he was asked to remain in his current position until certain projects were completed. Those projects involve Wang Fan traveling extensively outside of the country. It does not seem to me that Wang Fan can have really visited you or Diao Lijun!"

George tried to recall the few dates they had met him. "Whenever we met this Wang Fan he always told us you said this or that, General, just as Yi did. They both told us you were tied up but still involved." As the three added other statements made to them, supposedly coming from Zhu, they watched him shake his head in disbelief.

"So, General, this points to an important question, who was the minister visiting with us? What does Yi have to say about it, and where the hell is Diao?"

"We'll come to that shortly. The other day I was advised that Commander Yi and his assistant were in Datong interviewing three terrorist suspects. I called Yi and arranged to have a meeting earlier this evening in preparation for ours." At that point Zhu began to show his anger. "Yi did not show up for the meeting, nor did his assistant. The cell phone line to Yi is dead, and no one can locate him. Calls to the top leader of the Palace Museum reveal little of what Diao has been working on. The only thing the leader was aware of is that Diao and three assistants are working on a new display that the cultural ministry is privately funding and cannot not be discussed publically."

"Didn't the leader think that was a little suspicious?" Xiao Ping asked.

"He admitted it was unusual, but had no reason to doubt Diao's integrity, or the military commander that accompanied Diao when the project was discussed. The museum was especially grateful that funding had been put in place through a separate group to cover the costs. He told me their own budget had become more difficult to control in recent years, even though museum attendance has grown."

"From your earlier words, General, there seems to be more to tell us. Can't we be told what's really going on here? Or maybe we can guess already?" George paused as Cai and Xiao Ping nodded their assent.

"Of course, bear with me. There are in my mind, a number of questions I need answers to as quickly as possible." Zhu began counting them on his fingers. "Is this a cover-up for the theft of certain relics? Is Diao involved in a crime or is he a victim? Who is posing as Wang Fan and is he connected to Diao, Yi or both? Where is Yi? Where is Diao? We need to get over to the museum ourselves and look around!"

"We must, General. There was more treasure than you could imagine in the second coffin."

When Cai Levee assured him the items were priceless compared to anything ever found in China, worth an unimaginable fortune, George saw Zhu visibly stiffen,

Xiao Ping mentioned that she had a preliminary set of photos of the treasure pieces. It was not complete, but would show what Diao had. She flushed a little when she admitted that Diao had asked for all copies of the files to be given to the museum to assure confidentiality, but she had kept one set.

Zhu waved his hand in a gesture of "no matter" to Xiao Ping and asked her to bring a copy with her in the morning, but not to show it unless he agreed the time was right. He was beginning to be suspicious of a circle outside of Diao and Yi. Zhu looked at George, and for the first time since they had known each other simply addressed him by his first name. "George, this is serious, we have a flagrant robbery of relics that belong to the nation of China. We cannot let this succeed. We must find out if Diao Lijun is a part of this. If I can get my hands on Commander Yi we will find out the answer to everything. One way or another." The way Zhu said "one way or another" with such a cold look in his eyes sent a shiver down George's spine. The question was where was Yi now, or Diao for that matter?

As the meeting finished the side door opened and a government official walked in. He had obviously been watching and listening all the time. He was not introduced formally, but the way Zhu greeted him indicated he was highly placed, possibly a senior Party official. He shook hands and apologized for listening in to their conversation; he told them he had not wanted them to feel intimidated by his presence.

"I have to thank you all for the information you've provided, Professor Mathers. China appreciates your friendship over the years and the work your organizations have done together with Cai Levee and the university, especially on your so-called dragon scales. I hope we can call upon you all to help resolve this issue and assist us in bringing any criminals to justice. It will not go unrecognized or unrewarded." George was surprised to hear that he knew about the work they were doing.

"Professor, I want to reassure you that your work on the dragon scales, whether they simply document legends or not, will be fully supported by the government. I can't say Zhu or I are believers, but we do recognize this may be another legend of great importance from the past." This was good for George and the others to hear, but as always the minister added the proviso that the leaders would vet whatever they planned to publish.

Zhu and the official said farewell to one another in a manner that told George they were extremely close. Whatever the official said quietly to Zhu, George gathered he was being told, in no uncertain terms, to get the case solved and to do it quickly. George agreed to meet Zhu at 7 a.m. next day at the Palace Museum to join in inspecting the area where Diao and his team were working. A team of forensic experts would look at the area with them but Zhu was not expecting to find much.

———— ⁓⁓ ————

An early meeting had been arranged with Diao's museum leader, Chen Xing, who was anxious to learn more about what was going on. The team arrived outside the Palace Museum private entry at seven the next morning. Chen was already waiting for them to arrive. Zhu came in minutes later with a small team of military people and local investigators. They were led into the museum facilities after a brief introduction between Chen and Zhu. Once everyone was in the reception area they were advised of the museum layout and the secured basement labs where Diao's team had been working, Zhu emphasized to all in attendance that they were part of a highly confidential investigation. All information and associated actions were viewed as extremely sensitive and anyone found leaking details without Zhu's approval faced serious disciplinary action, even prison.

Zhu was careful to direct his comments to everyone in attendance including George's team and Chen Xing, but especially the forensic specialists that were there. As they approached the lab area they passed by a female assistant troubled by the disappearance of Diao and his assistants. She had little to add to various questions they posed regarding the activities in Diao's section.

Zhu took the woman into Chen Xing's office to talk to her alone. She told him there had been much activity to and fro over recent months but she had no access to the lab area herself. She had handled a number of things for Diao, but never actually been inside. Plain-clothed security personnel had been in place these past months with access denied to all but a few people. There was no documented record of visitors, but she thought perhaps the new closed circuit security system might hold a visual record. She told Zhu the last security guard, who had been there for ten days, told her the security blanket was being lifted, but that the rooms were still to remain secured at all times. Zhu asked when the guard left and was told just four days earlier.

Zhu pulled a file from his briefcase, took three photos out, and laid them side-by-side on the desk. "Do you recognize any of these men?" He asked her to take her time, as she seemed very nervous.

"Why yes, of course. That is Commander Yi." She then pointed to another photo. "He's the last guard working here who told me the security operation was complete." The third photo took more time. She took off her glasses, reached into her desk, and pulled out a large magnifying glass. After a few moments of silence she declared that yes, it looked like the gentleman who had visited Diao on occasion recently with Commander Yi, but it wasn't him. She pointed out the similarities and the differences she saw in the photo.

"Miss Li, why is your memory so vivid regarding this individual?" Zhu asked.

"Well he seemed to me to be an especially good-looking man!" she said, blushing at the admittance of his attraction. He thanked her and told her there could be more questions later.

George asked Zhu afterwards what photos he had actually shown the assistant. He smiled. "The first one was Commander Yi. The second was the assistant who was supposedly with him interrogating three suspects in Datong the day before. And the third photo? Well that was the real Wang Fan, newly appointed minister of culture."

⚬⚬⚬

They entered the secured lab area with the help of a lock specialist on the team; investigators had not entered before for fear of damaging any of the artifacts. Chen had tried his master key, but clearly the locks had been changed. The switch likely occurred at the time Yi heightened the security arrangements in that section. When they finally walked into the area they were asked to place covers over their shoes and wear latex gloves to avoid disturbing any evidence. Cameras began to roll and some of the people were asked to wait outside; the area was not big enough for everyone. Within a few minutes one of the technicians, who was busily dusting for fingerprints, commented that all indications were the room had been cleaned of any prints. They would continue to look closely, hoping the criminals had made mistakes.

As areas were cleared, lockers and drawers were opened for inspection. Chen was able to identify a number of collections that were designated for different displays in the museum. Some of them held projects put on hold when Diao and the assistants began their "special project" work. The second large locker the officer opened contained deep drawers revealed the dragon scales that had been sent back by the military for storage. Zhu asked the technicians to dust them for prints. He hoped these would not have been wiped too.

Xiao Ping and Cai Levee wondered aloud why none of the scales had been taken despite their apparent value. Zhu smiled. "If you were a thief and didn't know what could be done with them versus some kind of real treasure that you did, what would you choose to steal?" George agreed it was an easy choice as they continued their search. One large locker remained unopened and was the most secure in the room. It took the experts longer to get it opened. Every drawer in the locker was bare.

Xiao Ping confirmed to Zhu that this locker could very easily have been the storage area for the relics. They left the team to finish their search activities and proceeded to unlock file cabinets to search for any documents that could shed some light.

As Xiao Ping and Cai Levee joined Chen Xing in the search, a technician came over and asked Zhu to look at an area by one of the flat metal tables. After a few moments of whispering between them, Zhu asked everyone to stay where they were. They were going to switch off all the lights in the lab for a while. As the room went dark, a couple of technicians with UV wand lights used them to carefully cover a couple of suspicious area.

After ten minutes one of the technicians advised that the lights could go on; they would continue their work after everyone left. Zhu talked to one of the technicians, who said they had found blood traces on the table and floor, even though it had obviously been wiped cleaned. He hoped they could find some DNA. It was seconds later that another technician came running over. Xiao Ping cringed as the officer told Zhu they had found part of someone's crushed small finger wedged in a gap near an inside table leg. How someone who severed the finger missed it in the clean up was a mystery, but the slit in the floor was likely the reason. Zhu smiled as if to say someone's carelessness could betray whom he or she was and he wanted the blood and finger trace analyzed immediately.

The search of the file cabinets produced nothing of value. Chen was able to identify all the materials in them except for the numerous files still there on the dragon scales, something Chen wanted more information on, as he had not been involved in those. Two drawers were completely empty, while every other file cabinet in the room was crammed. A quick check by a technician verified it was the only file cabinet in the area wiped thoroughly on the inside. With that Zhu ordered the teams to continue to do their work and plan on meeting first thing the next day to discuss their findings. He told Chen and George that they needed to talk separately and asked for a private area to meet in.

On the way to the room Zhu's phone rang and he motioned for them to pause while he answered the call. He finished the call telling the other party to have the report sent to him in Beijing by e-mail right away. They all sat down in Chen's conference room with Cai and Xiao looking inquisitively at Zhu. He said, "I've just been advised that Yi's assistant has been located outside of Datong. He's dead. Yi is nowhere to be found."

In Chen's office Zhu reviewed events so far. Chen seemed to know little; he had been busy with major exhibits and several overseas exchanges for museums abroad. George and Cai Levee reiterated all they knew since the discovery of the second coffin. They omitted the fact that Cai had retained a number of the items. They discussed the visits by Diao and on rare occasions Yi and the individual posing as Wang Fan. Xiao Ping had brought with her a hard drive copy of the photographs. They included most of the photos taken in the hotel room in Zhangjiajie and e-mailed to Diao. She pointed out that Diao had asked her to handover any copies at the time, which she had done, but she'd backed up a copy on her hard drive. Chen asked to see them if he could, and Zhu nodded to Xiao Ping, advising Chen that no copies at this stage were to be made or mentioned to anyone outside of the group without his permission.

They waited for a few minutes while Xiao Ping and Chen set up a computer and projected the images onto a large digital screen in the conference area of his large office. As Xiao Ping flipped through the pictures, Zhu sat quietly taking them in too; Chen became animated, uttering words of wonderment at what he was seeing. When Xiao Ping finished, she glanced at Cai, then confessed they had not been able to complete all of them by the time Diao arrived with Yi to organize the transfer. These were to be finished in Diao's lab with much higher quality equipment. Zhu asked Chen's opinion of the items and their possible value.

"I concur with Diao's original conjecture that many of the items pre-date anything anyone has seen, some before the Xia Dynasty. The items are of a quality and value that would have been available only at the imperial level and produced by the finest artisans of their time." Zhu asked what value Chen would place on this collection. "I've no idea what individual collectors might pay for any of these, but a single one of these pieces would see everyone in this room taken care of for the rest of their lives. They're that valuable!"

Chen proffered that no one group could afford to purchase all these items except the government. If indeed they had been stolen, they would likely be sold off to individual collectors, and only the very wealthiest could afford them. The question from Zhu was how Diao might be involved. He told them his biggest worry was finding Yi as soon as possible. The longer Yi was on the loose, the more difficult it was going to be to find him. If he had stolen the items, he had probably left China already.

"Even if Yi has fled the country," George remarked, "It would require time to get these items out. They can't be hidden in a couple of suitcases and taken on a plane. The relics could already be on their way to whatever safe location was planned for them, either here in China or overseas wherever the collectors are."

Chen responded quickly, "I must point out, Professor, that the type of articles we are talking about would find a huge market in the rising Asian markets. Because of their historical value they would be highly sought after by very rich Chinese collectors."

Xiao Ping said that with the right publicity about the theft, collectors would be disinclined to purchase them.

Chen waved that comment aside. "My dear, there are so many billionaires and millionaires in China these days that many of them have private collections no one ever gets to see. They purchase masterpieces and items like these on the black market all the time!"

Zhu finally brought the meeting to a close after asking Chen to provide him a list of dealers and collectors he thought might be open to buying these items. Chen looked a little nervous about providing this kind of information, but Zhu reassured him that the source of such information would never be revealed. He reminded Chen they were dealing with a national treasure here; it was his patriotic duty to help in any way he could.

As everyone prepared to leave Zhu said he wanted them to work with him on the investigation but on an informal basis. He was not sure how exactly to use them, but since they were so involved, he valued their comments and questions. George assured him they would help; nevertheless he wanted Zhu's commitment that while they continued to work on the dragon scripts project they not be cut out of the treasure side again. Zhu assured him then, if possible, he would support them in that regard. He gave each of them a private cell phone number to call if someone heard anything or had an idea that could help. He had already instigated an investigation into Yi's departmental activities and accounts. Finally, he promised to keep everyone posted as long as they kept their discussions confidential.

CHAPTER EIGHT

Zhu headed back to his office knowing that he wouldn't get much sleep over the next few weeks. Like many others in China, he maintained a small bed and washstand in his office for such times. His assistant, along with others flown in by helicopter from the Datong area, met him as he arrived. There were no pleasantries as Zhu waved them over to his conference table. The lead officer promptly laid out several photos of the dead soldier; he was immediately recognizable as Yi's assistant.

Zhu was surprised that no attempt had been made to hide the body or try to make it difficult to identify. "So Officer Li, do we know the cause of death? There seem to be no injuries to the body in your photos."

"Exactly, General, but Yi's assistant Chang, based on our review of medical records, has a history of heart problems over the last two years. He was hospitalized twice for heart related issues. The initial assumption is Chang suffered some kind of problem in that regard resulting in his death."

"Well, I'm not buying that, Li. " Zhu sat silently for a moment, remembering Chang was not discharged from the military for this health condition after the intervention of Commander Yi. With Zhu's approval he had been moved to an office-based position under Yi.

"The initial thought is that perhaps exposure to the field operation brought a stroke on. I must say, General, while the official report will state this assumption, a local military doctor provided a second opinion. He was not convinced and felt that more testing was needed. He suspects that the heart attack was induced by something either Chang took or was administered to him."

"I'm inclined to agree with him, Li. Yi is still missing. It's just too much of a coincidence. Where is Chang's body now?"

"His body was loaded onto the same helicopter we took and is being sent to the forensic department for examination. I trust these actions are satisfactory up to this point. When receive a full autopsy report I will inform you right away."

"You have done well, Li, I want this kept under wraps for now. Take personal charge of this for me and make sure they do a thorough autopsy. I'm convinced he was murdered. Off with you and make sure there are no delays with the autopsy. And thanks again; you've handled this well!"

The officer saluted and left the building, heading over to the hospital right away to reinforce Zhu's request and be the first one to communicate the results.

Zhu called in other personnel and began to list actions that needed to be taken right away. He wanted a thorough search of Yi's office and effects for anything suspicious as well as a review of Yi's bank accounts. All phones attributed to Yi at work and home were to be tapped including those of his family members. A thorough audit of the sector budget and expenditures that Yi managed for Zhu was to be performed. Photos of Yi, full medical records including DNA, and any travel records that covered his activities over the past six months were added to the list.

He selected two of his personnel and told them they needed to contact the civilian security branch involved in this incident to assist them in one more activity. He wanted them to get with the authorities and go through the manifestos and photos of every overseas flight that had taken off from China in the days following the disappearance of Yi. Until Diao Lijun was absolutely confirmed as dead he wanted them checking for him, as well as the supposed "look alike" for the real Wang Fan. This was a big task, but Zhu told them it had to be done, to concentrate on Beijing and Shanghai, but to check International flights as well.

The alert needed to be continued in case the suspects were still in the country and planning to flee in the weeks ahead. Zhu further suggested they focus on flights to major cities such as New York, Chicago, San Francisco, Paris, Zurich, and Hong Kong. He told them he suspected a robbery of certain relics, but did not identify what they were. His teams were also to maintain secrecy regarding the operation.

Zhu received a call from the minister for an update of the investigation; he appreciated the actions under way and offered additional resources - military and civilian - should Zhu need them. Zhu brought the minister up to date with the death of Officer Chang, his health history, and his suspicion that Yi had disposed of him because he knew too much. Although the evidence now made it clear this whole situation was indeed a robbery, the minister advised that the government was continuing to keep public attention away from it. Zhu thought that perhaps there was an effort to avoid any embarrassing situation if the relics were never successfully recovered. At any rate he could feel the pressure mounting to get to the bottom of it.

The next day Zhu received a full report from the forensic team at the Palace Museum revealing more of the planning that had gone into the theft. The cleaning of the facility had been done very professionally; except for the cupboards and tables where the relics may have been worked on, all other prints were accounted for.

"Were these people that good, Officer Wong?"

"Initially we thought that too, General, but we did finally find something I think you will be interested in."

"That's encouraging. What is it?"

"At first we determined all the prints that had not been wiped clean included all the known players, and of course Commander Yi's prints were there in other areas. One print in the cupboard has not been accounted for. It matches nothing on file either in military or civilian records. It's a thumbprint on one of the scale things. It was also confirmed not to be from anyone involved in the scale research project."

"Okay, we need to keep the print out there for future reference." Zhu wondered if this might turn out to be the Wang Fan impersonator, unlikely, but it had to be considered.

"It gets better, General. We retrieved samples of blood from one of the floor cracks. We are still working on them as they were contaminated by the cleaner used. As soon as we have a result one way or another, they will be calling it in."

"You call that better, Wong?"

"No sir, sorry sir. I meant much better. As you know, we found underneath one of the table legs a fragment from a crushed fingertip. The forensics work on the finger remnant is conclusive, General!"

"Is it Yi's?"

"No. It definitely came from Diao Lijun's right hand based on medical documents and a small area of the print that forensics could examine. The conclusion of forensics is the nail was pulled and the finger crushed severely.

"Anything more?"

"One of the older lab technicians thought it could be consistent with someone having been tortured for information, but this is purely speculative, General. Oh, and the specimen is fresh; it's not been there very long."

Zhu immediately thought this had the smell of his associate's handiwork. That type of activity fit well with Yi's methods. Maybe he had used them on Diao Lijun in order to complete the theft of the relics. The big question was whether Diao was still alive.

The officers had also checked the security system installed by Yi when the relics were moved into Diao Lijun's area of the museum, but the news had not been good; all data records had been wiped clean of everything. Experts were trying to see if there was any way to recover the deleted material. According to the specialists involved, whoever did it knew what they were doing. Zhu was disappointed to hear this, but not surprised. He saw Yi's skills all over this theft.

There was, however, some other news to report; apparently a private entry to Diao's area used by the people working in the lab was not connected to the security system that had been cleaned. They had managed to pull some data from the location and worked with Chen Xing at the museum to rule out known personnel and identify anyone with a questionable need to visit there. Wong laid out five photos on the desk to show Zhu. They were of Yi, his assistant Chang, and another figure who closely resembled Wang Fan with two well-dressed businessmen.

Zhu could see the pictures were not perfect but the lab was busy enhancing the images and confident they would have better ones for him to work with. In terms of the two businessmen, Chen Xing did not recognize either of them. The other interesting images on the system were those showing Diao's assistants frequently taking roll-along cases in and out of the lab. Zhu couldn't believe Yi missed wiping this system, but he had to find out if the assistants were all dead - or involved in the theft.

The museum forensic team had nothing new to come up with. The enhanced security views of the two businessmen and the Wang Fan imposter were available, and while not perfect, could help in identifying them. The photos had been shared with other agencies. The word was out that these individuals were the subject of an ongoing investigation and needed to be tracked down. Someone wondered aloud if, along with Yi's photo, they should be using official or unofficial channels to contact the FBI in the U.S. or Interpol in Europe. Zhu told them to hold off until they had more solid information to go on.

The investigative team looking into Yi's departmental and private accounts finally had information to provide when they met with Zhu.

The leader of the team seemed nervous, which told Zhu there was something in the report he was not likely to appreciate. He gestured for the man to sit. "Tell me whatever you have found, good or bad. Do not worry, facts are facts."

The leader passed sheets of records over to Zhu and began to outline what they had uncovered. "On the personal account side we have found nothing suspicious. Yi's lifestyle, outside of the benefits his position provides for his family, reveals nothing out of the ordinary. There are no large deposits in his personal accounts, nor are there any unusual payments to third parties outside of normal family expenses, restaurant bills, et cetera. Nothing to raise our suspicions over his lifestyle, sir."

"But there is something, and by the look on your faces it's serious."

"Yes, General. I am afraid you won't like this!"

"There's nothing I like about this whole matter, so just tell me what you've found!"

The team leader passed over a second batch of papers to Zhu. "We've discovered a number of irregularities in the accounts of Yi's departmental finances and expenses. What do you know, General, about an entity that his department established called "The China Relic Preservation Company?"

Zhu became slightly embarrassed realizing this was something he was not aware of. "I am aware the department was partially funding the work of a Professor Mathers. They were investigating certain special items along with another government agency. I'm embarrassed to tell you I do not recall the amounts; I assume this could be it."

The investigator shuffled nervously. "Regrettably, I don't think that is the case. This entity has only been established in recent months, and there are other entries covering the funding I think you are referring to."

Zhu reiterated that he was not aware of this entity and wanted to know how Yi could have established it without his knowledge. A further set of papers passed to Zhu showed that every authorization in the process and payment request system had his own signature and personal "chop", legal proof that Zhu, alongside Yi and Diao, were active principals in the entity. Another set of accounts passed to Zhu showed significant payments issued to various parties in the course of recent weeks, in total a substantial amount. Of course in terms of the very large budget that Zhu controlled, it could pass through without raising too many alarm bells.

It dawned on Zhu that his years of complete trust in Yi were ill-founded. He had been too free in approving expenditures based on Yi's review and assurances. On the other hand, he was absolutely sure he had no knowledge of these specific payments; otherwise, he would have questioned them at the month end reviews.

Zhu asked for a five-minute break before resuming the meeting, and returned to his office. There he went to his desk and unlocked the bottom right-hand drawer where his personal "chop" was stored. The carved chops, used for centuries in China were still deemed a legally binding commitment to any form of contract or payment.

Zhu extracted the box containing his military seal and returned to the meeting. He passed it unopened to someone in the team. He wanted to know if the seal used to chop the papers and requests was indeed his, or if a copy had been used. He had picked up the box out of the drawer using pieces of cleaning cloth, and asked them to check the box and seal for prints. Zhu asked for these checks to be done right away. The final task Zhu gave was to track down the companies in the accounts as soon as possible. He expected these entities would turn out to be bogus accounts, but they needed to be followed up on anyway.

The review of the seal and the documents came back quickly, confirming Zhu's suspicions that the seal used on the documents was a copy. There were only Zhu's prints on the seal itself and the elaborate box it was stored in, but they had found one part of a single print underneath that indicated the box had been wiped at some stage. The print area available to the technician matched a section of a print on file from Yi's small finger.

Any remaining doubts about Yi's involvement as the mastermind of this robbery, or being one of its leaders, disappeared when the team leader responsible for monitoring transportation out of China came in around 6 p.m. with new information for Zhu. A report from the civilian services indicated that a person resembling Yi had been seen at Beijing's Capital Airport on the day Yi claimed to be in Datong. Yi had apparently left Beijing that day on a United Flight 851 for Chicago, flying under the name and passport of a Mr. Shane Shi. Surveillance cameras showed him in the airport going through customs and security. All of his documents had passed inspection with no red flags raised to security personnel. Under this alias, Yi flew economy rather than business or first class, likely helping him to melt into the crowd rather than be remembered. The ticket was paid for in cash according to Air China, the sister carrier for the flight; the address given by the purchaser was the Kempinski Hotel, Room 1302, in Beijing.

This turned out to be false, as was the phone number left with the airline in case of schedule changes. The ticket itself had been one way. Yi was also spotted on one of the surveillance cameras in the restaurant area on the departure level. He could be seen talking with someone briefly, but enough to make the analyst suspicious. After enhancement and enlargement, the man looked like Wang Fang. This led the team to further review the security records; they came up with a passenger name whose pictures seemed to be him. He had flown to Hong Kong and on to Zurich, but not on the same day. His passport had already been run through the system and was, as expected, false. The photo and name was sent to Zurich police, where the Beijing civilian police had good connections. They were hopeful fingerprinting of foreign nationals on arrival might generate something for them to follow up on.

"What information do we have on this Shane Shi? Is it a fake identity too?" Zhu asked,

"We have not approached authorities in the U.S. at this stage, but we did call the specialists in our own embassy there to make informal inquiries. Our contact in passport control tells us that Shane Shi is registered as Taiwanese. His China visa is multiple entry with a business work visa showing a green card and address in the U.S."

"So we know where to find him. That's promising!"

"Yes, General, it was quite easy to obtain an address and phone number. The embassy arranged for one of their personnel in the Chicago consulate to travel to the address and check out the occupants."

"How can you take action like this without talking to me first? Something like this could have disastrous results! I want Yi to think that we still don't know he has left China!"

"So sorry, General, it will never happen again under my watch. Our colleague from the embassy only knew there was a visa issue involved, that was all. He drove right away to the address on file that was confirmed by telephone records. When he was sure there was no sign of anyone answering Yi's description in sight he knocked on the door of the home. It's in someplace called Lincoln Park in downtown Chicago. He simply asked to see this Shane Shi."

"Was anyone there?"

"Well, first a woman answered the door. When advised he was from the Chinese Embassy to meet with her husband, she immediately asked if they had found his passport. He reported it stolen three months earlier. She described how concerned her husband had been because of the work visa for China in the passport, as well as the problems he had obtaining a green card to stay in the U.S."

"He didn't believe her story, did he? I hope he didn't expose us."

"The Chinese representative apologized and told the wife he had no news but perhaps he could talk to her husband directly. She said her husband was in the hospital and would not be home until the weekend. He had been sick for several months on disability and the doctors were still unsure what his problem was."

"Sounds like a story to me, Officer!"

"No, General, our man was smart enough to follow through. He offered apologies for bothering her and assured her there would be no future problem for her husband's China visa issues. He left and visited the hospital right away; he was able to confirm the wife's story."

"So somehow Yi found a group or organization that stole the real Shane Shi's passport and presumably modified it with Yi's photograph."

"Exactly, sir. The consulate in Chicago has asked if our people in Beijing need any more follow-up. We've told them to hold off for now."

Yi clearly was in the U.S., but Zhu did not want him alerted to the fact that they were on his trail. If they were going to track him down they might still need help from the U.S. authorities, but Zhu was not ready to involve them yet.

CHAPTER NINE

The following morning two officers arrived to be interviewed by Zhu and his key lieutenants running the investigating teams. The officers had been guarding the lab prior to Yi's assistant taking over. It took a couple of days to reach them as Yi had reassigned them to other projects in the western province of Xinjiang. Their stories were quite similar. Both were part of the original team that traveled to Zhangjiajie with Yi and Diao Lijun to pick up certain items and bring the locked trunks back. Neither was aware what was inside the trunks and were told at the time not to try to find out. They had assumed all along it was something of value and related to history since it was to be kept in the Palace Museum.

They confirmed that in the last months the three assistants in the lab traveled frequently and each time carried small cases, locked and cuffed to their wrists. They never knew where the assistants were headed; they simply checked them in and out of the area. Yi told them to make sure they passed through the detector and were carrying no objects on their persons, and that the cases did not require inspection if locked. They said Diao Lijun spent most of his time there, and also that the man in the photos showed to them was introduced as Minister Wang Fan; Fan visited the museum some three months earlier but infrequently. One of them had seen the two businessmen in the photos; he said they always arrived with Yi and he was told there was no need to register them in the visitor log.

After the two officers left the meeting, Zhu asked for full searches of the homes of the men who guarded the lab for anything that might help the investigation. It was time for Zhu to update the minister again; Zhu had growing concerns about the investigation before finally speaking to the minister between his meetings.

Zhu quickly outlined the latest developments and also broached the subject of possibly involving the Americans in the hunt for Yi. The minister was opposed to the ide.

"Not now, Zhu. You are doing fine. We have our own people who can continue the search for Yi there. Someone will call you soon for more information and he will contact the embassy in Washington. They will take it from there."

"As you wish, Minister, but finding him is critical. Also, I have to say this whole affair is outside my sphere of responsibilities after all, intelligence and security is what I'm supposed to be doing. This is not my work. There's no more military interest in the scales. What do I have to do with this treasure business?"

"I understand your feelings, Zhu, but the Party has faith in your capabilities. You are not getting younger; the Party has your future in mind too. You need to trust them in this matter Zhu, it's for the best, believe me."

"I do trust the Party, and I appreciate its concern for my well-being, but this case needs more involvement by civilian police with more resources on that side. If I am to be involved, though, I need full control, and I don't imagine the Beijing police would enjoy taking direction from me."

"I understand your concerns; leave it with me and I will talk to others. We'll find someone for you to work with who can be trusted.'

"Thank you, Minister. But please get back to me soon. The local police we've contacted so far are asking a lot of questions we can't answer right now."

"Understood. Give me a few days, old friend."

Zhu requested a meeting the next day with Chen Xing from the museum and George Mathers to discuss developments. They met in the conference room where Zhu worked after George and Chen were searched and cleared for entry. Zhu began to bring them up to date. "This investigation now involves robbery and murder, as well as a host of smaller charges related to falsifying passports and documents. These crimes will easily lead to the death penalty for the perpetrators. Take a look at these photos." George and Chen studied the photos Zhu put in front of them, but neither knew who the two businessmen were.

"I only met this Wang Fan once, I'm afraid. What about you Chen?" George asked.

"Diao never introduced us. I do know Wang Fan, of course, at my level. All I can say is the man in the photo does look like him."

"What about all this activity by the assistants, Chen? Did you review the paperwork I sent you from Yi's area?" Zhu asked.

"Yes, I did, General. My guess, based on this so-called Cultural Relic Preservation Company information and the photos of the assistants going in and out of the palace, is that Diao and Yi were either having the items worked on or copied. Based on the payments by your Relics Company, my view is they must have been having copies of items made, not just expert reviews."

"Don't you think these payments seem high for copies?" George asked, "Not really. The level of payment amounts would bring me to assume the companies involved were making extremely high quality ones. Perhaps the two businessmen here are with the companies involved, or part of the theft, maybe even potential buyers for the relics."

"You may be right, Chen, " George said. "It's still a mystery in respect to Diao though, and whether he's a victim or not. I'll continue to reserve judgment until more is known, but I struggle to believe he's involved in this. We need to track down who the Cultural Relic contracts are with and somehow find Yi as quickly as possible."

Zhu nodded in agreement, clearly frustrated at his lack of progress in finding Yi.

"Yes, we are very concerned. The trail is starting to run cold over in the U.S. The only way to work that angle may be to involve the Americans without causing any embarrassment to our side. I've talked to the minister about involving them directly but he won't permit it for now. We've tracked him through our people to Chicago, but the trail has died. He did not accomplish this on his own, I'm sure of that. He's had some very professional or underworld help in this."

Chen said he could begin contacting companies he felt had the capability to make high quality copies of the relics.

Zhu thought it was unlikely they would learn too much from them, other than whether the pieces had been duplicated or not. Chen doubted they could have all been completed based on the time that would be needed. More important was to discover if the two businessmen in the photos were with these companies or were known to be fences for stolen antiquities.

Zhu said the authorities planned to put a story out to the Party about Yi being involved in an internal scandal in the military, committing a potentially treasonous act before fleeing his position. The story would say he was last spotted in Shanxi province, that the suspect was still in China and actively being sought by the authorities. Zhu wanted to keep the knowledge that Yi was somewhere in the U.S. quiet for the time being, hoping security systems could monitor some contact by him.

As regards Diao Lijun, there were still opinions either way. Zhu erred on him being alive but still suspected the evidence was planted to mask his involvement. George and Chen told him they were sure Diao was a victim. He was more likely dead, like Yi's assistant. At best they hoped he was being held hostage.

George's cell phone rang as the meeting came to a close. It was Xiao Ping. She asked if he could talk or was still in the meeting. She told him she had important news if the line was safe to use. Zhu advised against it, and they were led away to a locked area controlled by a security guard; inside were three soundproof meeting rooms with secure outside lines. George used the speakerphone. Xiao Ping said another confidential message had been received that morning, after he left for the meeting with Chen and Zhu.

"Go ahead, Xiao Ping. We're all listening."

"Good morning, everyone. Sorry to bother you but I think it's important. We've received another of our mysterious contacts from the Black Knight. It's as brief as ever. It was slipped under the lab door, and no one saw who delivered it."

Zhu asked her to read it.

"Okay, it's addressed to Professor Mathers. It says, 'The objects of your search are still in China and intact. Yi is in the U.S. and making arrangements for their next step. You may have to enlist the Americans help. You need to find him. He's the key but not the mastermind."

Zhu wondered aloud if Diao would turn out to be that person, voicing his frustration in terms of who this so-called "Black Knight" was and how he knew what was going on. George wondered if the source was a step behind them, working from leaked information, or a step ahead?

"Is he here in Beijing or will he turn out to be some international spy or official? Is he a friend or foe of China? Is he even Chinese?" Zhu mused to the others. George shook his head. He had wondered before if it might even have be Zhu until confident he was not.

Xiao Ping made one last comment before ringing off. "Based on what I've seen of these messages in the past and the way the current one reads, I feel sure he's Chinese or at least a friend of China in many ways."

George could sense Zhu's growing frustration with the constant challenges from outside agencies and countries. "You know," Zhu said, "I raised my concerns with our minister friend and discussed contacting the Americans, but that sort of cooperation is not approved for the time being. In any event we know there is much to do in China, assuming the relics really are still here."

"If others are involved with Yi, the question is who and where they are." George said.

—— ⚬❀⚬ ——

George and Chen were about to leave later in the day when Zhu received an e-mail addressed directly to him claiming to be from Yi. It said Yi was in a hidden location in China but that Zhu would never find him.

"Listen to this, everyone! The timing with your communication is suspicious, but at last things are starting to move. It seems Yi has seen our internal documents circulating through military and civilian channels. He knows we are looking for him, but assures me we won't find him."

"What does he want then, General?" George asked,

"He claims his group has a very simple request that needs to be followed if the nation wants to see the treasure again. They know the relics are priceless but he says they are offered to the Chinese Nation at a bargain price, only one billion dollars. Can you believe that? He wants the monies to be transferred to several accounts, which will be identified at a later date, as will the method of transmission."

Zhu paused and George said, "What if the government refuses to pay that kind of ransom?"

"It says that if the government refuses their demands, the relics will not be disposed of on the black market as they are. They claim there is enough gold and precious jewels worth millions to be recycled from the relics. The choice is up to the government. Yi is giving me forty-eight hours to review the matter with our officials and respond."

"That's not much time," George said. "How do you get back to them? Is there a clue to help track them down?"

"They say we have to place an article in the China Daily under the title Ancient Relics; the article is to say that recent discoveries of ancient relics in Beijing are currently under review by the Palace Museum for authenticity."

"If there is no article?"

"Then Yi and his group will proceed with recycling them. The items will be lost forever in their present form."

Zhu asked Chen Xing if he thought it made any sense to recycle the items or was Yi bluffing. Chen thought it made no sense to ruin the pieces; there was just too much value in them based on their historical value, even on the black market.

"It's certainly possible to break a lot of them down into their valuable components." Said Chen. "Both Xiao Ping and I could see where their components would be worth a tremendous amount of money. She remembers that one of the jewels is set in a bracelet that's bigger than anything she's ever seen; the heavy bracelet in its entirety was solid gold."

Chen added that the sight of that one piece alone might turn someone into a crook, but commented that this entire operation must have come together quickly.

Zhu agreed. "As far as I'm concerned Yi did not drive this, even though he's heavily involved. As his mentor I know him better than anyone. Yi does not have it in him to fully plan and develop this robbery. He likely introduced the idea to someone with experience. I've assigned one of my investigators and their civilian counterpart to scour Yi's background and work experience for any underworld connections."

Zhu indicated to George and Chen Xing that he was talking to the authorities regarding the ransom being placed on the relics, but doubted they would agree until they figured out the next steps. "I've recommended we not reply in forty-eight hours. I expect another warning or two at least. The timing is critical in finding Yi and the goods."

CHAPTER TEN

Chen Xing requested an urgent meeting with Zhu. George was also invited and this time Cai Levee came along too. When everyone was finally together they could see Chen was excited, obviously quite proud of himself about whatever he had uncovered. Zhu told him to slow down, to explain carefully what he had found.

Chen told them he had ordered a thorough search of Diao's lab again, as well as all the support files maintained in a secure document area separate from the lab. One of the officers in the meeting indicated they had already searched the lab and found nothing helpful, but was clearly nervous that Chen might have found something this team had missed.

"You are right, officer. I agree that indeed nothing was found where you searched, but in the other document area someone misfiled a document that I was sure of interest and I followed up on it."

"I hope you have done nothing, Chen, to alert others and warn them off somehow!" Zhu said. "No one here is to go off his own tact without first contacting me or my lead investigators!"

Chen became very quiet and his face reddened. He apologized profusely for taking matters in his own hands and hoped he had in no way compromised the operation. Zhu visibly calmed. "I will be the judge of that, this is a very critical time and communication at every step is critical."

Chen began to tell them what he had discovered. "I asked my staff to search through all of Diao's back-up files in the secure document vault for anything related to contracts the Palace Museum had with antique merchants, sellers, auction houses, or specialists in renovations in the last six months. In the search we came across many different companies that the museum worked with. We searched in particular for any reference to the so-called China Relic Preservation Group."

Chen told them he thought one particular document looked suspicious, a blank folder titled "Potential Qualified Sources"; inside was a sheet of paper headed "Proposed Companies." "There were five companies listed but one company had a line through it with a note by the side saying the company was not to be used. The date of the handwritten note is this year and fits within the time period after the relics were installed in the museum." When Chen mentioned he had phoned each one of the companies Zhu shook his head. Chen immediately tried to put everyone's fears at rest, assuring them he was convinced no harm had been done.

"I'm sorry, but all I did was locate each of the companies on the list in my role at the Palace Museum. I contacted the owner of each company to check if they had contracts with the museum over the last few months. All of them asked where Diao Lijun was as they had not heard from him for a while. Four of them confirmed they had contracts with the China Relics Preservation Company. They understood this company was working on behalf of the museum and hoped their work had been well received. They also promised to continue to maintain confidentiality."

"What about the fifth company?" Zhu asked, impatient. "I did make contact with the fifth company on the list. They acknowledged they had been contacted in confidence about the project, but for reasons they could not understand had been rejected." Chen then provided everyone with detailed copies of the list and what he knew about each of the companies. All were deemed highly reputable and had worked for the museum in the past. Chen could not understand why the one company had been rejected. Zhu softened his attitude to Chen, who was clearly troubled. He thanked him for his efforts; and said he hoped Chen had not compromised the investigation.

Zhu asked Chen to take no further action on the listed companies without talking to him. Then he asked one of his officers to call the company owners in for meetings. Chen pointed out to everyone that none of the companies seemed to know others were involved. The work was definitely being parceled out to multiple companies.

Throughout the following day each of the four company owners was brought in for questioning. Each had the same story to tell and brought copies of their contracts with the China Relics Preservation Group. They related being told the project was to be kept confidential and went over the contract penalties for disclosure. They had all honored that commitment to date, payments had been received promptly for their work, and they were happy to have been involved. They wanted to know why they were being called in to be questioned in this manner. What was happening with the project itself? Could they now talk publically about their work?

Zhu told each one they were invited because of accounting irregularities under review, and that this meeting was strictly confidential until further notice. Each brought details of the individual items he had duplicated, still in the dark that other companies were involved. Zhu wondered nonetheless how much longer the information surrounding this case would remain out of the public eye.

As part of their meeting Zhu's team showed each owner the photos of people involved in the contracts - Diao Lijun, Yi, the assistants from the Palace Museum, and the military people used by Yi. All the photos were confirmed as being people they had seen or met at some point, each of the companies dealt with individual associates from the palace team for continuity and were visited independently by Yi. They were shown photos of the two businessmen accompanying Yi to the museum. One company owner thought one of them looked familiar, but could not place him.

Zhu called for the company that had been rejected to be brought in last. When the owner arrived Zhu had to put him at ease that he was not under any suspicion of criminal activity. The man seemed nervous with something to hide, but how far Zhu would pursue that depended on what he heard.

The owner, Mr. Yang Guiyu, was the fourth generation of the Yang family involved in the antique and restoration business, Yang Antiquaries and Restorations. They had been in business in Beijing since the 1800s. Yang was a small man, slightly balding, who despite his nervousness quickly impressed Zhu with his knowledge of antiques. His family business had survived through good times, but also had somehow scraped through the devastating periods of the colonial powers' plunder of Beijing and the Cultural Revolution. Yang knew the business side of the world of relics, its players, suppliers, and buyers better than any of others Zhu had talked to. This was so evident to Zhu it concerned him as to why Yang had not been chosen by Diao and Yi. Were they too knowledgeable perhaps?

In responding to Zhu, Yang outlined how Yi and Diao approached him in respect to a potential contract to duplicate certain ancient relics as close to museum quality as possible. "My former associate and I met a couple of times, both with Yi and Diao Lijun; then my associate held a second meeting with Yi only. I was out of the country at the time for an auction at Sotheby's in London. We were given a draft contract to look at without being allowed to see any of the pieces."

"And you or your associate were not interested in this opportunity? Was there any reason they did not award you any business?"

"Frankly, General Zhu, I did not like some of the legal terms. The payment terms were very good and I'm sure some company would jump at them. I wasn't too happy when my associate did not progress with Yi on the negotiations. In the end both parties declined to move forward on any agreement."

"Was there anything else that seemed strange about this arrangement to you?"

"To be honest I was nervous about this Yi character. I asked why the military was involved. I hope I do not offend you by saying I did not like the threats regarding keeping our discussions confidential in the future, even though no contract was signed. We are after all a business with a reputation beyond reproach, General."

"There are accounting irregularities at the museum and I've been asked to help the authorities. I appreciate your assistance and your willingness to hold our discussions in confidence." Zhu said, and then laid out the surveillance photos as he had done with the other four companies. Yang confirmed Diao and Yi were the only participants in the meetings. He knew Diao Lijun from various functions in the antique world and had cooperated in the past with him on certain projects. When Zhu showed Yang the pictures of the two businessmen with Yi at the Palace Museum lab, an expression of surprise spread across Yang's face.

"I recognize both men, of course, sir." Pointing to the tall man on the left he told Zhu that was Liu Ming, his associate manager and buyer. He had resigned just a few days after the meetings with Yi about the project. Zhu noted that the date stamp on the photo was after Yang's company had been turned down.

"Where is this Liu Ming now? Have you any idea?"

"I can only tell you what he told me. He said he was taking a break for six months and touring the world. If he came across any interesting items he would let me know. General, he has money. He made a small fortune in his own work over the years with our company. I tried to dissuade him from leaving. In the end I assured Liu a position would always be available for him."

One of Zhu's men immediately rose and nodded to him as he left the room. Clearly he knew they needed to find Liu without Zhu having to tell him.

Yang sat back with his finger on the picture of the second man. Zhu detected a sinister look on his face.

"I'm surprised no one here in the room recognizes this man either," Yang told his audience,

"We refused many years ago to do business with him. Let me think. Yes, that would have been when Liu Ming first joined us after completing his degree at Tsinghua University in antiquities. He must be in police files somewhere, definitely in Hong Kong where he comes from."

Zhu looked around the room at his men; his look said everything. How had his researchers missed this? It told him he needed civilian police working with him more than ever. He would need to call the minister again.

"So who is he?" Zhu asked.

"He's among the higher ups in one of the Triad groups over there. Definitely not a 'Dragon Master' as the top Triad leaders are called, but very close to the top. I can't remember his real name, Wang something or other. I do recall him being very knowledgeable about antiques and trying to get me to buy some old pieces of imperial jewelry from the Ming Dynasty. I declined as I suspected they were stolen. The price was too high anyway for my business to handle at that time."

"How do you know the man is with one of the Triad organizations?" Zhu asked,

"There is no doubt for me. He turned quite hostile when I turned him down. He made a veiled threat against my future business, said that I may need protection, which only his organization could guarantee. Wang's accent was clearly from Hong Kong. His manner was quite like that of a gangster. Now that I think about it, Liu warned me about turning Wang down. He suggested we try to work something out, but I still refused. I expected some kind of retribution from the affair, but nothing transpired."

"Do you think Liu and Wang did business together in the past without you knowing?"

"That's possible I suppose, General, but since Liu sometimes had his own separate deals it would have been hard to know for sure. Until now I suspected nothing, depending of course on what this meeting is really about."

Zhu excused himself and left to ask one of his men to get the civilian police and to communicate directly with the Organized Crime and Triad Bureau in Hong Kong. They needed to identify this Wang figure and track him down.

Zhu thanked Yang on his return for the input and asked him if he would be prepared to assist the authorities in a serious matter requiring absolute secrecy for a while. If he were willing Zhu would clear it with the authorities and meet with him and others again later that day. Zhu liked Yang. He seemed to him a more traditional Chinese in terms of guarding his honor and the incorruptibility of his company and its business ethics. No doubt he always drove hard bargains and was an excellent negotiator, but he seemed to be the type who would not knowingly cheat in his business dealings or his life.

Yang readily agreed to help, at this stage Zhu limited the amount of information being given to him, but was sure he could help the investigation.

CHAPTER ELEVEN

In Beijing Zhu had not responded for two days to the ransom request. The next morning an e-mail advised he had twenty-four hours to respond before the destruction and piecing out of the treasure items would begin. To show they were serious, a series of attached digital photos showed a large gold head band with gemstones around the outside in a unique design being taken apart carefully. The gold was then melted into a block, the individual gems lay out on a large jeweler's tray, and some large ones were shown mounted in presentation boxes. A further attachment showed a receipt for the items with certain information blocked out; the purchase figure of seven and a half million was circled for emphasis.

The e-mail said twenty-four hours was their limit of patience; buyers were now in line and it was up to the Chinese authorities to decide if they wanted to preserve the historical value of the relics. Zhu called Chen, along with George, Cai, and Xiao Ping to come over to his office immediately to study the photos and determine if they were genuine. Meanwhile he directed his cyber team to track where the e-mail may have come from. It was the only lead to the whereabouts of the thieves and the relics.

As soon as George and the others arrived, Zhu put the e-mail up on the main screen in the large conference room; Xiao Ping readily identified the piece. Zhu flipped through the photos showing the disassembly of the piece. Chen became very animated at the loss of such a piece of history. It was worth far more as an untouched piece than these people had seemingly sold it off for.

Zhu had thought a lot about their recent meetings and already made the decision to expand their group by inviting Yang, the antiquarian, to join the team. He felt Yang had access to the markets for these items, and he was a potential conduit into the black side of the business. He suspected Yang might be able to lead them to either a customer or a fence for these items, if the worst-case scenario did transpire.

He expressed these thoughts to Xiao Ping and Cai Levee in the meeting and they both agreed that this was a logical approach. Chen Xing told them he knew Yang Guiyu; he was an honorable man who he was sure would help all he could. The fact that somehow the Triad organizations were involved in this was alarming. Zhu knew their reputation for being able to reach out far and wide, not just in Hong Kong and Mainland China but also well into the heartland of the U.S. where Yi was hiding.

⊷∞∞⊷

Yang arrived back at headquarters as requested, a little flustered from fighting Beijing traffic; an accident on the third ring road had caused a forty-minute holdup. Zhu told Yang he had approval at ministerial level to talk to him about assisting in the recovery of a treasure of historical value that needed to be kept confidential for the time being.

"General, I'm sure you do not take me for a fool. I suspected something important was at the bottom of this!"

Zhu already had a formal document prepared for him on the conference room table; he slid it across to Yang and asked him to review and sign at the end.

Yang read through it quickly. "Signing such a document is not necessary, the word of my company and ancestors has always been good enough in my world, but if it makes your friends in the Party more comfortable I will sign it. I do hope, however, my services in this matter will somehow be rewarded in the future." Yang smiled slightly as he made his subtle request.

"I can assure you, Yang, the minister involved has told me to pass along the comment that your help will not go unnoticed. They are sure that the business of the Yang family will benefit in the future." Zhu knew how to handle Yang in this typical kind of agreement that Yang would understand could one day open a high level door, or render special assistance in some future matter for him.

Zhu brought Yang up to speed quickly. Chen finally leaned across the table and spread the photos of the first damaged piece. Xiao Ping at the same time passed him photos of the many pieces she had originally photographed.

"Frankly, everyone, I'm surprised to find out there are more relics at issue than I was aware of and that four companies have been copying them already. I agree these relics are amazing! Incredible! It's shocking to me to think they could all be damaged this way."

"I think we all agree with that, " Zhu said. But for me a billion dollars ransom request is very steep. I don't trust criminal forces as dangerous as the Triads if they are involved."

" Not steep, General, not at all! Of that you and our government can be sure. I agree with the observations of Mr. Cai and everyone. The potential buyers for these items at their price levels may be limited, but there are many rich private collectors today who would jump at the chance to own these. That may help us!" He studied the pictures on Zhu's computer screen in more detail and after some time indicated that he too believed the photos were not faked. The invoice in particular was genuine even though certain names and addresses were blanked out.

"Interesting, yes, most interesting. The format of the invoice is familiar, but I suspect the purchaser and not the seller generated this.

There is something familiar about it, but I can't put my finger on it right now."

He asked for copies to take back with him to compare with some of his invoices on file and make some calls. "The array of jewels they are threatening to sell would appeal to specific buyers who are very private in their dealings. I need, with your permission, General, to make some calls on that too."

Zhu reluctantly agreed to Yang making discreet enquiries, but cautioned him to be careful. He then drafted an e-mail response to the ransom note indicating the authorities had given him basic approval to negotiate an agreement to purchase the relics. It would only be on the basis that no more of these national treasures be adulterated and must include any copies made. The government considered the billion-dollar figure extreme. but was prepared to compensate the parties with a transfer of $500 million, on the understanding that the exchange be entirely confidential and completed within thirty days.

Zhu told everyone the authorities were ready to deal with the thieves but were still trying to buy as much time as they could. He expected this could result in further relics being destroyed but for "face saving" they needed to achieve something from the negotiation.

While everyone in the room, especially Chen and Yang, was alarmed at the prospect of losing more relics from the collection, the instructions from the authorities were clear and would have to be followed. Once Zhu finally hit the send button, cyber teams continued their efforts to track where the e-mail was going. They needed to move quickly knowing how difficult it would be with the blackmailing party using servers and networks through multiple locations. No one had illusions of a successful outcome; the perpetrators had money and apparently a high level of technical expertise at their disposal.

Within thirty minutes of the e-mail going out the cyber team leader came in to the meeting shaking his head in frustration. He said the e-mail had bounced out to servers in eight countries including China and the U.S.; many of them were obvious decoys to bog the trackers down.

They would continue their work but his prognosis was that by the time they could unravel this knot the criminals would have moved. It could be done eventually, but time was against them.

Yang gathered copies of the information he needed and left for his main office to begin searching his files for potential buyers. George drove the others back to the university to await further developments. Chen remained with Zhu trying to persuade him they could risk no more breakup of the collection.

CHAPTER TWELVE

George received a call from Zhu with an update. The news was not good. The response from the thieves included photos of a second piece disassembled into its respective parts, but this time in a way that it could be reassembled if needed. Zhu told him the billion-dollar demand was unchanged. Within twenty-four hours they would provide fresh photos of additional objects. They would all be in parts by that time. The deal would be off the table, and the relics would be shipped out, lost to history forever.

The others in the lab could see the concerned expression on George's face as he hung up and brought them up to speed. "Zhu is waiting until later today before sending off a response that they expect no further damage to any of the pieces or the deal will be off anyway. They'll agree to the billion dollars subject to agreement on how this was to be handled. The money would not be transferred before inspection of the goods by experts."

Cai spoke first. "Isn't it obvious to the thieves that Zhu is trying to pull them out into the open and then grab them?"

"Most likely it is, but the perpetrators are at liberty to determine how and where this will happen. Hopefully they'll reach an agreement and the trade will go ahead as planned."

Xiao Ping said she thought Zhu was getting frustrated with the lack of progress in the affair. "The poor man is working closely with the civilian police, his area of expertise is on the military side. Everyone seems happy to leave all the responsibility to him. If the operation fails Zhu will take the blame."

George answered another call, smiled briefly, and then turned to the others. "Let's go! Yang Guiyu left an urgent message to meet right away. Zhu thinks they might have a break!"

Zhu had to slow Yang down when he arrived and began to tell everyone what he had uncovered. George's Chinese was good, but not when someone was as excited as Yang.

"I went back through my records looking over sales invoices to see if any of the layouts or odd handwritten comments matched in any way. " Yang said. "I found four potential purchasers I have dealt with, but worked with Liu Ming as well. I placed calls to each one and talked for some time, before asking if they had purchased any precious jewels and metals recently."

Zhu grimaced.

"Don't worry General, I used the excuse that I had come into some items to offer at a low price, provided they could keep it confidential. Two of the buyers were ruled out as they were not in the market and claimed they hadn't bought anything in the last few months; capital is tight right now. Of the other two only one in my mind fits the profile of someone with the capacity to have handled it."

"What makes you think, that Yang?" George asked,

"His obvious hesitation, his excuse for not being interested in talking to me because he had made a large investment recently. I believe I've found the right one. Once I told him I had access to high quality items and could deliver them at a low price his greed overcame any reservations he may have had. I've arranged to meet him to discuss a potential sale and agreed to go to his house to meet him privately."

Zhu shook his head and pointed out how dangerous that could be to the operation, that Yang should have called him first, then sighed and waved his hand as if it was too late anyway. "Please continue," he said.

"The potential buyer's name is Deng An. He's an industrialist, made a fortune in steel over the last twenty or more years since the opening up of China. He's now retired. The company he founded was acquired and through various stages of consolidation through the years has become a part of China's largest steel producing entity. Deng survived his time in industry without any stain on his reputation as regards illegal activities or corruption - so far, that is. He used his relationships wisely to amass a fortune, which he is now expanding through investments and trading in the world of art and antiques. His wife of forty years is a jewelry expert and collector; he told me he just made a major purchase of jewels for an anniversary gift to her. He might consider other items if the price is right!"

"What else are you not telling me Yang?" Zhu asked as Yang's face reddened and he shifted nervously in his seat.

"Well, General, I'm sorry I didn't call you but I had him stop by my store this morning."

Zhu leapt to his feet unable to contain his anger. George and Cai Levee held his arms briefly to calm him, "What in the name of whomever got into you, Yang? Why would you do such a thing without calling me? Does no one in this room listen to me?" He slammed the desk with his oversize fist, the room echoing from the sound. Yang seemed to cower as if he was about to be hit across the face. It took a few minutes for Zhu to calm down and apologize for overreacting. He was learning daily he was no longer running a military operation.

"Go on Yang, tell us what happened," George interjected, trying to get the meeting back on track.

"My humblest apologies, General. I meant no disrespect. Let me finish, please. Perhaps you will be happier with me than you are now. I asked Deng this morning if he could come to my office to see the collection. I reiterated that I had something very special and attractively priced for him to consider. I told him I wanted to make sure that the stones I had to offer were not from the same seller. And guess what happened, General?"

"I have no idea, Yang!"

"Deng noticed all the photos of important customers in my office and right away pointed to one of the earlier ones. Guess what he said? He asked me if Liu and I worked together. He was Deng's recent seller along with a client he would not name." Yang seemed relieved when Zhu appeared much more positive.

"That's good news, Yang. That confirms your Liu Ming is in the middle of this. We need to get Deng to confirm the other man if we can from our photos. I hate to say it but you've done well. But please listen to me, I have to know what you people might do out there!"

"Thank you. For a moment I thought you were going to shoot me!"

"I was!"

"Deng told me the person he knew as Liu Ming was the 'expert' that certified the items and the other gentleman was the real seller's representative. Deng agreed to meet me again later whenever I would like." He smiled at Zhu and suggested that perhaps he would like to meet him too! Zhu thought for a few moments and then thanked Yang. This was a chance to see if they could get a link to the Triad organization, but they needed to get it done on Zhu's terms. He turned to one of his assistants and told him to arrange to pick up Deng and get him there as fast as possible.

"We need to have Deng get back to the organization and try to draw Liu Ming or the other man in the photo into the open where we can get a track on their whereabouts." As he described and discussed his ideas, Zhu became excited. He finally had something to work with! He walked around the table and almost lifted Yang out of his seat with his powerful arms and gave him a bear hug, thanking him yet again.

It took Zhu's men a couple of hours to track Deng down; he was in the Club 8 Spa alongside Chaoyang Park, playing mahjong with former executives from the steel industry, all retired and well off like him. The agents were told not to disturb him at the spa but to wait until he was alone. Zhu did not want others seeing Deng taken off the streets. There had been enough stories in prior years of civilians being bundled off to so-called black jails.

Later in the afternoon the group ended their games and left to be picked up by their respective cars and drivers. Agents had located Deng's Mercedes 500 parked in the back and surprised the driver, who was waiting to take him home. The agents advised the driver they were from the steel ministry and were there to ask Deng An to join a planning group working on finalizing special reports. They only needed his employer to assist them for a couple of hours. The driver said nothing to the agents but likely suspected these were not really industry people. It was better though not to challenge them. They had government IDs, which were enough to keep him quiet. As soon as Deng called the driver to tell him he was on his way the agents got out of the car, waited until Deng was close by before stopping him and telling him he was needed at an urgent meeting right away.

Deng told them he was too busy, but another government-registered Audi A8 pulled alongside advising he could come freely or be forcibly taken. He chose to go freely, wondering what this was about. He was given a couple of minutes to confirm to his driver that he was to attend a government meeting, then climbed in the Audi, which moved quickly out of the Club 8 parking area and back on to the busy Beijing streets. As the car sped down Chang'an Avenue on towards the intelligence buildings Deng knew he was not going to some industry meeting. The two agents with him declined to tell him anything, saying he would find out soon enough.

On his arrival he was taken to the conference room to meet Zhu. Yang was not there but both George Mathers and Chen Xing had been invited; by then Deng had a pretty good idea where he was being held.

Zhu quickly welcomed him and introduced the others. "Deng An, I have to apologize for the way you've been invited to this meeting, but it is a matter of national importance and highly confidential." Zhu pointed out to everyone that Deng was well known and respected by the Party. "Deng An has served the country well in developing its leadership in world steel markets." He further commented how well financially Deng had done, with just enough turns of language for Deng to understand that all of that could be at risk if he did not support whatever was about to be asked of him.

"Thank you, General, for your comments and your discretion in picking me up to come here. I must assure you that, as always, I am ready to help the Party in any way I can."

The Party - and me in particular - must advise you, Deng An, that you are here under strict secrecy. Any discussion of what you are about to be asked by your wife or associates will be viewed by the state as a criminal act and punishable by imprisonment and confiscation of your assets." Zhu mentioned all of this quite amiably and told Deng he was sure that it would never come to that however, and that the help he needed from him was not so significant in the greater scheme of things.

With that Zhu got quickly to the point. "Look at these photos of jewels and precious metals, which came from a particularly remarkable relic. Is it true that you purchased these recently?" Deng shifted in his chair a little and his face slightly flushed as he acknowledged that he indeed purchased them not long ago.

"Was the price for these around seven million U.S. dollars?" Zhu asked.

Deng at first said it was much less, and then was shown the copy of the sales invoice. Zhu followed up right away with the photo of Liu

Ming and the other individual. "Are these the people involved in your transaction?"

"Yes, General, they are the representatives I dealt with. This person, the one here on the left, is Liu Ming. He's the expert who validated the items as Ming Dynasty. The man to the right represented the owner and seller. He negotiated the pricing." Deng told Zhu they offered the pieces to him with an established value as ten million U.S. dollars. He was enough of an expert in the field to know they were probably correct in their estimate. The pieces of gold were significant in themselves, but the diamonds and emeralds were spectacular.

"Did you know these items were stolen, Deng?" Zhu asked.

"Oh my goodness, of course not, General! I am a reputable man; I have no need of that in my position. Why would I jeopardize my life with something so foolish?"

"Did you know, for example, that these were actually taken from the Palace Museum vaults and have never been displayed to date?

Zhu could see that Deng was extremely concerned as to what he had walked into in buying these items. Zhu softened his manner. "Look, Deng, there is a way out of this mess for you. The Party needs your help. I'm sure the reputable former steel executive, Deng An, will do all he can to help in this situation. Am I right?

"Most certainly, General, anything you need, anything! I am a loyal member of the Party. My reputation speaks for itself!"

"I'm sure it does, Deng." Zhu turned slightly to George Mathers as he spoke; the slight smirk on Zhu's face told George that Zhu thought Deng would not survive an investigation into his financial affairs. Deng missed the look between the two men.

"What do I have to do?" Deng asked.

"We want you to make contact again and have the seller come to your home or meet him somewhere. My team can take over from there. I also need you to give us the private cell number you have for the seller."

Deng sheepishly asked what would happen with the items he had already bought if they were palace property.

"What do you think? If your assistance allows us to get our hands on the seller and resolve this matter, the government will of course expect you to turn over the jewels and gold in your possession. They will then return your investment to you – in full. Of course, that depends entirely on your success in getting the seller to see you again and us getting your money back!"

As they talked others in the room went off to track down the cell phone number Deng gave them to see if they could put a tracer it. If it was one of the latest smart phones being used, they had a good chance of finding the user. It was likely though that the phone itself was simply a second phone and switched on only when needed for special calls. The number and the registered user were traced fairly quickly, but the location, as expected, turned out to be a false address. Now, all depended on Deng drawing the seller back into the open, the question being how that would be done. A request for more goods? A complaint that the jewels were fakes?

Zhu was in luck; Deng had a large holdback pending his own authentication of the goods, which was about to be paid based on a successful appraisal that week. At the time of purchase Liu Ming was the seller's authority that confirmed the authenticity of the items, but Deng had driven the bargain further to include his own authentication.

"This is good, Deng. You keep calling the seller's number until he responds. Tell him you have to discuss a slight problem with the goods and final payment, but that you two can clear up these two issues in a quick meeting." Deng said he was nervous about how he would handle himself without giving anything away. "There is nothing for you to worry about. No one will suspect anything, and the story should not alarm the seller. The final payment will be made in order not to raise any suspicions with whichever seller's group is involved."

A female undercover officer was then assigned to accompany Deng for the next few days, not only to make sure things moved forward but as added protection in case anything went wrong.

CHAPTER THIRTEEN

Yi was lying on his bed thinking about the past weeks of activity and what his future would be in the U.S. He was going to be a vey rich man and expected to live in comfort for the rest of his life, but he could never return to China. Yi hoped to settle in a mountain home and hike the trails, far from the polluted days of Beijing and its traffic congestion. From what he had read of the U.S. he liked the photos he saw of Colorado. He needed to be careful about the place he chose and not draw any attention to himself. They would be looking for him now. He read reports that he was being actively sought in China, and he did not underestimate Zhu for one moment.

His relationship with the Triad organization had been necessary, but not one he wanted to continue. Liu Ming had introduced the Triads to him after they were reunited. He had been thinking about how to benefit from the discovery of the treasure the moment he first heard about it. But it was Liu Ming, during the second night of reunion and after heavy drinking, who brought up the idea of stealing it. Liu Ming had long worked with the Triads. He told Yi that any plan the two of them came up with would require resources they did not have. They had moved surprisingly quickly in planning the theft, and Yi had shown no remorse over the killing of his closest associate on that day when he left Beijing in haste for Chicago.

The Triads had made all the arrangements to get him through passport controls on his arrival; everything had gone according to plan. If he had been tracked to the U.S. they expected the authorities to be looking for him in Chinese areas, as his English was relatively poor. The Triads therefore set up a house for him in Chicago and made sure it was well away from Chinatown area. He had arrived at night and to date had made few trips out of the house. The home was fitted with a nice recreation area and fitness equipment that Yi used to keep in shape; aside from that the Triads managed his periodic contact with Liu Ming closely.

Now that the negotiations were in process, the Triads had brushed off his warnings to be very careful in dealing with Zhu; Yi was concerned that they were not wary enough of the one man he feared most. The treasure itself remained in China, and Liu Ming considered it too dangerous to try to move right away. Kept in a secure location the pieces could be worked on if needed, as had been the case with the first two pieces. Yi and Liu Ming had anticipated a period of negotiation over the ransom so had not been unduly concerned when Zhu began delaying tactics. They were confident the historic value of the pieces would yield the prices they wanted but the Triads were much less sophisticated and pushing to break the collection apart and sell off the pieces quickly. It was Liu Ming and his advisor who continued to insist the treasure collection be kept intact.

The intent of the copies was also for potential sale, Yi had used money from his budget as well as investment by the Triads to fund the copies; the Triads were expecting a return on that investment too. The first $7.5 million sale of the one piece was to directly repay them; they were now pressing for the balance of that sale. He had already contacted Liu Ming to see what the problem was with Deng and his final payment. Liu had told him he was planning to get with Deng and resolve it right away, Yi told him to resolve the payment or there would be trouble, to kill him if he didn't pay.

In Beijing Deng soon received another call from Liu Ming, who arranged to come to Deng's house and discuss what was holding up the final payment. Zhu quickly arranged for agents to be located around the house to follow him afterwards. They would try to place a tracker on his vehicle if the opportunity presented itself. A female agent would also be assigned inside the house posing as a niece of Deng's wife, just in case anything went wrong. The plan was simple; after Liu Ming arrived Deng was to apologize and tell him he needed a second opinion on certain of the gems to confirm the original value assessment. Assuming everything was okay final payment would be released within forty-eight hours, and if Liu Ming could find more, Deng already had a group interested in acquiring them.

⚬⚬⚬

When Liu Ming arrived, surveillance reported two other people in his vehicle. The driver and passenger, who were confirmed as the other individuals in original photos from the Palace Museum, were most likely the Triad gang members involved with Yi. Zhu assumed the two were backup in case Liu Ming had a problem with Deng.

Two agents posing as road cleaners, one male and one female, were lazily sweeping the gutters along the quiet street outside of Deng's house. They swept a little, stopped and smoked cigarettes to delay their progress along the street. Once alongside the black Mercedes parked there, one of the sweepers knocked on the driver's window asking if the driver would be kind enough to give him a light for his cigarette. The driver obliged with some annoyance, telling the man to move along and get on with his job.

While the two men in the car were focused on him, his female partner bent down and picked up something as she attached a magnetic tracker onto the underside of the car. She came up and walked quickly to her partner shouting that she had found a ten yuan bill on the road. They both acted excited by the small cash find but argued over whose piece of the gutter it was found in. The driver again powered his window down and told them to move on before he reported them to their supervisor.

———⟨∞⟩———

Inside the house Deng thanked Liu Ming for coming. He had forced a couple of stiff drinks down beforehand to steady himself; he was able to seem natural as he asked Liu Ming to take a seat and offered him tea. The agent assigned inside the house took Liu's coat upon arrival and brought tea in for them; she was introduced as his niece visiting from outside Beijing. Liu Ming declined politely, advising he was rather busy and had people waiting for him outside as Deng waived his niece away.

"I'm sorry to keep bothering you, Liu Ming, but I do have some good news for you. Another expert has countered the first evaluation of the items; there are no problems. My concerns and those of my group have been eased. In fact the value of the items has been raised based on the last appraisal, that's why my group is interested in purchasing more items like them if they become available. Of course, payment for these is being processed and should be finished in one to two days for sure."

Liu Ming was clearly annoyed with him. "You contacted me for this? You could have called me by phone! I'm pleased to hear final payment will be received, of course, but those people outside are not going to wait much longer for the final payment."

"No worries, Liu Ming. It can be in your bank within a day, two at the most. I can assure you of that now."

"If we don't get this payment certain people will call on you, Deng, to assist in collecting it! And they won't be as pleasant to deal with as me." He also told Deng that he doubted more pieces could be available but that there might be an outside chance depending on current negotiations. In any event Deng was not to call him again. "I will contact you if the situation changes or the money does not show up as promised."

Liu then got up and told Deng he had to leave, telling him that perhaps they could do business again in the future. Deng's "niece" handed him his coat as he left and walked down the driveway, just as the Triad driver was walking to the house. Deng stared out of the window and saw Liu Ming waving the man back. He had the impression the man was stopped by Liu from coming to threaten him. He immediately began to shake as he worried about what he was now involved in, but relieved the meeting was over.

The Triads were not happy with the speed of negotiations with the government, even though the last communication had asked for details of how payment was to be made. They viewed the request for expert verification as not only another delay tactic, but also an effort to capture them. Both Yi and Liu tried to convince them there would likely be no billion dollars without some kind of examination of the goods.

Their idea was to divide the relics into four lots, which would be moved to different locations around Beijing. Payments would be made to four separate accounts in overseas locations in the amount of $250 million for each lot. The deal would be done in one day; lot one in the early morning, lot two in late morning, lot three in the early afternoon and the last lot late in the day. The locations would be revealed one hour before an onsite meeting. If anything went awry and a wire transfer was not made at that point then subsequent lots would be pulled and their breakup initiated right away.

The arrangement was communicated to Zhu after being agreed to by others involved in the theft. They soon received a positive response to the proposal but only based on verification of the items. The Triad main advisor indicated they should control who would participate from the government side. The final note sent to Zhu advised him that the persons involved in the certification would be held as hostage throughout the day and only released after all payments were received. The e-mail over Yi's signature also demanded that one of the experts be the original discoverer of the treasure and a foreigner, Professor Mathers.

The messages were being relayed from Chicago via Hong Kong, on to Beijing, and finally to Liu Ming. Yi was getting concerned about the communications as negotiations continued, but Liu said there was no way to track them and the Beijing side was under control and safe. The Triad leader in Beijing, however, was not so sure and pressed Liu Ming to accelerate things as soon as possible. He again recommended that Liu forget the government exchange and break up the relics; there was enough market in their own underworld to dispense of them and still make a lot of money. Liu and his other advisor fought against the easy way out. They wanted the money too, but did not want to see the treasure lost from China's history.

Liu had always been leery of Yi, who commented often that he felt they were not running the operation, the Triads were. Yi was not even sure the Triads would keep their part of the deal. They were both to get a large share of the proceeds, which now seemed to him a dangerous level to have argued for. Liu, for his part, knew he would have no remorse if something untoward happened to Yi. There would only be a bigger share of the proceeds for him and everyone else.

CHAPTER FOURTEEN

At a meeting with representatives from the Beijing Capital Metro
Armed Police Department, who were coordinating local operations under Zhu's leadership, George, Xiao Ping, and Cai listened intently as the general told them where they stood on various fronts. For
several hours they had been following Liu Ming and tracking his vehicle as it traveled from place to place. At every stop agents had moved
in to cover the location and determine its merit as a potential hideout
in Beijing. Zhu said he was convinced the relics were still somewhere in
Beijing; with a heavily populated city of some twenty million people it
was as easy a place to hide as anywhere else.

They were also tracking the man accompanying Liu Ming. He had
appeared in the Palace Museum photos with Yi. The two sometimes
traveled together, sometimes separately. Zhu acknowledged it was con-
suming manpower and resources to track them. There was also an in-
creased risk of them becoming aware of being followed, but so far the
thieves seemed to be confident they were still in the clear. All of this
continued in Beijing while progress in Chicago was slow. Yi's location
was still unknown.

George remarked to Cai and Xiao Ping that there were more intelligence and local security people in this meeting than before and
pointed out the number of screens now around the room with surveillance cameras showing several locations in Beijing. The group's focus
seemed to be on two of them, a large facility that George recognized as

being somewhere in the 798 Art District, and a large secluded house in an area called Kings Garden Villas, not far from the 3rd Ring Road and only fifteen minutes or so away from the art district itself.

Zhu pointed to the two screens again. The relics were thought to be in the 798 building, but some could be at the large house where Liu Ming seemed to be spending a lot of time. So far no parcels had been taken in or out of any of the facilities on the screens, the assumption being that the relics had not been moved yet – or had been moved earlier.

George finally turned from the screens. "What's the latest in the negotiations, General? Have you reached agreement yet? Time's running out, don't you think?"

"It is," Zhu agreed. "I'm expecting a strong response from them soon. We just sent off a communication that again alters the terms of the transaction. We want to make the exchange in two drops, not four. I've told them our internal processes would take at least twenty-four hours after they stipulate where payments are to be deposited."

"I doubt their patience will last much longer." George said.

"We know that. That's why we've decided to move today on these location, and why I invited you all here. We want you to accompany the different teams on their raids." George was alarmed about the police going in if the relics were not there, but more so with being directly involved.

"Don't worry, your people will only follow after a site is taken. I need some independent eyes there for security purposes. I doubt any of my men have light fingers, but I want someone who has handled the relics before, along with Chen Xing, to make sure they are secured properly and not damaged."

Zhu received a call on the cell phone he used for public purposes and motioned to George and the others to stay quiet. He mouthed the name Deng and listened intently for about five minutes. He thanked the caller, told him to express interest, and to call back immediately once a meeting time and place was agreed upon. Zhu then turned to everyone.

"It's not good! Deng has received a call asking if he is still interested in more items. They say they can have a similar group of items available to him if he moves quickly. They're sending him photos of the pieces right away. Sounds like more pieces are being broken apart. He's stalled them by saying he needs to check with his group to be sure the funds can be made available. He also said he can't make such a large purchase without inspecting the items."

"How much are they asking this time?" George asked.

"They want sixty million yuan, a little under ten million U.S. dollars, but this time they want the money in five business days. They didn't leave him a number to call but gave him an hour to confirm. I told him to go ahead."

There was now no time to lose. Zhu would definitely have to move. "I'm afraid, George, there is one small thing about the main exchange agreement I haven't told you about, or asked you to agree on."

"What are you talking about?"

"They specifically ask for you to remain with them until the exchanges and payments are complete."

George didn't know what to say. He stood there for some time, not quite sure he understood what Zhu had said.

Xiao Ping interrupted, "That's out of the question, no way, General. Absolutely not. He's not one of your army officers, or a policeman. He's just a professor, period. He's my husband and is certainly not going to be put at risk!"

"I understand your feelings, Xiao Ping. My hope is it will not come to that after we hit them today. I only ask that if it becomes necessary our country would like your husband to assist us in every possible way."

"Of course he will, General, but not at the risk of being killed."

George finally spoke up. "Okay, okay, let's not argue right now. Assuming your raids on these locations go okay, you shouldn't need me involved. Meanwhile I'll think about it, but it seems too risky just now. Your focus needs to be on making sure there are no mistakes today."

Zhu readily agreed and over the next hour plans and personnel were assigned to the two main target locations. Xiao Ping and George were asked to accompany Chen Xing to the 798 Warehouse locations. Cai Levee would go with others to the house where Liu Ming seemed be based. By the time assets were assigned to each location, the number of participants was well over a hundred, not counting all the back-up services and coordination that was required. Zhu had decided they would raid all locations at the same time. He contemplated going in during daylight hours but finally decided on eight o'clock, or as soon as darkness began to envelope the city.

⸙

Liu Ming was worried. The Triads had sent new warnings that there was no more time for negotiations. They gave him twenty-four hours to settle this once and for all, or the relics would all be moved, broken up, and sold to private collectors. Liu saw that they had no interest in the historical importance of the collection. The organization was not concerned about the security of its communication trails either, which bothered Liu even more as time progressed. If Chinese or U.S. authorities tried to access the systems without specific codes, sequences, or secret identification details, the whole system would move into full safety mode and alert the developers. They had already told him that numerous attempts had been made to unravel the codes and get into the system; full system destruction of any linkage by preset program logic had been initiated.

The Triads were confident nothing could be traced to their Beijing locations. Liu Ming was not convinced. He decided they needed to move the goods to another location the next day unless the Chinese government and this General Zhu stopped their delaying tactics and were ready to go forward. The side of him that originally wanted to preserve the historic value of the relics was leaving him, despite his advisor's pleas. He told his partners they should give the authorities one last chance to complete this transaction and that was it. Within twenty-four hours the relics would move, one way or another.

After those discussions Liu Ming placed the call to Deng, asking if he were interested in another batch of precious stones. He gave him an hour to make up his mind.

The next e-mail to Zhu was immediately thrown up on the main screen for everyone to see. George noted that the tone of the e-mail made it clear they had strung out the negotiations to the limit and would have to move that day. The senders attached photos of yet another relic in pieces, photos. Chen Xing said, "Whoever took this one apart has done it expertly; he must be highly skilled."

Xiao Ping recognized the piece, "That's one of the pieces I remember handling. I knew there was something special about it from the moment I saw it."

Chen agreed, but said the piece was not one of the oldest in the collection. "Its loss to the world is not so significant as some of the other pieces. It's relatively new in terms of originating from the Ming Dynasty, probably made around 1450; it is, however, one of the finest pieces of Ming jewelry I've seen. It surpassed those on display in the Palace Museum, or even in the collection taken to Taipei by the Guomindang when they fled in 1949."

George commented that there seemed to be someone in the thieves' camp trying to keep the pieces intact. "It looks to me as if Liu Ming is a major factor in that effort. Without Yi's support, however, he could lose that battle quickly. If you compare the e-mails, the language and pattern of phrases, it looks like the e-mails sent to us haven't been coming from Yi. They're presumably coming from Liu Ming with the Triads guiding his hand. To me the Triads are squeezing him to get this finished quickly or else."

Zhu was already drafting a response demanding that the sender keep the rest of the relics intact, or he would not agree to all the terms. The thieves had insisted that the fund information would only be given after government negotiators, including George Mathers, came to each site and inspected the goods. They would not be released until after the exchange and monies were transferred. The only concession made in the e-mail to Zhu was that they agreed to two transfers. The location of the transfers would be forwarded to Zhu the next morning at nine, with one hour to get there; the afternoon transfer would be at three.

Zhu placed everyone on high alert at each location in case any sign of moving the relics appeared on any of the screens. No one was to make a move or expose himself or herself without his approval. Zhu again tried to reassure both George and Xiao Ping that it was unlikely they would have to follow through on the thief's demands. He hoped the day's efforts would be successful. Neither George nor Xiao Ping was comforted by his words, especially his use of the word "hoped."

As plans were being laid out Deng phoned in. He had received a new call from Liu Ming. As instructed by Zhu, Deng confirmed his group of investor's approval to proceed quickly. If the items were as they seemed to be in the photos, payment would be made as requested. Liu Ming had told him to be ready to meet in one hour, promising to call with directions; Deng could bring his appraiser with him but no one else. He was advised to keep his cell phone on speaker while directions were given. When Deng asked why Liu could not just bring them over to his house Liu had simply told him it was not possible.

Deng seemed nervous and ready to back out of any further meetings. It took efforts by Zhu and the head of the Beijing police to calm him down and get his agreement to continue. An agent was on his way to Deng's house to accompany him and pose as an appraiser. He would be there to protect Deng while other officers followed at a safe distance. There would be no attempt by the authorities to arrest Liu at that point. They would simply follow him to wherever he returned. The authorities would take care of funding transfers, so Deng had little to be concerned about; it was more important that he not act nervous in any way. Zhu suggested he let the agent drive and have a couple of stiff drinks to calm himself before driving to the meeting. With Deng now in play everyone waited to see which location Liu Ming would come from and return to.

While waiting for Deng to get the call to move, teams set up to hit each of the key sites. Individual leaders were assigned to each of the locations. After about an hour there was still no call to Deng and video surveillance showed no movement in or out of the house Liu Ming was thought to be in, nor at the building in the 798 Warehouse district. George commented that perhaps they had become suspicious since Deng had agreed so readily to take more goods.

Zhu admitted he was concerned. The hour had passed and nothing seemed to be happening. Shortly after their conversation, Zhu's agent was on the line. The call had come in and Deng was asked if the appraiser was available to meet Liu. Deng had told him he could pick the appraiser up in thirty minutes and then meet him, depending on where the meeting was to take place. Liu instructed Deng to go ahead with picking up the appraiser and that he should head first to the main entrance of the Panjiayuan Antique Market. He would give him an hour to get there and meet him in the market itself.

The location for the meeting concerned everyone; it was Beijing's biggest antique market with over four thousand shops and some ten thousand dealers. The police could get there easily via the East 3rd Ring Road, but only if they had no traffic holdups. With the traffic delays in Beijing worsening, that might not be so easy. Also with an area in the market of nearly fifty thousand square meters and packed with thousands of tourists, keeping track of anyone would be difficult. The car that had been tagged earlier by the unit's GPS surveillance monitor was still parked at the house location. The agent accompanying Deng was asked to tag any other vehicle they came into direct contact with, if he could do so without raising suspicion. The agent carried two small magnetic transmitters to use if an opportunity arose.

———⚬⚬⚬———

Zhu ordered more officers to get to the Panjiayuan market as soon as possible but to stay out of sight. He was afraid of the team being spotted, or losing sight of their target amongst the throngs of people and in the noise of hundreds of people haggling over the prices of what were mostly reproductions. There was no sign of other activity yet from the screens around the operations center.

Before Deng left the house he was fitted with a small microphone and hearing aid so that Zhu could stay in touch and keep Deng from getting too nervous. He could hear the agent continually making comments to Deng to calm him. They took a circuitous route to pass the time Liu had given Deng to pick up the so-called appraiser, and to allow other plain-clothed officers to get in position at the market. Chen Xing had given the agent a short briefing the previous day and some typical appraisal tools so he could appear to know what he was doing. Two undercover police, who worked full-time at the market, were brought into the picture to look out for Liu in particular and for anyone with whom he might be working.

———⚬⚬⚬———

Deng arrived at the market around lunchtime and parked his car. He and the agent wandered around some of the street stalls outside the main entrance waiting for the next call.

Once Deng finished that call and passed the details to the agent with him, everyone understood the next steps they were to take. Panjiayuan consists of five general areas; they were directed to head towards the area where stores selling higher quality antique furniture were located. They were to find a coffee area near the Panjiayuan Exhibition Hall and told to wait there. One of Liu's men would take them to the dealer's location where Deng could examine the relics. Zhu told them through their earpieces not to communicate too much and relax. He told everyone to be especially careful; the gang was likely monitoring the area to see if anyone was following them.

Ten minutes later, Deng was approached by a young girl, who handed him a note to follow her. Deng read it aloud to the agent so others could hear exactly what was in the note.

Zhu didn't like the way things were developing and ordered everyone to stay alert. Liu Ming appeared on the screen, coming out of the house they were watching in Kings Garden Villas. At the same time his car pulled around to the front of the house to pick him up. He had no case or packages with him. The police transmitter tracked the vehicle as it left. It was clear the car was heading far away from the 3rd Ring Road and definitely not to meet with Deng. Zhu swore under his breath, turned, and warned everyone this was not turning out as he hoped. They were too far into this now not to follow through, but he worried that the raids on the known locations could turn up nothing.

Deng and the agent followed the young girl. They came to a three-story building that specialized in furniture, calligraphy, and paintings, not far from a restroom area where one of Zhu's men was watching for Deng's next move.

Two men were waiting to meet Deng and his associate. Both had the air of being very tough but politely welcomed Deng and guided the group upstairs to the second floor. A sign indicated the location of stores 23-46 on that floor. The girl led them to one of the stores midway along the hall. After knocking on the door they were let in. The two men remained outside for some time, looking around the area before they too went in.

Zhu advised all personnel to make sure they covered the front and back of the area the store was in, and to follow anyone coming out of the location with a package or briefcase after the meeting. He also wanted a sweep of the dealers in that area within an hour of everyone leaving. It had to be done quietly so as not to alarm anyone. They could pose as shoppers looking for something special. The two undercover security men who worked at the market were assigned to move among the dealers, as they were well known to everyone. They were to see if anything might have been going on that a dealer thought unusual.

Zhu listened to the updates as Liu was driven out to Beijing Capital Airport; this caused a panic among the pursuers. Perhaps they were all wrong and Liu was headed to where the relics really were, somewhere outside of Beijing. There was great relief later when Liu's car parked at the arrivals section of the airport outside Terminal 2 to meet a female striding out with carry-on baggage. The two embraced as she accompanied him into the back of the car. The woman was either American or European; from the images sent she was elegantly dressed and extremely attractive, turning the heads of men as she walked past them.

Liu's car was followed back into the city, his pursuers staying well behind as the vehicle transmitted location data back to the command center. Zhu was surprised to see the vehicle pull off the airport freeway and head down Juxianqao Road towards the 798 art district. Cameras monitoring the art gallery and area under surveillance soon showed the car arriving there. They watched the screen as the woman stood for a while gazing at the surrounding buildings before Liu finally seemed to be insisting that they go inside.

"So who is this?" Zhu asked. "Is this a buyer? Find out who she is and what she is doing there!" Zhu told his people it was critical to find out if this was someone he needed to be concerned about or not.

CHAPTER FIFTEEN

Deng and Agent Wang followed the young girl along the narrow balcony of the second floor landing. Midway she knocked on a particular door and was let in. They were led into a long corridor that ran along the back of the dealers' rental spaces. At the very end the girl knocked on another door and a young man opened it. He asked the girl if they were alone, then glanced down the hall for signs of anyone following. Seeming to be alone, Deng and his "appraiser" were welcomed into a storage room that was full of antique furniture, apparently being held for dealers in that area of the market.

In a quiet corner of the room two men sat waiting for Deng. There were no greetings other than Deng introducing his associate Wang to the two men. One apologized that Liu was not able to attend the meeting; he had been called to an important meeting with some other potential buyers that very hour. Each man had a metal briefcase discreetly handcuffed to his wrist. Now they both entered the combinations, unlocked the cases, and placed them on a table. Deng was given fifteen minutes with Wang to examine the goods.

Fortunately for Deng and Wang it was clear that the two men were nothing more than mules carrying the goods, likely Triad gang members who knew little about precious stones. This made it easier for Wang to appear quite knowledgeable as he and Deng viewed the pieces, sometimes expressing satisfaction, occasionally raising a doubt or two.

Throughout the examination Deng was amazed at the quality and size of the pieces. They must have come from a stunning necklace, and he wished he could have seen the original piece. He doubted that they were all the jewels from one piece either. He and Wang made a demonstration of discussing the pieces in front of the men, then asked if they could move to another area of the room to talk privately.

After ten minutes the men told Deng they had to leave for another meeting, but they placed a call to Liu and passed the phone over to Deng. Deng complimented Liu on the pieces in the collection and told him he had reviewed the items with the appraiser. He said that while most of the stones were excellent, several would be less marketable; those would take longer to sell. His group would therefore only offer eight point five million dollars for them.

Liu said he would consider nothing under nine point five. Finally they agreed on nine million. Liu would give him details on the money transfer and handover of the goods later. Everything was subject to the final payment being received for the first lot Deng had previously agreed to buy.

When Deng hung up, the young girl appeared at the door to lead him and Wang back to the main market. Zhu put everyone else on alert to follow the other two men once they reappeared from the building.

Inside, two women entered the room, took the items out of the briefcases, and placed them in packages that looked like any other purchases in the marketplace. They were told to wander around the dealer's showrooms and purchase some other simple items before leaving the area.

Two new gang members showed up and were given the two empty briefcases and told to leave the area in separate directions. The two men from the meeting changed clothes with each one and accompanied the women, posing as husbands as they toured the dealers' booths. The Triads were being far more cautious than before in their movements.

Once Wang and Deng were clear of the building, Wang doubled back as quickly as he could. He was the only one able to identify the two men in the room. He moved back down the aisles of jade taking the same route along the back area, pausing to chat to the agent who was lingering by the restroom area and watching the rear of the building. Unfortunately he was only able to see only the exits on the left side.

Wang had on a reversible jacket he often used on surveillance missions; he quickly took it off, reversed it, and put back on, adding dark glasses and a small hat that he carried in an inside pocket. He spoke quietly to Zhu, who hoped no one had been trailing him. Wang was quite sure he had gone far enough in the market without seeing anything suspicious.

While the two couples with their precious packages toured the other dealers, the two men with the briefcases left the building separately, one turning to the left and one to the right. Zhu sent out instructions to follow them both, splitting the watcher's resources right away as Wang whispered that he was taking the man on the left. The individual moved quickly through the crowd, pushing shoppers aside and waving away vendors trying to press their wares on him. The man reached the perimeter of the market and proceeded along the aisles reserved for those who did not have facilities or covered spots. Wang could see he was heading for the car park behind them, possibly toward the Huawei Road exit, another busy area where he had a good chance of losing himself in the crowds.

Wang stayed on him but grew cautious every time the man glanced back to make sure he wasn't being followed. He whispered that the individual was certainly dressed like the man he had met, but now he was beginning to think they might have a switch on their hands. Walking behind the aisles Wang had to be careful to avoid being spotted; the crowded aisles helped but made the pursuit tricky.

As the man passed a dumpster he placed a briefcase behind it, then walked faster in the direction Wang had expected. Wang quickened his pace, ran to the dumpster, and grabbed the case. He alerted Zhu right away that they had been fooled; the case was empty and the goods were likely long gone by now.

Zhu called off the chase and told Wang to put the case back where he found it. He didn't want to alarm Liu and the Triads. Wang said he felt sure that none of the thieves at the market were aware of what had just transpired. If no one came for the case, they could get it back later for analysis. Zhu told everyone to stand down and refocus on the site raids that evening.

————◦◦◦◦————

In the underground bunker of one of the 798 warehouses, Sally Meese was busy with Liu Ming. She had arrived two days earlier, directly from New York on behalf of her company. She was originally educated at Harvard but found a career in modeling that led to the role she now played. Sally had found favor some years ago with an executive from Sotheby's; she'd met him in a New York bar that catered to business executives. He had introduced her to people there who thought she would make a great model for jewelry items. She had the face and body of a first class model, but it was her long slender neck that made a perfect backdrop for many of the special jewelry items Sotheby's handled on auction days. It helped too, of course, when Sally soon began sleeping with the executive.

Over the years Sally had gained the knowledge and experience to become a senior sales executive who traveled the globe dealing with clients from around the world. Her looks opened doors and sealed relationships that few could match. She was intelligent and highly motivated to succeed, which to her meant money and the ability to accumulate nice things. Over time she had developed "special clients," in particular one she had met two years earlier at an auction in Hong Kong where Sotheby's had handled a Ming vase; it broke sales estimates with a bid of twenty-two million dollars. Sally was immediately taken with the purchaser.

James Xu was a self-made billionaire who was not only handsome but also charismatic. His real name was Xu Hong. He had amassed a fortune thanks to his father; he told her it was the privatization of certain state-owned industries that had paved the way for his family to prosper. His father had long-time Party credentials at the time and ready access to political figures. With advance knowledge of State plans he had been able to purchase various businesses. Over time he developed further "guanxi" relationships with important people, which helped the family make millions.

James had not been a true "princeling," as many sons of original Party members were called, but he'd used his father's influence to further enhance the family's enterprises on his own. He proved to be highly successful in his own right, and when his father died James was the automatic and overwhelming choice to take over. Sally heard rumors that his Hong Kong operation was also a tax front for other less public business activities that Xu had developed. She saw him as a risk-taker known to push his businesses to the legal limit—and beyond in some areas.

One of those "areas" was James Xu's penchant for collecting art and jewelry. He spent a fortune purchasing art from both Asia and the West. She had visited his apartment overlooking the bay in Hong Kong, as well as one of his largest apartments in the Palm Springs development across from Beijing's Chaoyang Park. Both were luxuriously appointed bordering on being art museums. He was unmarried but Sally learned he kept girlfriends available there and in other locations. He was also known for his so-called philanthropy, often loaning works of art to museums around the world—if there was a business benefit for him, of course.

Sally considered him the perfect catch at that fateful Hong Kong sale, and soon became his mistress in New York. She'd also traveled to Beijing and Hong Kong to be with him whenever possible. The couple never mentioned marriage, and when James bought her a large apartment near Central Park in Manhattan, it was kept in his name. She did have her own Jaguar XKF convertible, his gift to her along with a substantial wardrobe of designer clothes. Nevertheless, she was also acquiring wealth on her own by trading items independently of Sotheby. The practice was strictly forbidden as an employee at her level, but her colleagues—and her patron—turned turned a blind eye to her transactions. It was through this circuitous route that Sally came to be in Beijing negotiating with Liu for the sale of certain Chinese relics.

Sally found herself in a well-equipped lower room of a former factory building, painted white throughout with very expensive chairs and walls decorated with large artworks; an elegant atmosphere. The art had been purchased from other galleries in the 798 district and several pieces were being sold from there. She was introduced to Liu's young assistant, who maintained the facility and kept it stocked with fine wine, Chinese liquor, caviar, and other delicacies for Liu Ming's "special" clients.

That day Sally was there at James Xu's urgent behest to see items that Liu was going to make available to them. Liu told her he trusted dealing with James because of their prior business dealings and personal relationships, jokingly telling her they could both put each other in jail for a long time if they wanted.

The items were supposedly ancient Chinese relics and jewelry that Liu told James had no precedent in the historical or art world. Liu was intrigued by the photos of several items e-mailed to him, but was told they would only be available for a short time. She had left New York the very next day.

The two of them settled into the comfortable surroundings and Liu asked his assistant to leave them alone. A tray of welcoming treats was laid out and champagne poured before the girl left. Sally watched Liu walk over to one of the large canvases and move it to reveal a large safe in the wall. He entered the combination and opened the safe to reveal several drawers that were similarly secured; Liu unlocked one particular drawer, removed the tray and its entire contents, and set them in front of her. She gasped. "My god, Liu, where on earth did you find these?"

She recognized the uniqueness of the collection and carefully donned white gloves to study the pieces. She had been well trained by the professional appraisers at Sotheby's and knew what she was looking at. "What are you doing, Liu? It's not like you to try to pull a fast one on us! They're beautifully made, in fact exquisite, but these are copies!"

"I just had to see how skilled you were, Sally!" he said. Laughing he took the drawer from her and slid it back into the safe, locking the drawer again before removing another tray, which he brought over to her. "Now look at these!"

She picked up the first piece; turning it over she inspected it closely with the eyepiece Liu handed her. After looking at two or three more she sat back. "This is amazing! Wherever did you find them? Why are you smiling?"

"Sally, they are only a portion of what I have. Not even James has enough money to cover the entire collection. These are pieces my partners and I are willing to sell to James."

"Where did they come from?"

"We understand these were many of the jewels once housed in the Forbidden City. Over the centuries they were stolen by the emperor's eunuchs. They were likely originally stored in the palace's treasure house, the Palace of Establishing Prosperity. They were most probably taken in the years before the eunuchs finally burned down the building in 1923."

Sally nodded. "It was burned to avoid the thefts being revealed when the last emperor of China, Pu Yi, called for the updated inventory of all the treasures held there. That sounds a reasonable story for the items—if it's true, of course."

The pieces Liu showed Sally were all of the Qing Dynasty; whoever selected them had determined the category and time the relics were from. She knew they were extremely valuable pieces. "How did such fine copies make their way into your hands, Liu?"

"Simple; the collectors who owned them originally planned to set up displays in large museums; they had the copies made for the actual displays to the public. Since that time, however, they've decided to sell them all, including the copies. The plan is to invest the large sums they will generate in different ventures."

Sally knew the asking price for the items was going to be high; she had discussed it with Xu before leaving New York. He had given her a budget of a hundred million dollars based on the photos he had seen and the prospects that there might be other pieces to choose from. She knew the outstanding pieces before her were going to cost much more than that, but when Liu mentioned three hundred million she laughed and said it was time for her to leave.

Their negotiation over the part of the collection she picked out went on for an hour; figures were tossed back and forth, and the combinations of pieces changed. Finally a figure of ten million over her budget was agreed to. She was confident that James would approve it. It would be easy for them to move the pieces in the market and make a handsome profit, even if she had to find her own investor.

Liu told her he wanted 10 percent in his bank before holding the items for her. Upon payment of 50 percent they would release the items to James Xu. He trusted Xu completely for the balance within sixty days.

Sally knew that in the world Xu operated in, no securities were needed. Liu gave Sally the account details for the ten million dollar transfer; he told her he would be in touch as soon as the money was in the bank in order to arrange transfer of the pieces she selected. He said he would likely come to her hotel. Knowing that copies existed, Sally told him she would be checking the pieces very carefully to make sure no mistakes were made.

Sally was staying at the St. Regis Hotel; she told Liu she would be there for a week. She would specify when to bring the pieces there for final packaging and shipment out of the country by their "mutual friends." With the restrictions on exports of historical and ancient items, special handling was needed to get them out of the country and into the U.S. The so-called movers would insure that no loss or mishap occurred on the way, but the cost was likely to be quite high. Sally figured it would run about 2 percent of the price, but that was to be expected with these kinds of items.

It was clear to her that this operation was not being handled by Liu alone. James had told her what was really going on following several calls he had made and received. She declined Liu's invitation for dinner that night as she had a prior arrangement with a collector about a particular article she was trying to move. She also wanted to spend a little time looking at artworks for sale in the 798 art district. Liu offered to have his assistant, who spoke good English, to take her around; afterwards he would have someone take her back to the hotel.

———— ✧✧✧ ————

At six o'clock that evening two vehicles arrived by the main gallery at the 798, when most of the galleries were closing. Watchers at the site advised the operations room that one of the two drivers was on his cell phone to someone. Ahead of where they had parked there was a road previously used by the factories for moving items between buildings. It was now a pedestrian walkway but wide enough for a vehicle to pass through. Zhu ordered everyone to be on their toes; he suspected this could be an effort to move the goods. Once the vehicles left they were to be followed and intercepted. Anyone inside the building and the vehicles was to be detained for questioning out of the public eye.

———— ✧✧✧ ————

Liu was getting ready to leave his underground gallery at the end of a successful day with commitments for another 119 million dollars from

Sally and Deng combined. There were still more valuable pieces left to sell. He had told the Triads they needed to be patient in selling the relics over a long period of time; there was no way to move a billion dollars worth of items into the market quickly. Plus, he had pointed out that too much released at once would bring the market pricing down.

The pieces for James Xu would be neatly packaged and picked up after final review by Sally, then taken by the organization and moved to the U.S. as promised. Liu didn't know how the system worked or who would be involved once the goods were smuggled across the border into Hong Kong. He did know that the goods' first port of arrival in the U.S. was scheduled to be San Francisco. The local Triad group in Chinatown there would handle the forwarding; nevertheless, China still took overall responsibility and financial liability to the buyer.

One of Liu's associates received a call from the cars parked outside advising him the drivers were ready and awaiting his signal. Liu took a metal case containing the items for Sally, which would be shown to her as soon as the deposit was in their account; he would soon head for the bunker exit leading up to the roadway between the buildings. There was another case holding the jewels for Deng but he decided for safety to move them in separate cars, just in case.

Liu locked the heavy steel doors to the room itself and carried the cases with a colleague along the corridor past other storage rooms that were simple steel cages where various items were warehoused. His facility had been a special location in the factory's early days and was the main bunker for executives of the 798 electronics factory. He had spent a lot of money getting it readied, but it had proved its value over recent years.

He called the lead car confirming they were coming up. After passing through a friend's gallery they waited in a doorway for both cars to pull up. Each would jump in separate cars with a case and speed to their destination. This time Liu drove alone in a large black SUV with darkened windows; the other men took off in his Mercedes.

In the operations room the screen monitors revealed two cars drive out the back side of the building, one turning left and one right, heading towards different exits. Both cars were followed at a distance and information went out to other team members alerting everyone to the current moves. Zhu told his teams not to lose them, nor to intercept them yet. He wanted every action held back until the 8 p.m. target time for raiding every known location.

An assistant came in to tell Zhu that his "special phone" was ringing; he excused himself telling George and the others near him that it was likely the Ministry on the line. He was gone for a short time and looked puzzled when he returned.

He responded to George's questioning look. "Interesting . . . that call was from a minister I've never had contact with in the past. He had heard we have an operation planned to retrieve stolen goods and wants to know when and where it is scheduled for!"

To date the final timing had been kept under wraps as everyone was concerned about the risk of leaks.

"So what did you tell him?" George asked.

"I was highly suspicious. I told him Minister we are still planning and have not yet pinpointed an exact location. I said we are at least twenty-four hours away from any move." Zhu was clearly suspicious of leaks, even at the highest level. "He thanked me and wished me success."

George asked Zhu if there would be repercussions when he found out that the timing of our actions was in fact this evening. He just shrugged. "Only if we fail!"

Sally waited for Liu to arrive; monies had been transferred to the account specified. All that remained was for her to re-inspect the goods, seal them, and leave them with Liu for the delivery part of the process. Around 7 p.m. he called from his cell phone saying he would be at her door momentarily.

Liu entered her suite and after some pleasantries got down to business. He unlocked the case and allowed her to verify each piece for its authenticity. They were indeed the pieces she had selected. Once satisfied, she excused herself for a moment and went to her bedroom to bring in a larger suitcase and a slightly smaller one. She told Liu she needed to transfer the contents to this case for shipping purposes. The case was heavier than the one provided by Liu and appeared more secure. She did not tell Liu there was a tracking device inside that would monitor where the case was at all times during its journey.

She made sure the pieces were set in the case with the appropriate packing around them to prevent any damage, and then secured the lid with two combination locks. The outer cover of the case, which included the tracking monitor, was also closed with further combination locks. Sally smiled as she prepared seals for the edges of the lid. She melted the material and withdrew a special gold seal to impress her mark on them before turning the case back over to Liu.

Asked if she did not trust the organization, even though it bore the cost of the goods and guaranteed arrival or their money back, she simply smiled and told him it was just "standard operating procedure" with her boss.

Sally already had a delivery and sale notification for Liu to sign, which he waved aside as unnecessary, but she insisted saying James Xu would expect it. The bill of sale itself would never see the light of day. Any time Xu sold an item there would be other documents created to give them a legal right for sale. Official documents authorizing their export from China would be obtained through Xu's own sources if needed, even though Liu assured Sally the documents he provided would pass official scrutiny.

Liu invited Sally to dinner to celebrate the transaction but she told him she had calls to make. She thanked him for the invitation and the items purchased. Liu then took his leave after passing along his regards to James. He said he was confident the goods would arrive safely and promised to keep her updated on the progress being made. She told him that was fine. She didn't mention, of course, that the case was already emitting its signal and that their tracking had begun.

Sally knew that James was very interested to know what route the case would be taking; if he could figure out how this was done he would perhaps save himself a considerable amount in the future. Either way, he wanted to check the progress and verify where the goods were at all times.

Reports came back to the operations room that Liu was leaving the Regis Hotel but with a different case, more substantial than the one he had taken in. Sally had come down from her room and appeared to be having a drink in the lobby while on her cell phone with someone. Zhu told the onsite officers to get in her room and quickly check for any sign of relics. He expected that the goods, which everyone assumed Sally had been there to acquire, were likely now on their way to New York by some underground route. Sally would be left to continue whatever her plans were over the next couple of days, but they planned to pick her up at the airport before she left.

CHAPTER SIXTEEN

By 7 p.m. George Mathers and the others were headed to the various locations. They had contemplated pushing the raid back another hour to see where Liu was headed, but Zhu decided to have him arrested wherever he was.

George and Xiao Ping were in the lead van headed toward the 798 art district and the underground warehouse gallery along with Zhu; they were followed by Special Forces and a couple of explosive experts who were skilled in taking down any obstruction they might encounter. Cai Levee and Chen Xing were in a separate team car headed to the house used by Liu Ming. Three more teams were approaching other targets. They would meet with the onsite surveillance teams and wait for Zhu's go-ahead.

The evening traffic was worse than expected on the fourth ring road headed toward the Chaoyang District; despite using sirens and flashing lights their progress was slow. Zhu put all units on hold until the order was given. Eight p.m. was no longer practical at the pace they were going.

They finally pulled off the ring road and drove quickly along a lower road running parallel to the elevated airport freeway before turning on to Juxianqao Road. They had to double back on this road to get to the art district entrance due to the center barriers down the middle of the road. When they arrived it was closer to 8:30. Their evening arrival offered added cover for the teams; most were dressed in black fatigues, some heavily armed.

The ops room personnel kept the team leaders updated at all locations. To date there had been little activity other than Liu's excursion. No other packages had moved in or out of any location. After a brief conversation Zhu ordered everyone out of their vehicles and to travel on foot to the gallery. He wanted a tight cordon around all sides of the building, especially the entrances and exits that Liu had used earlier that day.

Positioning themselves across the square from where the gallery was located, they were hidden by small restaurants and some large statues; Zhu held the teams back to wait for the last one to arrive at its location. Others were still stuck in traffic, but were not headed to either of the two key targets; they were trying to reach a less critical location normally under surveillance as a Triad meeting place.

⌘

Liu was heading back to the 798 area and not to the main house. As he came down Juxianqao Road toward the art district he could see some police and military vehicles parked off in the side areas; they seemed to be trying to remain out of sight. Now more suspicious he entered the 798 complexes carefully, proceeding slowly along the main entrance street as he passed the bright red sign with large figures denoting the district as 798. Then he recognized a car following him, though was staying back. He also noticed other cars positioned at side exits, cars not usually there. Liu suddenly lurched forward and accelerated down the street, tires squealing as his vehicle raced towards the Fine Art Square and gallery.

Liu screeched into the square and headed straight for the narrow road that passed through the galleries. An unfortunate vendor had left a display cart on one side of the alley; Liu demolished the stand as he shot through the passageway with barely any space on either side of his SUV.

Display windows of the side galleries smashed as his rear end shimmied from side to side. He knew that at the end of the passage there were two blocks around ten inches tall to stop vehicles from entering. He simply shot over the blocks, the vehicle bucking and slamming down hard over them. Racing to the end of the alley past officers trying to stop him, he crashed through two more bollards at the end of the street before braking hard and swinging wildly into a left turn.

There were now two police cars following him. Liu doubted they were familiar with the width of the alley and would be cautious about hitting one of their own men. The two granite blocks at the end of the building would be a surprise to them, giving Liu precious seconds to get away.

In the underground gallery the individual waiting for Liu received a frantic call from him on his car phone. He screamed that there was a trap and the police were coming, that he should take what he could to the safe area right away. He could see the shadows of police starting to move from across the street on his computer screen; previously he'd had his men tap into the surveillance cameras covering the gallery.

With no time to save all of the remaining relics, the man gathered up the best pieces as quickly as he could and headed to the safe area the Triads had installed in the room. He set the case by the underground air-conditioning unit, knowing he had some time before anyone could get into the area. The old electrical plant walls were reinforced concrete, specially thickened originally with help from the East Germans in the fifties to protect it from bombs and earthquakes. He knew the thick steel doors would have to be opened with heavy explosives; this would give him enough time.

He pulled at the large air-conditioning and heating unit until the whole assembly swung out from the outlet grills it was attached to. He slipped through the access this provided after pushing the case inside first; finally he was able to swing back the entire unit and close it. Locks from the inside would make it extremely difficult for anyone to take the cover off and get behind it. The installers had always hoped this would convince any intruder there was no way anyone could have disappeared through a fully functioning air conditioning and heating unit.

The shaft opened up into a small area that could hold three people for several days. It had been part of the system of rooms for senior executives in the event of a nuclear attack. The Triads had stocked it with three days of supplies and some rudimentary sanitary capabilities. It would be uncomfortable but might give the organization a chance to get whoever needed to use it out safely. He closed the steel panel behind the air conditioner so that if anyone shone a torch inside, it would appear that there was no way to gain access behind the unit. He would open it only when necessary to listen to what was going on, or to get out when the chance arose.

He tried to use his cell phone but couldn't get a signal. He was sure that once the raid by the police was over his colleagues would come after him; otherwise, he could be in for a long and miserable wait.

⸺ ⚬⚬⚬ ⸺

As the chase for Liu went on through the streets and alleys of the 798 district, George and Xiao Ping followed the team to the road that ran through the target buildings. The officers found the underground entrance just to the right and a short distance along the passageway; they broke in the outer door with surprising ease. The ops planners had obtained the old plans made by the East Germans, so they had a good idea what they were up against. They knew the lower area was better protected and that they were going to have to blow the large steel doors open, hoping they hadn't been modified. They fully expected to find some kind of a warehouse that Liu Ming was using.

Once down the steps and moving along the narrow entry hall their lights were soon shining on the heavy steel doors. They could see right away the doors had indeed been modified with additional security systems. If anyone was inside, the team knew that they were already exposed to the occupants. They placed explosives in key locations to blow open the heavy doors, and ordered George and everyone to stay well back and away from the blast. The noise when the charges went off was deafening.

The outer doors had moved only slightly, so they used the small opening to place a second series of charges. The doors finally gave way, swinging open on huge hinges. Parts of the jambs and wall were gone with steel reinforcement bars sticking out from the blasted area.

The first officers into the area wore gas masks and had automatic weapons at the ready but saw right away that the room was empty. They were surprised to find some kind of upscale gallery instead of a simple warehouse. Several paintings were destroyed from the effects of the second blast and every one of the glass cabinets in the room was demolished.

As the air unit began to clear the smoke in the room the team leader signaled to George and Zhu they could safely enter. They still had to use flashlights for a while, but it was clear to everyone that no one was there. George heard Zhu calling in the forensic guys to start work right away, thanking the Special Forces for getting them. He asked everyone to be careful not to disturb anything.

The raids on other locations went according to plan. For once there were no mishaps and the element of surprise helped minimize any serious losses on both sides. A total of thirty-two Triad members were taken in; four had escaped. Two of those arrested were gravely injured; ten sustained injuries that were not life-threatening and the rest suffered minor injuries. The Special Forces officers suffered only minor injuries, the biggest being perhaps more pride-related since four of the key players had managed to get away. Someone had apparently alerted them to the raids.

George listened as Zhu told everyone to get the prisoners out of the locations right away; he also asked Chen Xing and Cai Levee to get over to the 798 district as soon as they could—unless they found something. He instructed all team leaders to search each facility carefully; other forensic specialists would soon be involved in working through each location.

George called Cai Levee when radio and phone silence was lifted, asking if they were okay and how things went at their end. From their conversations it sounded like George's team had a more exciting time of it than Cai; there were only two gang members in Liu's place. Cai said that when the Special Forces team went in as quickly and noisily as they did, both gave up right away. The police were going through the house, but there seemed nothing of significance in the rooms they had inspected. Cai said it seemed like a normal, lived-in place, except for a safe in one of the bedrooms that a specialist was trying to open up. George told Cai about their entry, that they were in a bunker and beginning to see what was there; he hoped they would be able to get over there too.

The underground room was a mess, a large wall painting hanging off hidden hinges; the top of it was folded over on itself, revealing a walk-in safe. The team set to their next task of opening it while Zhu inspected the rest of the room. Forensics began fingerprinting the area. Zhu's phone rang constantly with activity updates, especially reports on the race to catch Liu.

The local Triad leader listened to Liu's open car phone as Liu looked for a place to ditch the car and run; he could hear Liu yelling about cars chasing him. The Triad leader urged him to get away at all costs; he could not risk Liu falling into the hands of the authorities. He was unconcerned about his own Triad members; they would die before saying anything to the police, and they knew only portions of the business anyway. They would never reveal his identity, nor his position as Dragon Master of the Triads in Beijing. Liu, on the other hand, was viewed as an outsider who would cave quickly under pressure. With his intimate knowledge of the theft and Triad leaders Liu was a danger to them all.

———⊸∞∞⊸———

Taking a left, after clearing the bollards, Liu had turned left yet again and driven up a one-way street looking for a way out as police road-blocks went up. He took a gamble and turned back onto the entry road and drove up the street as fast as he could. He had already passed the second exit on Juxianqao Road covering the D Park area and other factories in the 798 area, but they were heavily guarded; ahead he spot-ted only a small crew remaining at the main entrance. Police were busy trying to move bystanders away from the area. Liu decided this was his way out.

He approached the exit blocked by two police cars as officers waved at him to stop. He slowed down at first, but then pressed the accelera-tor pedal to the floor. He lowered his head as much as possible to avoid being shot, bulldozing his way through both cars. He swerved right as officers ran to their cars. Armed police briefly withheld fire due to the number of onlookers surrounding the scene. One officer ran into the road trying to keep his shots low and take out the vehicle's tires, but cyclists and pedestrians prevented him from firing many shots.

Speeding along Liu swerved around a number of vehicles, hitting several of them; the drivers parking their vehicles in the road created an even bigger mess for pursuers. Liu made a hard right turn onto the Airport Expressway; the police must have expected to contain him in the art district, as he could see no roadblocks to the freeway. He moved into the fast lane trying to outrun his pursuers.

As Liu sped towards the airport he was frantically trying to get help from the Triads and decide what to do next. Sweating profusely, he pushed and weaved his way through the lanes, horns blaring as taxi drivers and trucks screamed at him for his insane driving. Several more cars were clipped as he raced along but no serious damage was caused. Often as not Liu ended up driving in the emergency lane of the freeway, worried that if he ran into a traffic accident ahead escaping would be impossible.

———— ◦⊱⊰◦ ————

Airport security personnel were alerted to the fugitive on the freeway heading their way and told to shut down the freeway traffic as fast as they could. Three security vehicles with sirens and lights blazing left the airport area; once they reached the freeway they drove down the exit ramp against the flow of traffic. They forced their cars out across all the lanes effectively shutting down the traffic flow.

Several cars that were following to close to those ahead ended up in rear-end collisions; the effects of these accidents was that traffic quickly snarled on the freeway. Many of the drivers on the road that night were used to trucks breaking down and minor accidents, but none had experienced being in the middle of an effort to catch a fleeing criminal!

———— ◦⊱⊰◦ ————

Liu saw brake lights go on in every lane ahead and was forced to slam on his own brakes. He was immediately blocked in on all sides; at that point he was in the fast lane by the dividing barrier. Fortunately for him, the pursuing officers found themselves blocked too.

Liu opened the door as did other drivers and looked back down the highway at the entanglement of traffic. In the distance he spotted a couple of armed officers leaping from the two lead pursuit cars. With guns drawn they ran toward him. He was no more than five hundred meters ahead of them.

Liu had no choice but to abandon the car. He kept his phone line open as he jammed the cell in his shirt pocket, grabbed a handgun from the glove compartment, and jumped out. Running around to the trunk he pulled the case of precious gems out of the vehicle and raced to the center barrier, scrambling over it as best he could. The case was going to slow him down but he could not leave it. Despite his yelling to whoever could hear him on the phone, there was no response.

The traffic heading back in to Beijing from the airport slowed to see what was going on. Drivers sounded their horns, screaming at his apparent stupidity as they went by. The traffic slowed to some degree but no one heeded his request to stop. Liu waved his gun at several drivers but they swerved around him. His only choice was to make sure someone stopped by firing his gun at them. It took only a short time before the traffic ground to a halt alongside him opening up an empty freeway into Beijing.

Liu looked at the cars in front of him and ran toward a Porsche Cayene, which he knew would have the speed he needed. The driver looked petrified as Liu approached. He waved his gun at the man, wrenching the driver-side door open and literally dragging the him onto the road. Jumping into the Porsche he flung the case across the passenger seat and set off as fast as he could, this time with an open road ahead of him.

⚬≈≈⚬

Zhu was getting ready to leave the 798 district and told everyone to complete the search of the underground bunker; he was growing angry at their failure to capture Liu. He already had a police helicopter with a powerful searchlight in the air over the freeway, determined not to allow Liu to escape this time.

Since the 798 area was close to the freeway, by then fully jammed, there was no way get to the outbound side to the airport, so Zhu had his assistant race him over to the inbound side to downtown ahead of where Juxianqao Road fed into the freeway. Zhu and two cars following him then forced their way onto the freeway against the traffic flow, a highly dangerous move. If the reports were correct a hole in the traffic would open up to the Porsche with Liu coming straight at them.

———— ∞∞∞ ————

Liu pushed the Porsche to its limit, looking for a way to get off the freeway in the inner city; he hoped to lose his pursuers in a narrow alley. He soon became aware of the helicopter flying above him and could see the outline of a searchlight through the vehicle's moon roof. Over a loudspeaker he was being commanded to stop and he continued to yell for help on his cell phone speaker.

Liu knew he was trapped and told the people listening that his only choice was to stop the car and throw the case over the embankment. It would be up to the Triad to recover the case. A voice asked where he was on the freeway, then told him they would get there as soon as they could. He drove close to the side barrier hoping the overhanging trees would prevent those in the helicopter from seeing him as he flung the case from the Porsche.

———— ∞∞∞ ————

The helicopter was soon hovering almost on top of the vehicle. With the headlights of police vehicles driving straight towards him, Liu knew that any chance of evading arrest was lost. He hoped he had created enough distance between him and the case so that the Triads could get to it. All of that mattered little now as he stopped the vehicle and dispose of anything incriminating. He stomped on the cell phone and threw it to the other side of the freeway where other cars would finish the job. He hurled his gun over the embankment, hoping the police would never find it.

CHAPTER SEVENTEEN

It took specialists a while to get the walk-in safe and locked drawers open. Chen, Xiao Ping, Cai donned latex gloves to inspect the contents. Xiao Ping had brought along photos of the relics to determine if they were all there. Meanwhile, everyone was asked to be very careful; fingerprinting and DNA forensics experts were still covering every inch of the room.

Their inspection revealed that a number of relics were missing, but it seemed to George and Xiao Ping that the case Liu was carrying could not contain all of the pieces that their rough count indicated should be there.

George called Zhu and told him the best and most valuable pieces were likely not there. The team couldn't assess what Liu took out in the case; they needed to find it or get Sally Meese to tell them which items she purchased. Zhu agreed and ordered his men to pick her up for questioning. George could hear another person on the line with Zhu saying he was concerned that Sally Meese was a U.S. citizen, but Zhu ordered him to proceed; he would take any recriminations that came out of it.

Zhu's men were instructed to put her in an office, not a cell, keep her comfortable, and tell her that a General Zhu would be coming to talk with her. If she refused to go with them, they could forget being careful and use force if necessary. She was not to use her cell phone; it was to be taken from her and examined. If she needed to call someone she would have to use the unit's monitored lines. Any attempt by an embassy person or a lawyer to support her would be allowed, but only after Zhu had interviewed her.

Sally Meese was in the bar when two officers walked up and asked to speak to her privately; as soon as they showed her their official identification badges she became alarmed. The officers told her she was "invited" to a discussion with a certain General Zhu, who wanted to ask her some questions; he was currently on the way to his office and needed to see her right away. She offered to come in the next day as it was getting late; she needed to get to bed after calling her office. One of the officers advised her politely through his colleague that it could be done later; it was better to clear things up by coming with them now and cooperating fully.

She continued to hesitate, becoming more agitated about leaving right away. "Look here," she said. "I'm a U.S. citizen and must insist I talk to the embassy. I can surely come to see this Zhu fellow first thing in the morning."

The younger officer who spoke perfect English winked at his colleague and took Sally off to one side. In a calm and soft voice he whispered, "Miss Meese, it's my recommendation that you come with us right away. You can be assured that no harm will come to you. We've been instructed to have you wait in General Zhu's office for him to arrive. This is not some dark cell of the sort you've probably read about in newspapers." He didn't tell her what this was about, but said he suspected she was unwittingly involved in something very serious.

"General Zhu will explain everything in his office," the officer said. "It's in your best interest to cooperate. We don't want to see this to turn ugly, do we? To be frank, Miss Meese, under China's laws we are legally entitled to take you in as an arrested person and put you in a cell. But I assure you that won't happen if you cooperate."

Sally considered her situation; she already had a pretty good idea what this was about. She would stand by the story that she had done nothing illegal in Beijing and was simply purchasing artifacts that, as far as she knew, had been approved for export. Reluctantly, she nodded her assent. "Okay, but I need to gather some things to take with me. Am I at least allowed to do that?"

The young officer agreed, turned to his colleague, and confirmed that she was coming with them—of her own free will. He accompanied her to her room to allow her to pick up a few things, including a coat, and led her out to a waiting car. Zhu had told them not to worry about blindfolding her until they were close to the headquarters, and they were to treat her with kid gloves until he got to her.

When the young officer asked her eventually to wear a blindfold over her eyes for a short time, she became quite frightened.

"I can assure you, Miss Meese, this is only to protect an official government office location. You can even put it on yourself."

She didn't believe him but complied, her hands shaking. When she was finally in the headquarters, the blindfold was removed. She was taken to a comfortable office but again become alarmed when her cell phone was taken. She was advised that she could make calls from the office, but they preferred that she hold off until General Zhu arrived.

A female officer brought her coffee, a tray of Chinese snacks, and a copy of *China Daily* printed in English. She was told where the bathroom was located and that the door to the office was not locked; anytime she needed to use the facilities she could do so freely. Another female officer sat looking over some paperwork, clearly there to watch over her, but offering a comforting smile each time Sally glanced her way.

Sally began to think through her story. She was sure this had to do with Liu but wondered why this situation involved the military, not just regular police; the building was definitely a military one. She began to regret agreeing to come and tried to contact the U.S. Embassy from the phone she was allowed to use. No one prevented her from using the outside line but the number was continuously engaged, as were all overseas lines!

———— ◦◦◦◦◦ ————

As Zhu and his cars approached Liu, the helicopter hovering overhead used its loudspeaker to warn the suspect to kneel, put his arms over his head, and place any weapons on the floor in front of him.

Zhu and his officers moved cautiously toward Liu but soon saw he was in a submissive position. Zhu smiled, seeing that Liu was surprised that both regular police and a high-level military man were approaching. He motioned Liu to stand up before being handcuffed.

The officers made sure there was a clear area for the helicopter to set down on the freeway; it kicked up a swirl of dust from the embankment as it landed. Zhu ordered Liu into the helicopter and climbed in with him. They would be flown back quickly to the operations center. He left orders for the area along the freeway to be searched carefully. There was no case or phone in Liu's car, nor the gun he reportedly had in his possession. They were to search through the night, blade by blade of grass, inch by inch, on their knees if needed. Orders went out for additional officers to join the search, which would begin immediately. They could not wait until dawn.

By morning the search team reported finding the handgun in some bushes down an embankment, but the case was not found; there was evidence, however, that something had landed on the lower embankment not far from the suspected drop-off area. Marks on the ground indicated something like a case had been dragged a short distance before it appeared to have been picked up. Tracks nearby indicated that some kind of small vehicle, perhaps a three-wheeled cart used by workers to pick up trash might have been used to take it away. The local officer from the neighborhood knew most of the local scavengers; he sent groups of officers off to find the ones who worked the area with their pedal-driven carts.

———— ◦◦◦◦◦ ————

The men sent by the Triads to locate the case got to the site Liu had described on his car phone, but when they reached the area police were already arriving. They abandoned their search, calling in to their master that they were too late; with the number of police arriving they expected the case would be found quickly.

One of the Triad members called various "friendly" officers to learn if they had found what they were looking for. It took some time, but eventually they found an officer who said they were still looking "for some kind of stolen case"; so far they had only found a weapon. He was asked to keep the caller updated.

The officer called later to tell them it looked like someone, a poor beggar or trash collector, had made off with the case. The search was being broadened to find that person. He was thanked for the update and asked to keep passing along information regarding any new developments; he would be well taken care of for his help.

The search for the case was concluded rapidly, thanks to one local officer who knew the area where the peddlers parked their carts and often congregated. When they approached a small alleyway not far from the freeway embankment, the officer could hear a hammering noise; he motioned to his partner to stay silent as he headed toward the location the sound was coming from. As they moved among piles of junk and rubbish they carelessly knocked over a large can of trash, which caused a loud noise.

Realizing that whoever was doing the banging might have heard them, the lead officer ran down to the end of the alley and spotted a light in a small shack. He slammed his way through the door to find the hauler of trash and goods sitting on a blanket. He was clearly trying to shove a chisel and hammer under it.

The officer kicked the items away from the man as his partner came in. He asked the junk collector where he had been that night, and if he had found anything special. The man shrugged and claimed he'd found nothing, but her couldn't explain the hammer and chisel on the floor or the banging that had been going on. Nothing he described working on made any sense.

The officers pulled the old man off the blanket and ripped it up; there was the suitcase thrown aside by Liu. They could see that the man had been hammering away at the locks, trying to open the case but to no avail. They called the team leaders to say they had found the case and were directed to bring it to Zhu at headquarters. No one was interested in the man who found it.

They left quickly after one of the officers advised the man that he'd come close to being arrested; he should report anything suspicious like this in the future. While he was speaking, his partner stepped away from the area and placed a quick call to his contact in the Triad. He told them the case had been found and was in police custody.

The man waited in the hidden underground bunker until he was sure the room was vacated, then opened the shaft access to the underground gallery. He needed to stretch and move around, but recognized he had to be careful not to disturb anything in case they returned. He squeezed out of the safe area and quietly eased his way towards the doors to the safe and looked around with a flashlight. He could see that the safe and drawers had all been opened and their contents removed. Moving beyond the gallery room to the main doors that had been blown to gain access, he climbed the stairs. Outside he could hear muffled voices of police still guarding the area; there would be no way out that night.

Zhu was back in headquarters after midnight. The officers had given Sally Meese a cot to sleep on while waiting for Zhu in another area; they continued to prevent her from making any meaningful calls until Zhu got there. He told the officers not to disturb her; he wanted to wait until the suitcase was at headquarters. He planned to confront her with it as soon as he talked to her. He would be firm but not overly aggressive, unless it came to that. Liu Ming was also to be brought to headquarters and kept in a high security cell until Zhu was ready for him.

Zhu lay down on the overnight cot in his office, telling his assistant to give him an hour before waking him up. If the suitcase was not there by then, they were to let him sleep until it came.

The suitcase arrived in an hour and was rushed up to the operations room; Zhu was wakened and told it was there. None of the others were around, as George and his group had already gone home shortly after midnight. Zhu called the officer who tracked down the case to congratulate him for his diligence, and finding it so fast.

After washing his face, Zhu went to the conference room to meet the officers waiting for him. He quickly inspected the case, saw that someone had struggled to break it open. He noticed the torn seals around the lid, evidence that someone had tampered with the case. Rather than continue efforts to open the case he preferred to see if Sally Meese had the combination; either she had it or knew who would have it.

CHAPTER EIGHTEEN

Zhu watched the monitors as a female officer shook Sally Meese awake and told her it was time to meet with him. It was around 3 a.m., and she appeared groggy. It was clear that she had slept poorly and was startled—exactly the way he wanted her to be. The officer led her to an interrogation room that was by no means as inviting as the office she had been in; it stank of stale cigarettes and body smells that hung in the air. Zhu was outside calmly watching through a one-way mirror weighing her demeanor before entering the room.

When he saw that she was becoming more agitated, biting her well-manicured fingernails, the time seemed right and he stormed into the room. He grabbed the interrogator's chair facing her and stared straight into her eyes. "I am General Zhu. You have two options to choose from, and quickly. One is to open the suitcase that I am about to have brought in, and file a complete and truthful report of everything that has happened since your arrival in Beijing; then you can leave China sometime next week."

"I'm afraid I don't know what you're talking about, and I demand to have someone from the U.S. Embassy present before I answer any questions!"

Zhu saw through her attempts to sound in control; she was quivering to her core.

"The authorities and I know more about this than even you do, Miss Meese. As long as we gain access to the contents of this case, we are willing to make your situation much easier."

"I have nothing to say," she half-whispered.

"You need not worry about Liu Ming," Zhu said. "He is in a cell in the basement and will be going to jail for a very, very, long time."

"You said something about two options."

" Well, Miss Meese, your alternative is more complicated. If you do not agree to my first proposal you will be moved to a cell alongside Liu Ming, interrogated until a confession is obtained. You will likely spend years in a Chinese jail for smuggling artifacts."

"We haven't smuggled anything, I'm a legitimate buyer and seller of antiques around the world. Our dealings are always legitimate. I've done nothing wrong here!"

"I see. I suppose in your United States you could perhaps convince a jury there was reasonable doubt since you were unaware the goods were stolen. Here there will be no legal consideration of that possibility, even if your friendly embassy is present."

Zhu suddenly exited the room and spoke to the female officer, who had been watching through the one-way mirror. He asked what she thought, and she complimented him on his approach. She believed the American woman was ready to crumble.

Sally's head was spinning after Zhu's sudden exit. She did not want to spend any more time in this place than she had to. It was important for her to let Xu know what was going on. Someone monitoring the suitcase's location would know it was still in Beijing, though they might not know where. She had no idea what the company contracted to handle the shipment would be doing now about the loss, but she determined to tell Zhu everything she knew—with the exception of the Triad involvement.

Zhu's manner was gentler the second time he entered the room. Another officer carried the somewhat battered case to the interrogation table and placed it in front of Sally. Zhu stared into her eyes with a harsh expression, but before he could even ask the question she spoke out. "If I may be allowed to return to the U.S. I'll provide you with a complete statement of everything I know."

"That is most wise, Miss Meese. This is the best approach for you and I think I can agree to it. Trust me, this is unusually lenient in terms of normal protocol in matters of this nature. Now, tell me what you know and what your relationship with Liu Ming is."

She seemed to relax somewhat, and took a deep breath before speaking. "Liu Ming approached our company about the sale and purchase of certain relics; we didn't question the origin as we were assured the paperwork was in order. Liu Ming was to handle the shipment to the U.S. and payments were to be made to cover that. We provided this particular case to ensure there were no losses of items along the way. We took additional security measures such as tracking the case, adding more locks, and sealing the lid to monitor if it was opened en route. It's as simple as that!"

"I hope it is indeed that simple, Miss Meese. Assuming your detailed statements check out, you will be free to board a plane next week for New York after your passport is returned to you. We will have to report this to the U.S. authorities due to agreements between our two countries. Once your statement is typed and signed, you may return to the hotel. But you must wear a small tracking device until you leave the country."

Zhu motioned to the suitcase. "Please open this for me as quickly as possible." She began to spin the combination wheels on the locks to open the lid; inside she entered another two combinations. When the cover was released the goods were finally visible to Zhu. He tried not to disclose his surprise at the beauty of the contents. While he knew little about ancient artifacts, he certainly understood the value of these items. Inside the case was also the bill of sale for the items as well as certifications of their origins and export licenses for them. Zhu called assistants in to take the papers away for analysis. It was important to find out if other officials had been involved with Liu in forging the documents.

In the corner of the case sat a small transmitter with two lights flashing, which Sally confirmed to be the tracking device. Zhu ordered his officers not to disturb it. "I must warn you, your phones and movements will be monitored once you return to the hotel. In the meantime you are to keep the recent events secret. If anyone asks you, simply say the last time you saw the case was when Liu took it away from the hotel for shipment.

"You are to maintain this story with all your partners until you are back in New York. If you break this commitment while in China I will know about it and the agreement we have will be voided." Zhu glared at her for added effect. "Then you will be immediately arrested. I feel sure you don't care to find yourself in a Chinese prison with little chance of getting out."

He went over this again to make sure she understood what he was saying. The metal case was closed and removed from the room. Sally was told she could return to the office she had been held in previously to prepare her statement. Outside the room the officer asked Zhu if he was taking a big risk agreeing to release her. He replied that he was now more focused on the "bigger fish" and recovering all the stolen items.

Since Sally was American he could already imagine the wrangling between the two countries that in the end would serve no real purpose; release would be likely anyway. Zhu told the officer to take Sally to the office for her statement; meantime, he would talk to Liu Ming. The officer was to call George Mathers and his group as well as Chen Xing to be at Zhu's offices early in the morning to check over the relics and ascertain what was missing.

───❧───

The next day George Mathers and the others arrived at the headquarters early. They were shown to a protected area where the recovered case was being kept. Forensics had finished their work and Mathers' team was free to handle the pieces. They all donned white gloves and began to inventory the pieces.

Cross-checking them with the earlier inventories they determined that they were indeed original pieces. Chen pointed out that they were not the prime pieces in the collection, but were worth over a hundred million dollars in the current market for Chinese antiquities. They dated from the early Qing Dynasty period—quite rare and exquisite. George wondered aloud where the fugitives were. Yi was somewhere in the U.S., but so far Diao Lijun's body had not been found. Would this Liu Ming finally tell them what had happened? More than ever he believed it was the work of the Triads; they could never have appreciated a man like that.

The questioning of Liu Ming had begun in earnest soon after he was incarcerated in the basement prison; security had been doubled around his cell. Zhu had apparently received a second call from the same minister, asking why the time for the operational assaults had changed and why he had not been informed. Zhu simply told him the events forced him to move. If this was a serious issue he would be happy to outline the sequence of events for him and his colleagues.

Zhu was certain that this minister was passing information on and was now embarrassed. He knew the Triads reached into the government from many angles; quite often a source would have no idea that his information was headed to criminal groups. The minister must have realized he was incriminating himself by pursuing the matter; Zhu had listened patiently until the minister's tone changed and he congratulated those involved for a job well done.

Zhu's key concern now was where the significant items were. His best interrogators were sent to deal with Liu Ming. Zhu told them he would join them later, but for now the methods of questioning were up to them; nevertheless, he did not want a dead body on his hands.

Sally Meese had been given paper and pen to write out a detailed account of all that had transpired since her arrival. She emphasized to Zhu her position as a buyer of artifacts in the fullest legal sense and outlined the transaction she and her partner James Xu had entered into. She claimed no knowledge of Yi. She claimed to have never met or heard any mention of a Diao Lijun in any meetings, all of which had been with Liu Ming. She remained concerned that she was not allowed to contact her partner, James Xu; a large deposit had already been paid for the goods and there could be a risk of not getting it back.

Once completed, several officers including Zhu reviewed it and asked for a few clarifications and some rewriting. Finally, the female officer then typed out the formal statement and Sally reviewed it one more time before signing it. She was then advised she would be staying as their "guest" for one more day before being returned to her hotel. Her guard took her to an area where she could shower; then she would be taken to a rest area used by female officers. A monitor was attached to her wrist and verified to be functioning before the room was closed off and a guard placed outside.

George and the others were going over the relics when Zhu finally showed up to take a closer look at them. Chen described why the pieces were a significant find. None of them had a clue where the key pieces were and Zhu reported that so far Liu was saying nothing about them; he was claiming that someone must have taken them.

George and Cai were mystified; they had monitored the gallery closely and nothing had been moved out, other than the two cases with Liu. The search was thorough yet nothing had turned up. George thought perhaps those items had never been there in the first place. Cai suggested they be given a chance to talk to Liu, but was told politely that would not be allowed. The interrogation process was under way, and they could be sure that Liu would reveal everything. George grasped what that meant when Cai raised his eyebrows and grimaced.

———∝∝∝———

A forensics team leader came into the area asking to see Zhu. He glanced around nervously; he said something strange was going on and he needed to consult with him right away. Zhu waved away the man's concerns about others in the room. "It's fine; they can all listen to whatever you have."

The leader then came over to the table and started laying out dozens of photos of fingerprints taken from the gallery. "We've identified many of these prints, but what intrigued me were those we found in one place and nowhere else. All of the other prints including Liu's and Meese's and those of the staff are all over the room. That tells me this person has been careful to avoid leaving prints behind. But in this one instance he has slipped up."

"Where did you find them?" asked Zhu.

The investigator pulled out a larger photo with an arrow pointing to the location. "Here, right here . . . on the edge of the air-conditioning and heating unit."

Zhu asked if the unit had been thoroughly checked out again. A quick call ensued and the report came back that it had been. The grill was fixed solidly and the unit was fully operational. They had pushed light probes in behind the unit to see if there were any items hidden there but saw nothing.

The investigator then took a deep breath. "There's more, General." He paused as Zhu urged him to get on with it. He laid out two more photos of fingerprints. "Look at these; they are the same. Don't you agree?"

Everyone looked closely at them. The photos were enlarged, and areas on the prints were highlighted to demonstrate why they were unique. Zhu grew impatient with the overly studious man leaning over the photos. "You're the expert. So who the hell is it?"

The man pulled out another file from his pile, shaking his head.

"Well, who do you think it is then?" George asked.

"It is without doubt Diao Lijun!"

George and the others appeared shock and looked at one another. Zhu muttered "Gou niang yang de!" (son of a bitch), then ordered them all to follow him. He yelled to someone to double the guards at the gallery until they got there. As they jumped in their cars Zhu told George that the prints made sense; there was only a thumbprint and three fingers on the grill. Diao must have given up his small finger hoping it would convince everyone he was a victim. The "son of a bitch," as he called Diao, was not an accomplice; he was the real leader, not Liu Ming.

—⊗⊗⊘—

Cai, Xiao Ping, and George were still reeling from the news. Diao was not dead and everything that had transpired may have been driven by him. George thought back to how upset the family and everyone who knew him had been at their loss. He hoped this was not true, as they had liked Diao from the beginning; plus, he was undoubtedly the best in his field in China.

Zhu called his headquarters as they sped through Beijing traffic to the 798 gallery. He gave them the information he had, and said to use that with Liu Ming as they extracted his confession. George overheard the officer on the other end saying they needed to give Liu a break for a while to recover, but Zhu told him not to go easy on Liu just yet. Xiao Ping looked at Cai and George huddled in the back. She grimaced, as if to say she would not want to be sitting where Liu Ming was right now.

—⊗⊗⊘—

The Beijing Triads were in disarray after the police raids; four of the key leaders had been able to get away, however, thanks to tips from their contacts. There had been little time for the Triads to do much more than get these key people away from the targeted sites. Needless to say, losing thirty or more members was a problem; however, they were confident that most of them would be back on the streets within days with the help of their contacts.

The Dragon Master ordered an urgent meeting in a quiet hutong house close to the canal area of Houhai. It was surrounded by shops and restaurants, an ideal place to get people together and remain hidden from prying eyes. The Triad master told the members present that although they had suffered major losses there was still an opportunity to make something of it.

Through his informants he understood that the most valuable items in the collection were still missing and that their main man was still holed up in a safe area of the gallery. They would have to move quickly, though. Liu Ming had been captured, along with a portion of the collection. He did not believe that Liu Ming would hold out very long before telling the police about the safe room.

They could not wait; a team needed to get to the gallery and find a way to bring the man out, along with the relics in his possession. It would be risky but the last reports from the 798 showed heavy crowds of tourists were still in the area—with the exception of the cordoned-off location near the gallery. There were only a few police standing around. None of them looked to be Special Forces and their weapons were light.

They planned to go in heavy, to get in and out as fast as they could. If there was trouble, two men would be assigned to grab hostages. The leader left the meeting after ordering members to mobilize near the 798, dressed as tourists with their weapons well hidden.

As they dispersed, the master wondered if this would work. This whole operation was interconnected with Triads in Hong Kong and New York, and he had already lost considerable face amongst his peers. If he could not turn this situation around he had a pretty good idea what might befall him. He would need to quickly make arrangements to leave if his plan went awry. He would head to the Capital Airport and be ready. The first leg of an exodus would be to Laos, where he had property the organization was unaware of. From there he could decide where to go to disappear—if it came to that.

———— ❦ ————

Liu Ming was being interrogated relentlessly, as much through mental torture as physical beating. The interrogators outlined what they knew, saying they had been on to him for a long time. Once Liu heard that they had retrieved everything and knew about Diao Lijun he caved. They did not have to abuse him further.

He told them how it had started innocently enough, with Yi drinking and discussing the possibility of stealing the relics for themselves. They had floated the idea to Diao Lijun while at a banquet—after plying him with drink. They were both surprised when Diao reacted favorably to the suggestion. Liu had brought in the Triad contacts he had dealt with in the past and things moved quickly from then on.

Diao himself came up with the idea to sever his little finger and leave it in the lab to make it look like he was a victim. Diao would arrange things on the inside of the Palace Museum. Working with the Triads, Liu Ming made the contacts to dispose of the goods. The Triads would provide the muscle; Yi would manage the police side of things, making sure Zhu didn't get too close to what was going on. Several plans were considered before the final one was adopted; it had played out well to a point, but now Liu Ming could see it was unraveling.

———— ❦ ————

The interrogators reported directly to Zhu. They said Liu was somewhat protective of Sally Meese; he claimed she knew nothing, that she'd simply been offered cultural relics that were licensed to be sold.

The interrogators guessed he was lying but decided they had enough from him. They told Zhu they would leave him for a time to see what else was found before continuing.

Liu was physically in considerable pain and his nerves were shot. They knew that dragging him from his cell the next time would require none of the physical inducements used before; he would be putty in their hands. They did place a suicide watch on Liu; they did not want to lose him at this stage. What he chose for himself later was not their concern. He would either go to prison forever or be executed. Zhu thanked them for the update, but suggested they not leave Liu Ming for long before finishing their work.

Sally Meese was finally released and accompanied back to her hotel where numerous messages awaited her. An officer stationed at her hotel room handed them over to her. Most of them were from her partner, James Xu, but there were calls from others that the police would have already followed up on. Earlier calls from Liu Ming did not bother her as he had been arrested anyway; she could only hope he supported her story. She guessed a couple of other calls might have been from the "organization." She decided not to call them, and would continue to deny she knew them. She finally placed a call to Xu. Her phone had been given back to her, but she was reluctant to use it. She assumed it had been copied and was now likely bugged. James told her he was relieved to finally hear from her and wanted to know where she had been.

For the benefit of the listeners she expected were tuned in, she told Xu she had been traveling to a remote area, out of phone range. She assured him she was okay when he asked her if anything was wrong. She said no; it was just that she had "broken the jade goddess."

He told her not to worry about any breakages and asked when she would be back in New York. She said her flight was for the next week and he wished her a safe trip.

James Xu put down the phone and swore, calling in his associate who knew the dealings of the company intimately. "Jack, something is very wrong over there!"

"What do you mean? Is Sally all right? Is the deal done?"

"I'm not sure. She used the code I gave her to use if there were ever problems and she couldn't talk. Get on the phone right now and find out what the hell's going on. If there is something, then why haven't they called us? Do it right now!"

Some twenty minutes later Xu's associate came back looking anxious. "It's not good, James. Sally was taken by the police but was just released. According to our contacts in Hong Kong things have gone awry. I'm told you need to call them right away."

Xu soon spoke directly with the Dragon Master in Beijing and was filled in on what the organization knew at that time; somehow their operation had been compromised. They didn't know how but what they could tell Xu was his "shipment" was now in police hands. Xu by now knew a precise location but declined to tell the master for fear he would not be trusted in the future. His main question was when he would get his ten million dollar deposit back, and why no one had called regarding Sally's arrest.

He was assured that they would have called but that currently the Beijing organization was scrambling to recover. Things had moved too quickly for them. Liu Ming was in custody and thirty of their members had been arrested. It was only recently they'd received confirmation that Sally had been arrested but later released. They tried to call her but she had not responded; the police were likely monitoring her. They had heard she was cleared to leave the country the following week.

Xu was told his company would be refunded, but that kind of currency transfer was going to take some time to organize. They had to be careful to evade the banking watchdogs and police looking for money laundering. There would, however, be a 10 percent fee for Xu to get his money back.

Xu was boiling with rage at that comment—and the loss—but knew that arguing with a Triad master was futile. It would also jeopardize future dealings with the organization. He was rich enough that a million dollars here or there was of little consequence; nevertheless, he was still fuming when he got off the line and took it out on those around him. Likely, Sally would be chastised as well when she returned.

Now Xu would have to phone three U.S. private collectors to tell them the articles they were buying were no longer available. He had just lost some twenty million dollars. .

CHAPTER NINETEEN

The 798 art district was bustling with tourists, although the area surrounding the underground gallery on Fine Art Square was cordoned off. Three armed officers on the perimeter were there to ensure no tourists or locals ventured near the passageway through the galleries. The sellers of mostly Tibetan trinkets in the gallery halls were also barred from the area. Those without licenses stayed well clear, except the woman whose cart had been smashed by Liu Ming as he fled through the alley.

Somehow the weathered old Tibetan had pushed her way through the police perimeter, screaming at the officers and demanding to speak to someone about the loss of her cart and goods. Tourists stopped to watch, and the police did their best to prevent them from taking photographs. There were not enough men on duty to handle the growing crowds, but those present tried to placate the woman and persuade onlookers to move on.

The two officers in the bunker gallery climbed the stairs and opened the door to hear what was going on. They knew Zhu was heading over, so they called operations to advise him that an altercation was developing and they needed help; meantime, they would lock themselves in and stay clear of the fray.

The Triads dispatched to the gallery traveled in a large van with dark-ened windows. Driving into the 798 entry road they could see a few po-lice standing around, lazily vetting vehicles as they came into the area. They appeared to have little interest in checking anyone thoroughly; if they did, the blue van had been stolen only that morning from the airport and its theft was unlikely to have been reported as yet.

They drove to the gallery taking care to stick to side roads. Gang members climbed out at different locations to make their way on foot. Dressed casually they carried backpacks slung over the shoulders hid-ing weapons, explosives, and masks for when they were ready to act. The van driver parked, waiting for the call to rush to pick up every-one—if they were successful. Some of the members thought the at-tempt was too risky, but had made their oath to uphold orders; their families would be well taken care of if anything happened to them.

Four of the Triad members strolled amongst the crowds until they reached the area around the gallery, then moved to recessed doorways to don face masks as if to guard against pollution; two moved to the outside of the crowd. Those two scanned the crowd carefully; they were there for backup should anything go wrong. They had separate tasks to perform if given the go-ahead but they needed to find the targets and be ready. The group received an urgent call; they needed to move quickly as more police were on the way. They likely had only twenty to thirty minutes before the area was swarming with police.

The old woman had become so emotional she was ranting. Her pres-ence was the perfect distraction for what the Triads needed to accom-plish. They quickly pushed through the crowds, which parted when they spotted men with weapons. There had been enough terrorist

troubles in western Xinjiang and everyone assumed the men were terrorists. By the time most of the crowd realized what was going on the
Triads had grabbed the three officers guarding the perimeter, ripped off
their phones, and pulled small weapons from their belts.

The crowd panicked. The sight of men waving guns and attacking
police officers sent everyone running off in all directions. Shots were
fired in the air to further intensify the confusion. Cell phones were being used to call out to friends, relatives, police, and even the local news
station. It was pandemonium outside the gallery.

The reports from the gallery filled police and military radios as their
vehicles raced towards the scene. Zhu suspected what was going on and
urged the drivers to forget safety and do whatever it took to get there
quickly. He warned all cars and their occupants to be ready, to make sure
they had protective gear on and weapons in hand. He told George and
the other outsiders to stay well back; once they arrived they were not to
get involved until called upon. He feared this was about to get ugly.

An approved broadcast on the main Beijing TV station announced
a terrorist attack underway in the area; the location was off limits to the
public. Internet coverage was already breaking out overseas through news
reports and social media posts. Nevertheless, after the initial phone calls
and messages went out, all outside communication lines were shut down.

Zhu responded to calls from other leaders that he was en route to
the art district. He emphasized he did not consider this a terrorist attack, but a continuation of the stolen relics matter, likely a last-ditch
effort to retrieve certain high-valued items hidden somewhere in the
gallery. He did not mention Diao Lijun's name or waste valuable time
giving them details. As they headed along Juxianqao Road with lights
flashing and sirens blaring they could see people fleeing the area while
other gawkers congregated to see what was going on. As they passed
the red 798 Art District sign, police were doing their best to control the

mayhem. Zhu muttered to George that this would be exactly what the gang was hoping to accomplish.

———— ∞∞∞ ————

Panic swept the square. Triads dragged the officers with them into the gallery entrance, breaking through the door to the stairs below, yelling for whoever was down there to hold their fire. Thrusting the officers in front of them with guns to their heads, the two officers in the gallery surrendered quickly; they had no stomach for causing fellow officers to be shot. Once the gallery was taken over, the occupants were gagged and tied and the pair of gang members with AK47's took up position at the gallery entrance. The leader phoned the black van to get to the entryway as quickly as he could.

They knocked on the heating grill and within minutes a tired and disheveled Diao Lijun worked his way out from behind the heating assembly, swinging the entire unit clear. He was told they needed to leave right away; a van was on its way to pick them up. Diao scurried back through the opening to drag out the case containing the most valuable parts of the treasure collection. One gang member tried to take the case from him; Diao waved him off insisting he was hanging on to it himself.

———— ∞∞∞ ————

The driver of the black van started to pull out of the side road he was parked in, but panicked visitors were streaming past, some dragging small children along with them. It took him time to get out to the main street without hitting anyone. As he moved towards the Fine Art Square he could hear sirens blaring and called his colleague to tell him a heavy police and military contingent was arriving. He had no chance to get through to them, so he would pull over where he could and wait for their call. Once parked, he climbed out and opened the hood, standing by the vehicle as if checking the engine out. He did not want an officer trying to move him away.

As two of the Triads holding the perimeter heard the police arriving they too backed up all the way to just inside the entrance of the alley between galleries and parked. One of them went in to discuss the situation with the gang leader, who was flanked by a disheveled Diao Lijun. They phoned the Dragon Master and advised him the situation was changing; they had lost the element of surprise and reinforcements now surrounded them. They would have to negotiate their way out.

As Zhu and other vehicles arrived at the square he could see the crowds were thin but not cleared; police officers were nowhere to be seen. A few diehard onlookers and foreigners seemed mesmerized by the confusion and were snapping photos and taking videos on their smart phones.

Zhu shook hands with the local police commander, who pulled up at the same time, and discussed the situation briefly. Now that Zhu was present a swarm of Special Forces suddenly appeared. In the alley to the underground gallery, a gang member was holding his machine gun at the ready, the door behind him slightly open. The commander told Zhu there were now at least five terrorists in the gallery as far as they knew.

Zhu was suspicious and feared they had walked into a difficult situation. He ordered his team of snipers to focus on the man in the doorway. He planned to approach him and try to find out what they wanted. He suspected it would involve allowing them to get away, presumably with Diao Lijun and the remaining treasure, if indeed Diao was down there.

At this stage the story of a terrorist attack was being maintained; the authorities preferred it that way since this had become international news. They couldn't completely hide what was going on, but they were shutting down websites declaring that this was not the work of an outside terrorist organization. The remaining onlookers were being dispersed and police were checking their cell phones, hoping that no images had already made it out of the area.

Zhu put on a bulletproof vest and passed his weapons to the commander, advising his sniper to shoot the man at the door if he looked like he was going to use his weapon. He told everyone else to hold their fire; no one was to get trigger happy—yet.

Zhu raised his hands and walked slowly across the square in front of the gallery. George Mathers, Cai, and Xiao Ping stayed well back, sticking close to a wall near other galleries. As Zhu approached the alley the man ordered him to stop some four or five meters from him. Zhu asked to speak to his leader. The man told him to just talk to him directly, but Zhu sensed he was a low-level gang member. He demanded to speak to whoever was in charge. Apparently being prompted from someone inside the door, the man repeated that Zhu could address him.

For the time being Zhu refrained from referring to them as a Triad gang and only used the word "terrorist," and asked what they wanted. He had a cell phone in his hand that he wanted to hand over so they could communicate directly if needed. Pausing for a moment to catch instructions from behind, the man told Zhu that was okay but not to come closer, to kick the phone over. As he picked it up Zhu signaled with his right hand for no one to try to shoot him while he was bending down and distracted.

The man warned Zhu that they were holding officers as hostages. They wanted the police and Special Forces to back off and allow them safe passage; otherwise, they would kill the officers one by one. For now he said Zhu needed to back up and they would talk more by phone. Zhu told him he would discuss their request and call them on the phone, but emphasized he had them surrounded and would have no compunctions about killing everyone inside if it came to it.

Zhu walked back across the square slowly; sharpshooters had the man's head in their sights. A few minutes later Zhu's own phone rang; it was one of the ministers. Zhu explained the situation briefly.

"Zhu, it's entirely up to you whether you decide to negotiate or attack the gallery directly," the caller said. "If you lose the hostages, that would be terrible; however, we do not want to bend to the will of terrorists or these gangs, whoever they are. That would set a dangerous precedent. The eyes of the world are now on this incident, and we expect you to handle matters with the local police and Special Forces prudently. That's all for now. Good luck!"

Zhu called the number of the phone he had passed to the gang, knowing as the gang members had certainly guessed that the lines were being monitored. A different and far more self-assured individual answered. When asked why Zhu needed to call him, he gave his name as "Zhang," a common name, no doubt not his real one.

"We have no time here to mess around, Zhang, or whoever you are. What do you expect to achieve from all this?"

"We want safe passage out of here! Very simple for you to arrange. That way you get all your officers back alive."

""Not so simple at all. Why do you think the authorities would agree? This is China. Not some weak foreign government. You know how we deal with people like you."

"If they don't agree we'll begin shooting your friends here one by one. It really is that simple. We know foreigners are out there watching this. How do you think that will play out? The foreign press love stories like this."

"That's the last thing we want, but perhaps we can avoid it. I do have a deal to offer you if you want to leave the area alive." It was then Zhu told him that they knew Diao Lijun was in there. He said all they needed to do was release the officers and Diao Lijun, along with certain stolen goods. If they did that Zhu would allow the others to walk away; otherwise, he would have no choice but to take them all—one way or another, dead or alive.

Zhang objected vociferously. "This is not a negotiation! You don't understand what's going on here! Things are not as they seem. Your superiors have more to consider; that's all I'll say for now!"

As the man rang off, Zhu's immediate thought again was that something else was out there, a bomb perhaps? It was not likely limited to the gallery, whatever it was.

———

Within ten minutes Chinese authorities were patched into the local commander at the art district to ask what was going on. He told them there were a number of officers inside the gallery being held hostage, no one else. Zhu's hostage cell phone rang again and he motioned for silence around him, suspicious that something else was going to happen soon, but continuing to wonder what it might be.

It was Zhang demanding an immediate answer on their request to be free to leave.

"You must be joking!" Zhu told him. "I'm still waiting for higher authorities to let me know whether or not to proceed to take you and the others out alive or dead, regardless of the officers inside."

Zhang swore at Zhu. "Don't be so stupid! I said things are more complicated. Set your watch for two minutes, then you will find out what complications await you the longer the delay in letting us walk out of here."

With that the phone clicked off; an ominous echo remained as he held the phone away from his ear. He sensed right away it could be a bomb, but where? The effort to move civilians away from the area intensified. The arrival of extra police and military personnel helped move more of them through the main exits but not as fast as Zhu knew was needed.

After two minutes one of the police officers was thrust through the outer gallery door. Staggering forward, bound, gagged, and blindfolded, he collapsed within feet of some security personnel. Before Zhu could warn other officers, three men rushed to assist their comrade. The explosion that greeted them immediately killed all four of them. A second but larger explosion came from the direction of the main entrance. The cloud of ugly smoke rising above the run-down structures of the galleries told Zhu he had a lot more to worry about than the mess in front of him. It took much of his iron will to hold other officers back from storming the gallery then and there.

Zhu received an update seconds after the second explosion; it was not good. A bomb had been detonated near the main gate just as people were being led through. It was chaos with security and civilian casualties. Added to the misery was news that part of a U.S. tour group had been seriously injured with some deaths still being tallied. This was now very much an international incident.

Zhu quickly briefed the local Beijing commander and advised him to call the Foreign Ministry. The commander rolled his eyes, as if to indicate this was not a call he wanted to make. He reached his headquarters and quickly told other officials what had just happened. The authorities were not happy with the situation at all. When he finished the call he turned to Zhu and warned everyone that the premier was now being called, as were the Americans in Beijing. For now, they were to continue referring to this as a terrorist attack.

Zhu discussed the situation with the commander, who seemed happy to defer to him. Zhu knew that in the end, if anything went awry, the blame would be on his shoulders alone.

CHAPTER TWENTY

After a few minutes of discussion, Diao and Zhang decided it was time to call Zhu again. Diao had been surprised to hear the police knew he was not only alive but in the bunker; they most likely knew he had key pieces of the treasure as well. He assumed the police had obtained the information from Liu Ming and wondered what else Liu might have told them.

Diao began to take over activities in the gallery, standing just inside the doorway with Zhang as Zhang phoned the Dragon Master. Later he listened in as Zhang called to demand an answer from Zhu. The bombing was not something Diao would have done but he had limited control over arrangements the Dragon Master made. Zhu was continuing to stall but Zhang told them to acquiesce or he would bring out another police officer and kill him. As before, Zhang said another surprise would be set in motion unless they were given free passage out.

When he hung up Zhang told Diao the police had asked for five minutes to reconsider the situation. Diao warned Zhang to be very careful and to do nothing more without the master's approval, but Zhang simply smiled, telling Diao he would do whatever he had to.

Zhu asked if anyone had other ideas before he called back. Xiao Ping told him to give them what they wanted, that somehow the relics would show up in the market and Diao could not hide forever. He smiled and glanced at George, saying he wished it were that easy. He told the Beijing commander he had a plan that would free the hostages but they could lose their current advantage over the criminals; however, it might limit their ability to resolve this to everyone's satisfaction. Zhu went over it in some detail and then left the commander to organize his men. It was critical that the thieves did not get away, and that the hostages were released as soon as possible.

Zhu made one call before proceeding; the authorities were divided over simply going ahead and risking more loss of life or allowing Zhu to play his idea through. By the time he finished the call he knew he was on his own; if he failed, his career would be over, perhaps worse.

Zhu called Zhang while George and the others stayed quiet. "This is General Zhu. I'm telling you again, we do not negotiate with terrorists. I have one offer to make before ordering an assault; if everyone with you is killed then so be it, but I will personally do my utmost to try to take you and Diao Lijun alive." His voice hardened. "Then I will ensure you two have the most miserable deaths imaginable without any trial and to hell with the consequences for me personally."

"You might frighten Diao Lijun but I couldn't care less! What's the offer?"

"Your vehicle will be allowed to travel to the square and depart but not with all your hostages. When the van arrives you release two of the officers. When you reach the 798 exit, two more officers are to be released. The remaining hostages are to be released prior to the turnoff to the airport; there we stop following you."

Zhu was surprised when Zhang asked for a few minutes to review the proposal. His response to George Mather's quizzical look after the call was to shrug. He had no idea what was going on with the Triad, and readied his men to storm the gallery.

———— ∽∾∾ ————

Zhang and Diao discussed the offer directly with the Dragon Master. As long as they could safely get to some preplanned destination, other members could be waiting to help get them or the treasure away from the police. They would actually be better off without hostages to deal with.

Diao pushed for preventing the police hostages from being shot at this stage; they were the only advantage they were holding. Zhang argued for his plan to shoot another officer in front of everyone, and continue to do so until they received an agreement that allowed them to get away scot-free. The master told them he was under pressure from the organization to resolve the incident, news of which was spreading among their leadership. The situation was attracting far too much attention; a full-scale assault on the organization by the authorities would be a disaster, especially for some of their people inside the police and government.

———— ∽∾∾ ————

After a few minutes Diao called Zhu. Zhu's response to hearing Diao's voice was cool, his disgust obvious. Diao told him they could agree to Zhu's proposal, but with a few slight adjustments. Asked what they were, Diao indicated they would release the hostages as requested, but beyond the turn to the airport expressway two of the hostages would remain in the vehicle. Assuming they made it safely to the Houhai Lake area they would be released unharmed, just outside the canal area along the Dianmen Xi Dajie Road.

"No police are to follow us after we enter the freeway," Diao said. "And if there is any sign of a helicopter overhead the hostages will be shot and dumped on the road. We'll allow one police vehicle to await the drop-off at Houhai. If any more police than that are seen in the area they will be killed."

Diao then told Zhu that despite what he may think of him, it was he that convinced these people not to just kill the hostages and fight it out to the end.

Zhu took a few seconds, then agreed. "But I need an hour to clear everything," he added. "I don't want your thugs to see a police or military vehicle in the area doing its usual job and overreact. And, again, I need to tell those above me what is going on."

Diao ended the call with a deadline of one hour before the first officer would be brought out and shot. They would contact their driver with details a few minutes before its arrival so police would not try to stop it. He then called the master and made arrangements for the next phase after they reached the Houhai area. It was important to have everything in place in order to pull this off.

After hanging up, the master finally envisioned an end to this debacle, and decided to immediately leave the Capital Airport and get back to one of his safe houses near the Houhai district.

Zhu turned to the commander and between them orders began going out. They had to clear all official vehicles out of the path of whatever vehicle would come to take the Triads to the Airport Freeway and on into Beijing, all the way to Houhai. Zhu wanted plain-clothes police positioned where the hostages were to be released, and ready to be in full pursuit.

The two men agreed that the thieves were heading for Houhai to get lost in the narrow hutong streets and alleys, where cars couldn't gain access. Zhu called his military contacts and asked them to send a small drone over the Houhai area and remain there. Their initial reaction was negative, but they soon changed after he gave them a superior's name and phone number. Zhu said, "Please call him and explain why you won't be able to assist in this rescue mission."

As Zhu set to work on logistics of the operation, two Americans arrived with a representative from the Foreign Ministry as observers.

As Zhu was busy with the commander, he asked George to brief the Americans on what was going on. The government representative was surprised that Zhu turned to some foreigner to do this, but Zhu told him not to worry, Mathers was being helpful and fully understood the situation.

Zhu whispered in George's ear to tell Cai and Xiao that under no circumstances were they to refer to the Triads as anything but "terrorists"; he was personally accountable for any reports to the contrary getting out. Zhu overheard George relay the message to his colleagues and then proceed to talk to the observers, explaining how terrorists had attacked the area, that police hostages were still inside, and in general what Zhu and the commander planned to do.

As their questions began, it was clear that the two observers were not diplomats but security specialists; they had close-cropped hair and bulging necks. Zhu recognized exactly what they were the minute they climbed out of their embassy vehicle. They both demonstrated fluency in Chinese, claiming they had been on assignment in the so-called "commercial section" of the embassy for three years.

The Beijing police commander wanted to ignore them, but with the deaths of American tourists his superiors had approved the visit. The instructions passed to both him and Zhu was that the diplomats were not allowed access beyond the perimeter of the operations, and under no circumstances were they to become directly involved.

The police had been scanning the art district for a large van parked somewhere in or approaching the district, and they suspected the vehicle was already there. They cautioned that no one was to approach any suspicious vehicle, only to report its whereabouts at this stage. There were five potential vehicles parked inside the area away from the square, but only three had drivers hanging around them. They were well away from the police cordons but were now under close watch.

A few minutes before the hour was up, Diao called to advise that a large black van would be moving to the square; any attempt to stop it would result in someone losing his life immediately.

Zhu in moments received another call saying that a large black passenger wagon, Chinese made, was pulling out from its parking place. Its driver was spotted wearing a face mask as he closed the engine hood and get into the vehicle. Within minutes the van was edging its way through the cordon of officers; the commander charged one of them with getting a tracker on the van if he could.

The tracker was easily attached under the rear bumper as the vehicle edged through the final cordon. It pulled up in front of the gallery entry blocking out any views down the alley. Zhu was immediately on the phone, this time with Diao, asking for the first hostages to be released. Shortly after, two police hostages were released; their arms were bound and tape covered their mouths, but their legs had been untied. Once the freed officers reached their colleagues, they were debriefed quickly. They described their capture and said the dead security people were still lying in the basement of the gallery.

After several minutes Diao appeared alongside the van and shouted to the police to hurry up, claiming he could "only control these people for so long."

———— ∞ ————

The captors forced the remaining police hostages, who were tethered together, into the black van. Diao was determined to honor his part of the bargain with Zhu, as he wanted no more blood on his hands. He ordered that the ropes attaching the hostages be removed, but told them their hands would remained tied.

Diao brought the large treasure case to the side of the van, out of view of the onlookers and made sure it was safely inside where he could control it. With five captives inside the van as well as the gang members it was a tight squeeze. The hostages had to suffer a little longer with being jammed in with their captors, most of whom would have had no compunction about putting a bullet through their head.

Diao apologized to them over Zhang's derisive remarks. They had been in the wrong place at the wrong time, but he was confident now they would all be safe. He told them that if their fellow police officers and the military did nothing foolish, they need not worry. One young officer, shaking in terror, thanked him saying he hoped he could be back with his family soon.

The van exited the gallery area and slowly headed left and up the street toward the main road, Juxianqao Liu. At the exit they stopped but the police stepped back to allow them through. The uniformed officers were doing their best to keep onlookers at bay but it was proving difficult. They had also tried to clear the crossover just outside the art district entrance; nevertheless, the media were there trying to understand what was happening.

The van's blacked out windows prevented anyone from seeing what was going on inside. The driver removed his terrorist mask but donned a baseball cap pulled down over his eyes, and put on sunglasses. He would be hard to recognize even if someone was able to get a photo of him.

⸎

Zhu and the others were following the van at a distance when it drew to a halt, just before reaching the entrance. The side door of the van slid open and one young officer was pushed out to the ground; the two remaining inside the van appeared to be alive. Officers jumped out of Zhu's vehicle and ran towards the released policeman. He was immediately led to a separate vehicle to be checked over by a medical team.

Zhu and his team followed the van out of the area, then turned right toward the airport expressway; their next turn should be a left into Beijing. All cars stayed well back so as not to alarm anyone in the black van. Zhu and Diao remained in contact as the journey progressed.

———— ∞∞∞ ————

The gang in the van continued to watch for police tailing them, other than the entourage following to retrieve the hostages. Once they were on their way, Diao advised Zhu not to follow them any further; the only vehicle they expected to see next was the one at Houhai in the canal district, waiting to pick up the last two police officers. As the van reached the Airport Freeway an argument ensued between Zhang and Diao. Zhang insisted they simply shoot both officers and be done with them. Fortunately, Diao held his ground, but he expected there would be a score to settle with Zhang if they survived.

———— ∞∞∞ ————

Zhu talked to the released officer but learned nothing new, except to confirm that the only man without a mask matched the photo of the person called Diao, and that he did have a suitcase. The officer told him the van was in constant contact with someone on the phone helping to organize their escape.

Zhu instructed everyone to head toward the Houhai area with extreme caution. He did not want to alarm the gang into doing anything to the hostages, but needed to be close enough to try to capture them after the release. Zhu was a realist; he felt the two officers in the van had little chance of surviving the journey to Houhai; if they did it would surprise him.

———— ∞∞∞ ————

As they raced towards Beijing, Diao asked a Triad member in the van to give him his backpack, the largest one that had been used to conceal one of the AK-47s. He pulled the suitcase from behind his seat and transferred the relics that were inside, asking for one of the gang's jackets. He was given one with a hood, a baseball hat, and sunglasses. Diao handed his own jacket over and passed the suitcase back with instructions that once they got out of the vehicle they were to throw the case somewhere difficult to get at. Diao noticed Zhang looking over with a wry smile as he relocated the treasure pieces. He had no illusions regarding what the master may have told Zhang. Ensuring that they got their hands on the treasure was more important to them than his survival.

The van continued downtown, finally turning right onto the Second Ring Road; they continued to report their position as they sped towards the turn-off at Deshengmen Inner Street heading south. They turned left suddenly on Dranmen Road, slowing as they approached the Canal District. They continued until they could make a U-turn, positioning themselves on the pedestrian side of the canal entrance, just down from a Starbucks and restaurants farther along.

They anticipated plenty of tourists there and hoped to take advantage of any confusion they could create. The roads were crowded as usual but the van made the best progress it could, unhindered to that point. Diao and Zhang had no illusions they were safe yet; they were surely being monitored, though no police vehicles were in sight and no helicopter was buzzing overhead.

The operations center in Zhu's crisis room continued to feed everyone on the progress of the gang. The tracker was working fine but more importantly the drone Zhu had commissioned for assistance was in operation around the Houhai area awaiting the van. The drone would give them the best view of the gang's attempt to lose their vehicle and escape.

Trying this was a huge gamble on Zhu's part, but he felt he had no choice if he was to save the hostages. He also knew the consequences if he failed to retrieve the stolen items.

As the gang approached the southern end of Houhai Lake, Diao watched out for police; other Triads were already in place in the area. Diao spotted the lone police vehicle parked in the specified area with just two officers in the front seat awaiting their arrival. Diao told the driver to move slowly along the street in front of the canal. They were not to stop until they found an area where there were plenty of tourists. He ran over how he wanted this handled so that everyone would be prepared.

Reports confirmed the van had arrived at Houhai and was in front of the canal entryway. They had not cleared the area as this would have been too obvious to the gang that the police were waiting for them. The two officers who were to receive the hostages expressed concern over the radio that too many tourists were milling around. Suddenly the door of the van facing the road was opened wide and the two remaining hostages were pushed viciously onto the road. Several cars slammed on their brakes or swerved to miss the two men lying on the road.

With the van moving forward slowly Diao spotted a larger crowd of foreign tourists that had just arrived by bus. They were being led by a Chinese interpreter, a yellow flag raised above him, and his loudspeaker blaring. Diao told everyone to get ready and directed the driver to park alongside the tour group.

As all eyes focused on the officers lying on the road, Diao slipped out of the van and into the crowd wearing the ball cap, glasses, and backpack. He kept low as the crowd became onlookers to whatever was causing the commotion on the road. To stir things up even more, shots were fired around the hostages. The van soon sped forward to the first corner and took a hard right towards the hutong area and narrow alleys, passing rickshaws parked along the street waiting for customers.

CHAPTER TWENTY-ONE

Two officers rushed to the hostages' aid as soon as they were pushed from the van. They were shaken but clearly relieved to be free. Zhu and others arrived shortly after the van had raced from the scene, and rushed over to them.

Once the hostages were secured, the chase was on for the van as it sped into the hutong area of old dwellings and narrow lanes full of tourists on foot or being ferried along in rickshaws. Plain-clothed and uniformed police appeared from nowhere in active pursuit. Two vehicles tracked the van using location feeds from the lone drone operating in the sky overhead.

In the operations room a technician reviewed footage of the hostages being ejected while shots were fired into the ground. One of the hostages had reported that one of the thieves had changed clothes in the van and emptied the contents of a suitcase into a large backpack. The technician who was glued to the monitor on his computer was growing uncomfortable with what he was trying to see. He enlarged the footage and slowed it down. Continuing to run it back and forth he grew more suspicious each time, and was finally convinced someone had sneaked away from the van during the incident.

After reviewing it with his supervisor they concluded he was right. They had all missed it; their focus had been on the two men on the ground. They called it in and were patched straight through to Zhu and the commander. They reported fleeting footage of the man as he disappeared into the crowd, heading up the side of the canal and farther into the hutong district.

———✖✖———

Zhu swore; he knew right away who it was. He slammed his fist on the dashboard, yelling out to the commander that he was sure it was that "son of bitch" Diao. He asked the caller what the guy was wearing and if he had a suitcase with him. The technician said the man was wearing a baseball cap and dark hooded jacket but carrying no suitcase; on his back was what looked to be a heavy oversized backpack. Zhu turned to George and the others, exclaiming again in foul Chinese his frustration. He was sure it was Diao, and they had lost him. Word went out in no uncertain terms to everyone who could hear that it was critical the terrorists were captured alive. Zhu particularly wanted to get his hands on the man called Zhang.

———✖✖———

Diao had moved quickly along the canal after exiting the van. When he reached the end of the canal area, past the many restaurants by the lake, he was waved over to a rickshaw waiting for him. Inside, he drew a leg-warming blanket over the backpack on the floor; he removed his baseball hat and jacket but left his sunglasses on. The driver lowered rain covers on the side of the cart to hide its occupant further.

Before the rickshaw pulled away, a young Chinese woman walked up, nodded to the driver, and climbed in. She put her arm around Diao and used a camera to hide his face as they were pulled through the streets. They looked like hundreds of other Chinese hutong tourists listening and nodding as their driver described the district's history.

The woman pulled out her cell phone and called the Dragon Master to advise him all was well; they were on their way safely with the goods intact.

The driver of the gang's van sped towards a predetermined street that narrowed to the point where a vehicle could not pass between the dwelling walls. The police were close behind. Turning into the specified alley Zhang told everyone to be ready. Within two hundred meters of entering the alley the van began scraping the walls of dwellings; its wing mirrors ripped off and sides started to crumple as the wide van jammed itself in the narrow alley.

Zhang was in the passenger seat wildly kicking at the front window trying to break it out. Once the van was at a standstill, the window was gone and the gang members scrambled. Within minutes the two police vehicles skidded to a stop behind the wedged-in van. Officers broke open the rear door of the van but saw right away what had happened. They immediately called in to headquarters to confirm what operations people were already reporting from the drone overhead: the terrorists had escaped through the front window of the van and were fleeing down the alley.

As gang members scattered, Zhang raced into a restaurant and through the kitchen into the next street. He hailed an approaching rickshaw and told the driver to get going as fast as possible, promising a big tip in return. Within minutes he was surrounded by police and under arrest. Unfortunately for Zhang, and undercover officer had been pulling the rickshaw. Zhang vehemently denied he was anything but a tourist, even after weapons and a mask were pulled from his backpack.

Word reached the Beijing commander that at least one of the terrorists had been captured. Zhu ordered that the man be taken right away to headquarters for questioning, not knowing he had Zhang in his clutches. In the interim gang members and police created quite a melee in the alleys and streets nearby, the end result being two police officers seriously injured from gunshot wounds; three terrorists had escaped but two were captured, and two killed.

One of those who escaped was carrying the suitcase and wearing Diao's jacket. Although he had been spotted, Zhu did not believe for a minute it was Diao. When the fleeing suspect flung the suitcase over one of the walls, officers pursuing him paused, deliberating over who was to retrieve the case as the other kept up the chase. The short delay allowed the man to slip into a courtyard home where he hid under a covered stack of roof tiles behind a row of old bicycles. The police lost him but found the suitcase, only to discover—to their embarrassment—that it was empty.

Zhu made his way back to the operations center knowing full well Diao had escaped and taken the relics with him. The police officers held hostage were saved but the remaining treasures lost. He needed to figure out his next move, although he suspected he would be removed from the case.

News reports were formally released shortly after the capture of the terrorists. They revealed the attack in the 798 area, gave details of how police were taken hostage, and hailed the efforts of the Chinese military and Beijing police, who had not only secured the release of all the hostages, but also captured some of the terrorists. Further details would filter out through unofficial channels, but by then the media would have moved on to new stories.

Needless to say, the happiest people at that time were the hostages. The Chinese premier, nonetheless, was pleased to get a call from the U.S. president, who praised his taking actions to minimize American casualties. He also expressed his sympathy and condolences for the officers killed in the rescue operation.

The call from operations and the switch the officer had seen in the van on the way to town confirmed what Zhu had surmised. He was not happy they had allowed Diao to slip through their fingers again so easily. He half-expected to be called back to more normal duties now that the case had reached this stage. They had recovered a good many of the artifacts despite the loss of the main items, arrests had been made, and the Triad organization dealt a blow in Beijing. Zhu assumed it would now be turned over to the Beijing police to launch a massive manhunt for Diao and the relics.

The Beijing commander, in the meantime, praised Zhu to his superiors and appealed to the authorities to allow Zhu to continue assisting him in the operation. Zhu declined recommending further involvement by Chen Xing, Xiao Ping, Levee, and George Mathers in the hunt. He told the commander they knew the relics well and Chen could provide access into the underworld of the art trade if the thieves tried to move the artifacts.

George and the others returned to the lab at the university feeling somewhat lost. The excitement was over. They knew Diao was out there with the relics, likely helped by the Triads, but they would not be involved further during this phase. The police and Zhu had thanked them profusely for their efforts and assistance. Zhu acknowledged to George he doubted he would see them again, expressing again his anger at letting Diao slip through his fingers.

CHAPTER TWENTY-TWO

The Dragon Master was relieved but not happy. Diao had returned safely with precious relics likely worth $500 million or more. They were the prime pieces but his organization had suffered losses. The whole affair had drawn a lot of attention to his and other criminal groups, not to mention a few people in high places. He was still in control in Beijing, but his peers' criticism had been harsh. None of them cared much about this Diao Lijun, but they expected something to be done about the revenue from the relics in a short space of time.

Diao became angry when the master ranted about the failure of the operation and the burden he was carrying.

"Look, I gave up part of my hand for this!" he shot back.

"Oh yes, let me see, Diao, a part of your small finger. Without my protection you would not have your head!"

" Maybe that's next, is it? What in the name of the gods was I doing giving up a good life and an important position in my field. I'm a wanted man now. I doubt the authorities even know who you are, but they certainly know who I am."

The master waved the comment aside. "No worries, my friend, I can change your face anytime you want and line you up with new papers. Once we are paid, of course."

"I hope that won't be necessary, but I suppose it might be," Diao said. "I do know we need to move the relics. But acting too quickly could easily expose us. We need to spread the movement of the items into the market over time. It could take two to three years to get rid of them, but we'll get more for them that way."

The Dragon Master grabbed Diao and slammed him against the wall. "You idiot!" he shouted. "I have six months to move these before my neck is on the block."

Diao had not seen the master lose his composure to this level. "Okay, okay. I'll work with you to do what I can. We need to wait a few days and we'll contact our customers."

"That's better, Diao, the sooner the better."

"I hope you and your colleagues understand that the prices will be below what they could be."

"Let me worry about that, Diao. Just find us buyers, and make it fast!"

They both agreed that they might need to talk to Deng and to James Xu. They hadn't returned Xu's $10 million deposit as yet, but Sally Meese had at least been released and flown out of Beijing. Diao needed to get to work on the problem and enjoy the rewards that were coming. The master had already provided a beautiful young woman to assist him. Although she did even more than assist him, Diao knew full well the woman was assigned to watch his every move.

Sitting in the lab George Mathers struggled to get started back on the scripts. Xiao Ping was still tired and yawning from lack of sleep. Cai lay back in his chair with his feet up on the desk as if wondering where to begin. George was still trying to get his mind off Diao and the relics. Cai reminded everyone the scripts were not some made-up legend; there was a treasure out there waiting to be found that would make what had already turned up look like costume jewelry.

"We need to take stock of where we are with the translation work," George said. "I know it's a lot more work than any of us anticipated but we need to start bringing it together. What's your assessment, Cai?"

"I know what you mean, George; it's even more difficult as we peel back the layers. This story was written in at least three distinct periods. It's likely that this whole legend is, as always, woven around a thread of truth. The rhythm of writing that's been analyzed clearly indicates several writers through the ages. The story of how the first dragons appeared in China is to me something like your Adam and Eve tale. Later, though, the theme of warring factions, supported by different dragon forces, starts to strengthen the validity. I'm convinced the latter portions that describe the establishment of the Dragon Keepers and the tithing to the dragons is plausible based on the small part of treasure we've seen. What about you, Xiao Ping?"

"I agree with Cai, but our progress is slow. We need more hands, George, but so far neither the university nor authorities will give us any more than we have. I think they are short-sighted; too many calling this just another legend."

George concurred. "I can't understand it, when they have the dragon scales as evidence. And surely the treasure already found should get their attention!"

"You have to understand how the Party looks at this," Xiao Ping said. "In their world these stories are just that. Look how long it's taken them to even open the door to religion. Yes, they see evidence of a treasure, but tales of ancient dragons and treasures? That doesn't fit their world at all!"

"You may be right but they'll certainly take any treasure we find! Realistically, how far along are we with the translation of the whole thing? Cai?"

"I'd say halfway, but at least we have a cross-sectional thread emerging. What do you think, Xiao Ping?"

"Maybe a little more than that. The challenge is putting the translated symbols into sentences that make sense. It's coming together, but very slowly. I agree with you, Cai, that what we have seems more fanciful in the earliest writings. The story of the first dragon egg and how it's raised alongside the boy certainly is. That it could communicate with him seems unbelievable.

"The later stories of the warring states, and the impact of the dragons on this grown leader seem less fanciful. The description of the endowments of treasures to the dragons fits with what we have found. Without that and the other scales and treasure I would have said it was time to wrap up a nice legend—as you always thought, George. Now I can't do that. To my mind there's more to find, including evidence of other dragons and a treasure."

Cai sat up straight in his chair. "I agree wholeheartedly with Xiao Ping, George. Let's carry on. Once they see what we really have here, they may give us more help."

George decided to leave it at that for the time being and continue their work. He did lower his voice and ask Cai what he planned to do with the relics he had quietly retained and hidden away. Cai flushed as he always did when this was brought up, mumbling to George and Xiao Ping about not being sure. One day they would either join the collection or might even fund their research into the rest of the scripts and treasures if it came to that.

Xiao Ping and George both warned him he was playing with fire by not turning them in now. They hoped he would not get burned, nor them too by the fact they knew but didn't speak up.

Cai simply shrugged, then told George not to worry; he would cross that bridge if it got to that point. George declined Cai's offer to tell them where they were hidden. He did not want to know, which would further implicate him.

———— ✲ ————

George suggested they get a little exercise, walk across campus to Cai's favorite coffee shop. It seemed a welcome excuse not to start working on the remaining scripts. Locking the door behind them they headed down the corridor and out of the building. They passed Professor Deng, who smiled and whispered to George as he shuffled by. "Dragons, I told you; dragons it is!"

George ordered straight espresso coffees; everyone was bleary-eyed after all the excitement over the last few days. They discussed again their shock in discovering Diao Lijun had turned into the villain he had. Cai thought it was a simple case of greed. Xiao Ping thought it was also his opportunity to spice up a relatively dull life centered for too long on his activities in the Palace Museum.

Cai smiled. "He certainly received a load of professional accolades, but I wonder if he had ever done anything unorthodox before. Perhaps he craved excitement of a different kind!"

"You mean like George Mathers here?" Xiao Ping asked.

Laughing they settled into their coffees, then George's phone rang. He spoke for some ten minutes before finally saying thanks and good-bye, followed by a comment the caller would see him soon.

Xiao Ping looked at him, puzzled. "Who was that?"

George stood up. "Let's go, we have some unfinished business to tend to."

"What on earth are you talking about?" asked Cai.

"Zhu's back on the case. He needs us!"

Cai smiled and jumped up. "What are we waiting for? The scripts can wait!"

CHAPTER TWENTY-THREE

They arrived at police headquarters to find a large meeting in progress with Commander Xi and Zhu and Chen Xing also there. They were cataloging the recovered relics and needed everyone's final overview to be clear just how many pieces might be in Diao's and the Triad's possession. Xiao Ping was able to clarify that in addition to the two pieces dismantled they still had a large number that were certainly the most spectacular and valuable. None of them mentioned the ten items Cai Levee had in his possession.

Commander Xi reported on the status of the hunt for Diao and the questioning of their various prisoners, especially Liu Ming and Zhang. "This so-called 'Zhang' has revealed much about what transpired, but the whereabouts of Diao is unknown to either him or Liu Ming. It is certain that he and the relics are under the protection of the Triads in a very secure location. Our teams have continued to monitor all known or suspected locations, but so far no sighting or activity related to Diao has surfaced."

Zhu indicated he would talk personally to the prisoners again; in the meantime they needed to explore other avenues to track down Diao. He threw the meeting open for suggestions and moved over to a large white board to work through any ideas.

Most of the early discussions centered around the manhunt itself; some ideas were written off as impractical, some put on the board. Zhu began to list out the actions on the board.

"First, a number of Triad sources need to be run to ground and brought in, and suspected Triad locations must be mapped out. Second, the Houhai alleys where the gang dispersed must be searched again for hideouts unknown to us. Several locations there are already being monitored. Third, known high-level gang members should be put under surveillance, their communications hacked where possible. Fourth, our particular focus will be the leader of the Triads in Beijing, our so-called 'Dragon Master.' Anything on him, Commander?"

"We aren't certain who he is. There are five prominent leaders in Beijing below him; that we know of. He seems to have kept himself off our radar."

Zhu instructed the teams to continue surveillance of the other suspected leaders but they should not bring them in yet. "I want them to continue working with Diao Lijun on moving the relics until someone makes a mistake."

Turning to the back of the room, Zhu and Xi introduced George's little team formally. Some leaders in the meeting knew them from the events at the Art District; many did not and probably were wondering what civilians were doing there, especially someone like George, the "lao wei" (foreigner).

"What do my friends back there think?" asked Zhu looking directly at George.

"Well, General, in my view we need to follow the money. There will certainly be an effort to move the relics into the market. I think Diao Lijun is an antiquarian who would have the patience to sit for years to move the goods, but the Triads will only be in it for the money. You've secured a fair part of their original haul but the best ones are still in their hands. I suspect they'll try to move them sooner rather than later."

Chen agreed with George, pointing out that the market for these items would be special; only collectors with significant funding available and who keep their collections very private would be approached by the Triads. The items would never find their way into a public auction, collection, or museum—certainly not in their lifetimes.

George continued. "There are two channels we know about right now, one through James Xu and the Meese lady, the other through Deng. When Liu Ming moved the two cases out of the gallery that day he left in one car. I don't recall what transpired with the man who left with a case. It would seem that those goods are still at large.

"Won't the Triads try to contact Deng to deliver the precious stones for the final payment? Shouldn't Deng be trying to call someone—if he has any numbers or names—to find out where his new goods are?"

Zhu thanked George for bringing up a point that was on his mind well.

When all ideas were exhausted Zhu went through them, confirming several to be handled under Xi's direct control. Zhu was planning a 'serious discussion' with Ming and the Zhang character. From the look on his face George could tell the interviews were not going to be pleasant for either of the prisoners!

Zhu asked his team to work directly on the line to collectors. He would try to obtain potential buyers' names from Liu Ming; he wanted George and Chen to focus on the James Xu and Deng avenues.

Xiao Ping suggested they find a way to get the word through to someone like Xu, or other collectors that came to light, about a fabulous treasure in the hands of the Triads. She thought that might make James Xu and Sally Meese try to communicate with the Triads again.

Cai shook his head. "Not likely," he said. "They've been caught at it once. They'll see it as too soon to try something like that, especially after Meese almost ended up in prison."

Commander Xi joined the conversation and said they might be surprised. In his years of dealing with criminals it always amazed him how people jumped right back into whatever activities they had been caught at.

George agreed. "This James Xu is known to be dealing on the black market even though he's not been caught at it. He'll be careful now, and I doubt he'll use Sally Meese as a go between again, but he could be tempted with the right carrot."

" We need to handle this James Xu carefully," commented Zhu. "What do you think, Chen Xing?"

"I suggest we use our friend Yang Guiyu, the dealer, to work on getting the word out to him through the right gallery people and underground merchants."

" Good plan; work with George and the others on that angle. The one person who is still missing is Yi; if we could find him that might help. We still have no clue where he is in the U.S. or if anything has happened to him."

Zhu advised they could use the police headquarters from now on as the main operations center, although he and others would also work out of his headquarters as needed. Specific prisoners would be interviewed in interrogation cells in his headquarters prison and not by the police, by him personally. The comment brought smirks and smiles to the faces of other officers. George realized at that point the interrogations were not going to be anything he would want to know about, and likely painful for Liu Ming.

Arrangements were made to talk to Deng and Yang as soon as possible. Before Zhu left to "interview" those arrested they talked about how to handle Deng. Commander Xi would stay behind and sit in on the discussions with Deng and Yang Guiyu, who might be of help in the fishing expedition to set out a line for Diao and Xu.

When Deng was brought in they questioned him as to what had transpired over the last few days regarding the jewel acquisition. From tapping his phones the police knew there had been no calls, but left him to confirm that. They assumed all the events of the last few days in the Art District had occupied the Triads fully.

The jewels sold to Deng were missing; even though the police had traced the other car leaving the gallery with Liu to another location, nothing was found in the raids there. It seemed likely the jewels and precious metals disappeared with the four leaders who escaped during the raids. Deng was to try calling the number he had been given and ask where his goods were. He was to tell them the funds were available and he waiting for instructions. Once he had the jewels in his sight, he would call the bank and send them the final payment.

Deng had only the one number, which they hoped was a Triad number. Deng dialed the number, and they could hear the phone ringing endlessly on the other end. He was about to give up but Xi motioned him to let it keep ringing. Eventually there was a click. "Wei," a muffled voice answered. Deng, clearly nervous, asked to speak to Liu Ming.

"Who is calling?" the Chinese voice asked in a rough non-Beijing accent.

" This is Deng An; I'm calling about a special transaction. Who is this? Is Liu Ming there?"

" He's not here. My name isn't important. Who are you anyway? How do you know Liu Ming?"

"Is there a problem with Liu Ming?" Deng asked from the hastily written note handed him by Xi.

"No, no problem. He is on a business trip right now. I'll call Liu Ming right away. Someone will get back to you that knows about a transaction with a Deng An."

With that the phone went dead. George muttered "Bingo!" and Xi smiled. Deng looked rather stunned.

They could not believe their luck; the line was still open. The person had been cautious but it indicated the Triads still controlled the line. They called Zhu with the news; he was pleased to hear it but cautioned everyone to be careful and continue with all assignments.

Zhu looked through the cell portal; Liu Ming was pacing in his cell. Zhu imagined Liu was mulling over what he had told his interrogators and what he wanted to be sure not to disclose. Zhu had the guards forewarn him that a military general, no less, was coming to interview him personally. The interrogators had, per his request, warned Liu Ming no one else would be present but this General Zhu, who had a reputation for brutality.

Zhu was a great believer in the power of suggestion as much as physical violence; in his early years he had been a practitioner of such methods that were supposedly no longer allowed. He could still perform them but had been far more successful using the prisoners' minds to convince them to talk. He was not sure with Liu if one method would work or if he would need to combine them.

When he arrived at the cell he discussed the preparations he wanted made. He asked the two interrogators to go back into the cell and make a display of preparing Liu for the meeting. He was to be stripped naked and secured to the seat with cuffs and chains. One of the interrogators was to prepare a trolley with instruments from the storeroom that were used in the old days. Trolleys dated back to the days of the revolution and were used against Communist Party members.

The officers laid out all the instruments of brutal torture for Liu to see. They brought them in slowly. A shivering Liu sat manacled to his chair and watched as they set them in front of him.

Someone else came in per Zhu's instruction and laid a large plastic sheet under Liu Ming's chair. One of the interrogators calmly commented that the last "poor bastard" Zhu had interrogated made such a bloody mess that the general had ordered them to cover the floor. They wished Liu luck and told him Zhu would be coming soon.

⁜

Outside the cell the interrogators chuckled over the scene before them, while Zhu focused on Liu Ming's facial and body movements. He decided to leave him a little longer to anticipate what may lie ahead. After five minutes they noticed Liu's anxiety growing as he began to shake. Soon after that he urinated and defecated right where he was sitting. Zhu turned to his colleagues and with a slight smirk said, "He's ready now!" and motioned he was going in.

───❦───

Zhu's facial expression darkened before entering the cell. He paused to prepare the image he wanted Liu to see and experience. He turned to the interrogators, who looked shocked at the change in Zhu, the pure evil his eyes and face projected.

Zhu was advised that Liu Ming seemed on the verge of tears; his anxiety level appeared at its limit. At that moment Zhu flung the cell door open and stormed in. He strode up to Liu and immediately kicked the chair sending Liu and the chair onto its back. Grabbing the trolley and pulling it over he stood by Liu Ming. In a menacing voice he demanded to know if Liu was going to tell him everything he needed to know or not! Liu was sobbing; he screamed that he would tell Zhu everything, but in the name of all the Chinese gods not to hurt him.

Zhu turned to the window in the wall and smiled. Two hours later he had finished with Liu; he had everything Liu could give, much of it confirming what he knew or had guessed. He left with full details of how Liu had propositioned Yi, how they lured Diao into their plans, and how the involvement of the Triads came about.

While Liu did not know the Dragon Master's name, he gave Zhu phone numbers, addresses where meetings took place, everything. He also supplied the names of eight private collectors whom they were targeting for the initial sales; Zhu was pleased to see that Xu and Deng were on the list. But he expected that with Liu now in police hands many of these trails would now be cold.

As Zhu left the room he warned Liu he might be back, thanked him for his co-operation, and closed the door behind him. He advised the interrogators to clean Liu up, get a doctor in to check him over, then put him in a half-decent cell for the time being.

After the meeting, the interrogators smiled at each other. "He hasn't lost his touch," the older man said.

CHAPTER TWENTY-FOUR

About two hours later Deng received the call they were hoping for. It was a different voice from the earlier call; it was female and she asked Deng a number of questions to verify his identity.

"We're sorry for not calling back. We've been busy the last few days but pleased to report we have some even finer items for your consideration if your investors are interested."

Xi nodded for Deng to say he was. "I'm sure we will be, but we still need the items already purchased. When can we expect delivery?"

"When we receive your final payment!" she said and told Deng it should take no time to finalize the current transaction. "We do want a deposit, however, for any new transaction in place before viewing those items. It must again be private; your appraiser may be present, of course."

"What deposit are you talking about?" Deng asked.

"For this new business we require a good faith deposit of one million U.S. dollars before any meeting; the items are that special. If you are interested, certain terms can perhaps be negotiated."

Deng thanked her for the call. Glancing at the paper pushed in front of him he also told her he now had buyers for the items already acquired. "We need delivery soon, so please let me know where to make the final payment and where the final exchange will be. Considering our past dealings, I do wonder why we need to pay just to see more items?"

The woman promised to review the issue of the deposit with her principals, as well as to get back to him regarding delivery of the sold items.

The police pinpointed the call as coming from inside the Solana Shopping Center near the Chaoyang Park District. Finding the mystery woman would be difficult but officers were assigned to visit the stores and check all video monitors to see if they could get a look at her.

Deng was sent home while officer Wang was called in again to reprise his appraiser role; the others were told to keep a distance from Deng for a while. Xi expected the Triads to be careful in dealing with him now. There was no indication the Triads had detected being followed when Deng was at the antique market, but it had been close; Wang was lucky not to have been spotted when he followed the decoys. All the police could do now was wait for another call.

The Dragon Master, Diao, and the woman argued over moving the stolen relics. The master wanted quick money from the Deng sale, perhaps to move another piece through him if they could. He also wanted to get in touch with James Xu again before others did. Diao was against it; the police had Liu Ming and he suspected they knew about James Xu. He pushed for using other channels he had in mind. It would take time but likely be safer.

To keep the operation moving the Triads badly needed a boost in funds. The master told Diao they must deal carefully with Deng, even as if he was working with the police. If a further million dollars came in, then fine, they would proceed with a new transaction; if not, they would avoid future dealings with him.

Xu was another matter entirely, according to the master; he told Diao how James Xu was connected to high-level Triads, and that if they needed to use Xu they would.

Diao and the woman were charged with dealing with Deng and the other potential dealers on Diao's list; the master would call Xu himself. There were two other good customers on their list in the U.S. aside from Xu, three more in Hong Kong, two in Russia, one in Paris, and two in Singapore. Potential clients in China, other than Deng, would be avoided for the time being.

❦

The next morning Zhu went over Liu Ming's full confession with everyone; it was incredibly detailed. He could see that Xiao Ping was wondering how badly Liu Ming was tortured to get it out of him; he turned to her and explained what he had done and how he had not touched him physically in any way. She looked relieved and one of the other officers commented to her that this was one of Zhu's special talents. Cai Levee smiled, reminding everyone of their own interviews with Zhu and Yi the first time they met. But Zhu told Xiao Ping in no uncertain terms he would have resorted to tougher questioning if he had needed to.

Zhu passed out lists of locations and people highlighted in the interview with Liu Ming and initiated follow-up as soon as possible. He said he expected that some or all of the locations had been vacated. Chen and Yang soon arrived to discuss how to set the trap lines for the relics. They compared the list Zhu had from Liu with the people Yang and Chen might know of to develop a strategy for getting information on the street about certain relics now being available.

Zhu was particularly interested in the mystery woman. She likely moved about more freely than others in the master's inner circle and might lead them to Diao. Later in the day word came back confirming Zhu and Xi's suspicions; locations for the most recent meetings between the Master and Diao had been vacated in a hurry two nights before. Police searching for clues verified the occupants had done their best to wipe the places clean in their haste but had not done a perfect job; among the prints they were able to retrieve was Liu Ming's, those of Diao Lijun and a female.

Nothing in the police database gave any clue as to her identity. Interviews with the owner of one location turned up an agreement with a woman's name and registration, but further examination showed the entries to be false. The woman had paid six months' rent in cash so there was no bank or credit card information to track. The owner's description of her was "medium height, slender, an outstanding figure, and long black hair." He said she always wore very large sunglasses and kept any dialogue to a minimum. Her clothes looked expensive and she always had a Louis Vuitton bag with her, never the same one and definitely not fake.

The detectives sent to the Solana Shopping center to look through security tapes finally came up with their best suspect: a woman in a phone booth but clearly using her cell phone. She had on a headscarf and large sunglasses. They were able to determine that after the call she went shopping further. They visited a number of women's stores to check their security systems. They focused only on the high-end stores based on the input that she had expensive tastes, finally finding her in an Italian fashion store. Their video showed her entering on the second floor level and removing her scarf and dark glasses to look at a specific dress in the window. The staff easily remembered her; the dress was the most expensive in the store and fitted her perfectly.

Not only had she discarded her disguise, but used a credit card to purchase the expensive dress. The lady who checked her out recalled her well; men in the store could not stop ogling her, and one customer got a slap from his wife for staring at her lustily. Minutes later there were clear pictures coming in to police HQ, several photos with and without her disguise, as well as copies of her credit card details.

Xi called Zhu with the news; both were surprised the woman had been so careless. Zhu doubted that the address and phone number on the account would be genuine. A plan quickly emerged for an officer to pretend to be a bank official and ask her to come to the bank as someone had used her card surreptitiously. They needed her to personally review the information at the bank before her credit card was hit with another very large sum. The officer was to be at the branch of Bank of China in Sanlitun to discuss a made-up error, and other officers would be ready to follow her to wherever Diao and the relics were hidden.

When they placed the call it took a while for anyone to answer. Detectives on the call assumed she was using two phones, this one for personal calls. They listened intently while the officer explained to the woman on the line that a serious problem with her account had to be resolved in person. The bank provided the officer with sufficient information on her account that her suspicions eased; she agreed to come right away.

There was a scramble by patrol officers to get to the branch and look out for her arrival. The credit card name was Lin Li, but the real Lin Li was quickly located working for a machinery manufacturer in Beijing. She was younger and nothing like the woman in the surveillance photos.

⎯⎯⎯◦∞◦⎯⎯⎯

The woman was seen arriving with a man by taxi at the main junction in Sanlitun before walking along the outside stores of the Village Shopping area toward the bank. The officer who spotted the woman and her accomplice get out of the cab held his station, while others trailed her to the bank. Reports went out she was on her way and to be careful; she had a bodyguard with her. She still wore dark glasses and scarf.

Officers watched her reach the northern corner of the Village stores. Her bodyguard was scanning the area for any signs of trouble.

An officer saw her stop to fumble with the large designer bag slung over her shoulder. It took a few minutes for her to find her cell phone, which she raised to her ear and listened. She was seen to lean over to the man beside her, who nodded calmly and held her closer to him. As they passed one of the main doorways, the man suddenly pulled Lin Li into the doorway for the emergency stairs into the lower level garage. Before an officer could figure out which way they had gone, they were driving out of the exit. An attendant was screaming at them to stop as they broke through the flimsy exit barrier.

The vehicle was found a few blocks away; inside the woman's scarf and glasses lay on the front seat. The area was crowded with people and close to a bus stop and waiting taxis; the couple was gone.

At headquarters word reached Xi and Zhu about the sudden escape the woman and partner had made following the phone call she received. Zhu was furious; clearly someone on the team had betrayed the mission. He wanted to know by whom within twenty-four hours, or he was taking the case away from the civilian team. He would not stand any more leaks like this.

—— ∞∞∞ ——

At the next briefing the issue of leaks was discussed. Zhu and Xi warned that anyone found letting any information out to the media or the organizations they were fighting would face severe consequences. At that Xi nodded to two detectives at the back of the room who left the room for a few moments. They came back in with a fellow police officer dressed in a prisoner's orange jumpsuit slouched in a wheel chair; he had a trace of blood at the side of his mouth but no other apparent injuries. Quickly it was understood the man was in fact in incredible pain and could no longer walk. Whoever worked on him had not been kind; he could not speak yet so the officers explained who he was.

The two men who wheeled him in had uncovered the source. The task of exposing the leak had been given to them by Xi, unhappy that one of their own might have betrayed them. They explained on the officer's behalf how a woman known to him by the name "Deco" had approached him some time ago; she had seduced him and eventually produced compromising photos and information that tied him to a Triad group. She demanded he provide information to protect the Triads. In exchange they would keep his indiscretions quiet and pay for information provided.

The officer confessed that there might be others involved inside the force but he didn't know who they might be. He swore he had given no other information out prior to this and had been threatened recently for not warning of recent police raids. He had hoped the information he provided would keep them from ruining his marriage and out of trouble at work.

Zhu thanked the detectives, asking how they uncovered him. They told him they knew the time of the call made to the woman and went through files of officer's calls looking for a match. A little friendly persuasion had then convinced their colleague to confess. Looking at the man in the wheelchair Zhu told everyone to get him cleaned up; he would pay for his treachery later but what had happened to him was a lesson for everyone else in the room. Zhu told them it was time to use this channel to their benefit. He suggested they wait and see if there were more calls to the officer for information; when the time was right they would use him to deliver misinformation.

Xi asked the dejected officer in the wheelchair if he understood what they wanted him to do and if he agreed to cooperate fully. The officer nodded showing he was still in pain, but that yes he would help. He had no choice.

Chen Xing and George's team of Cai and Xiao Ping met with Yang, the antique dealer, to discuss the lists of collectors obtained from Liu and how they would get the word out to the collectors without alerting the

Triads. Yang suggested not contacting the collectors directly; he proposed finding some interconnected channel for a pipeline into them. Yang knew some of the collectors on the list by reputation, but not all; Chen knew two of them because they were highly reputable dealers, familiar names in the business. Yang would find second tier collectors who often fed into the big money dealers; he would use them to funnel information to the underground market.

The information leaked would be that a newly discovered treasure trove of ancient Chinese jewelry had been stolen and sold through questionable sources. The police were offering a huge reward for information leading to their recovery. The groups confirmed this step with Xi and Zhu and they gave their approval, warning them, of course, to use extreme care. Xi would focus Deng and Xu's channels. These efforts were shots in the dark at this stage; the underlying goal was not to alarm the thieves and lose them completely.

When Liu Lin and her bodyguard returned to the new safe location there was concern over whether they had been followed. The bodyguard, a former security specialist, assured the Dragon Master they had evaded detection thanks to the warning call she received from her inside man. For some time she was subjected to a barrage of questions about her movements in an effort to understand how and where she had been detected. She slowly realized the police must have tracked her activities in Solana. She knew if she told the master that part he would be furious, especially since she had used her credit card so foolishly. She simply suggested they must have hacked her phone. Suspecting otherwise the bodyguard grabbed her phone anyway and crushed it under his heavy foot.

She voiced her concern about maintaining her "source" inside the police and how he would contact her now. It was important to get a number to him in case there was new information to report. Another stolen cell phone was given her to call the contact back, thank him for the information, and provide a new phone number to use for future calls. She was to be careful to talk briefly as a precaution against anyone trying to pinpoint her location.

———— ∞∞ ————

The cell phone rang where the officer was being held; one of the two men guarding him rushed to get the phone to him and alerted others to listen in. The call was from a new number; the woman's voice came on the line. "Yin, is that you? This is Deco here. Is everything all right?"

He responded quietly, "It's me. I'm fine. What about you?"

"Everything's okay, thanks to your call."

Using notes written in front of him Yin asked why she was using a different number.

"We need to be careful. Use this new number in the future; the old one is no longer valid. My friends are extremely grateful for your help and they will take care of you."

"When might that be, Deco? When will I see you?"

"Soon if you're good!" She urged Yin to call her with any valuable information; perhaps if it was really special she might see him. In the meantime she would see that he was paid. She asked him point blank if he was involved in an operation to recover stolen goods. He answered that he was not directly, but he knew there was an effort under way. He promised to listen for anything he could about it and get back to her.

She softened her final words to him. "Look, you've been a very special lover, like no other, but my friends think our relationship is strictly a monetary one. I still think about the times we met though. Perhaps we will get together soon."

As she said good-bye the officers took the phone away. Yin was bright red. One of them leaned over and in his best impersonation of Lin Li sarcastically said, "A very special lover, like no other, ooh, maybe again soon!"

The officers taunted him by wondering out loud how his wife might enjoy hearing about his escapades with this Deco woman.

Zhu and Xi had also listened in to the call; they were happy a line was open again. The trick was to keep it that way. They told the officers to watch for any cash payment being made to Yin, although they doubted she would deliver the payment herself after what happened at the bank.

Zhu directed the two officers to supervise Yin for a few days. He would need clothes and such, as well as a reason to give his wife for being away. Zhu did not want the wife alarmed just yet. They asked Zhu to let them back into the mainstream of the effort rather than being assigned to a babysitting chore, but Zhu assured them they were there because he knew they wouldn't fail him.

It took two days for Yang to get feelers out to the underground collector world. It didn't take long for wiretaps to pick up several conversations about what the precious relics might be and where they could have come from. There was open speculation they were from the Palace Museum; a number of them knew Diao Lijun and were aware he had disappeared.

The police were pleased that rumors were starting to fly, especially when second tier dealers were admitting they'd been told the items were out of their league. All the police could do after that was wait and see if the bait was taken.

James Xu received a late evening call in New York from his "special friend." He left Sally in the main living room of his penthouse suite; they had been out to dinner and were relaxing to music before going to bed.

He told Sally he had a few things to talk to some people about, to relax on the sofa. The phone itself was located in his panic room, a secure place if trouble ever developed. It was well equipped. He waited about five minutes before the call came in; the Dragon Master was soon on the line and after pleasantries an update of the current situation was exchanged. Xu was told he could purchase some of the key items the police had not retrieved; these were far better than the items they had originally allowed him to buy. The master said it was important to get this over with so the Triads could get back to their normal business; then, hopefully, the police pressure would abate.

James Xu was apprehensive about getting further involved but his collecting obsession and greed again got the better of him.

"Look, Xu, the items are worth more than five hundred million U.S., guaranteed. If you can raise the funds and agree to say three hundred fifty we can make a quick deal." He added that Xu needed to transfer fifty million to the master's private account in the Cayman Islands as his cut.

Xu argued about the price and the size of payoff to his friend. What would the master's colleagues think if they were told about that part of the deal? The immediate description of what would happen to him if he did something like that sent chills down Xu's back.

The relationship between Xu and the master went back many years; in fact, their dealings had been one of the drivers behind Xu's success, a fact the master would not let him forget. "It's time for you to make good on all my help by assisting us in getting rid of the treasures we're holding. At three fifty it's a steal; you'll make a small fortune out of it!"

"Three hundred fifty will take a little time, my friend. It's not that easy. I'll have to talk to others. I need photos and details of the goods to work with my clients to get commitments. I can agree right now to my earlier figure of one hundred and ten million dollars myself, but I need to pull others in to cover the rest. And by the way, nobody has returned the eleven million dollars I deposited for the last deal yet!"

He told the master he would need access to someone in China that was an expert on the pieces; he could not send Sally Meese again.

The master said they had a real expert Xu could use, but only in circumstances where a deal was positive; this expert would only be available in special cases. James Xu still was concerned about Liu Ming's arrest and how that may have jeopardized whatever was going on. Certainly Sally had been terrified by her experience. The Dragon Master brushed off the issue of Liu's arrest; they had adjusted their plans accordingly, and they had people on the inside who would help them. What Liu knew about their activities was already out of date.

The call ended and James returned to Sally. He would need her help with his clients but knew once the discussions came back to more of the items in China she would balk. Nevertheless, he knew how to move her to agreement through her personal greed. She would receive several million dollars in the offshore bank account he knew she maintained.

CHAPTER TWENTY-FIVE

Deng received the call from the woman regarding the delivery of the pieces he had bought and final payment details. She said the settlement was long overdue and that their second transaction also needed to be completed as soon as possible. "The new items are under offer elsewhere and likely sold, but perhaps we can release something for you if the current deal is settled quickly. I doubt, though, that you can raise the funds to cover these special pieces."

She told him she was sorry but that to view the newest items would still require the million dollar deposit, which other buyers were making to demonstrate their capacity to invest significant funds.

"Can't I at least see the pieces with my appraiser first?" Deng asked.

"That's not possible; we'll only show them to committed buyers who make the requisite deposits, not even to those we've dealt with before like you."

She wanted to know if he needed time to arrange their final payment. They wanted payment in full to an offshore account at the time of transfer of his items; that is, once he had verified the goods were as purchased.

"I'm sure you know that transferring those kind of funds out of China poses some logistical problems for my group. We could have run-ins with the government and the State Administration of Foreign Exchange over such a large transfer. We do have other channels outside of China, of course, but I'll have to confirm them with my group."

"You have twenty-four hours to get back to me. That's it."

"Okay, that's tight but let me talk to the group about the other items as well." Before he could say more the line clicked dead.

Officer Wang had coached him during the entire call; Deng had been nervous at first but settled down with Wang by his side. A conference call followed with Zhu and others in the operations headquarters. They discussed the response to her request for payment as well as the million dollar deposit for the "special items." Zhu and Xi agreed to talk to their superiors and try to obtain approval to release the existing transaction balance and the million dollar deposit if they needed to. They would argue that unless they continued to bait the hook with Deng the fish would soon be off the line.

Zhu was not yet ready to lose Deng in his efforts to draw them out of their hideout in Beijing, but his superiors were nervous about more funding, pressing Zhu and Xi to get the relics back quickly. They promised to review the request right away.

———— ❦ ————

James Xu received two calls over the next few days from private collectors he had dealt with in the past. They were fishing to see if he knew anything about Chinese relics, rumored to have been stolen from the Palace Museum in Beijing. Their information had come from reliable sources in their network. They assured him the people involved were trustworthy, but the last thing they needed was authorities looking into their own activities.

Xu told them he had options already on the relics, and if they were interested in taking a position he could include them in his group of investors. He warned them these were very special relics with extremely high values, likely out of their league. The buyers, both from Hong Kong, seemed offended by the comment. They told Xu he could count on them to match him. Xu admitted he was in for a hundred ten million on the basis of photos and valuations; he also told them one of his associates had already viewed them in Beijing. They were a little surprised at the prices and back-pedaled a bit. When they asked what kind of return the items were expected to fetch, he told them his expectation was to at least double, maybe triple, his money. The items were just that incredible. He said he already had commitments, sight unseen; if they wanted in it was up to them.

The two were private collectors, a real estate billionaire and the owner of a large contracting company with multi-billion yuan projects in Africa and Hong Kong. They argued back and forth before committing to match each other at fifty million dollars each, but only after seeing the goods. Xu indicated that might be possible but they would have to visit Beijing to do so; the goods were "fresh on the market" and many precautions would have to be taken. Assuming they were "in" he told them the people involved would need a 10 percent deposit in an overseas account right away. He promised to phone them back quickly regarding when they could see the goods and where to transfer the deposit.

Xu now had commitments for two hundred ten of the three hundred fifty million. He felt confident he could pull in the other hundred forty with a little more work.

The master was in a better frame of mind when Xu called; Deng, dispelling Diao's suspicions, was already seeking approval to deposit the million dollars. James Xu had good news for him too, not only a commitment that very day for another hundred million, but as a sign of good faith a ten million deposit would be transferred soon to the master's special account offshore. The problem was his clients would not commit the balance without seeing the goods as soon as possible. The master thought he could arrange it but would need time to work out a secure way. They were on the police's radar screen and needed to eliminate any risk; he wanted James to travel with the buyers too.

Xu said he would have liked to be there but couldn't see how that was possible. His assistant, Sally, had barely gotten out of China, and he was likely a marked man if he showed up there. The master assured James the organization could get him into the country under a different name; it would only take a week assuming he could travel to Mexico City. They would handle the paperwork there; then he could fly to Shanghai and take the high-speed train to Beijing. Xu agreed it might work, but it still sounded risky. He was sure the two buyers and whomever else he drummed up for the buyer group could easily travel independently. The two Hong Kong executives would have plenty of other business reasons to be in Beijing. As the two argued back and forth, the master finally told James he would reduce his fifty million fees to forty and James could keep the rest or refund portions to his buyers if he came along too. That was all it took to convince James Xu to travel to Beijing.

⚬⚬⚬

Diao told the master he was totally against Xu and others seeing the relics so soon; he felt it far too early with the police breathing down their necks. He could see that the master was growing increasingly irritated by his constant challenging of plans. He feared that the time would soon come when the master might be rid of him, adding Diao's share to his own. Diao had no illusions about what could happen to him and began trying to figure out ways to get out if necessary. In the meantime he decided it best to less confrontational moving forward.

Diao's work on all the items in their possession was completed. He had created a catalog describing the items and highlighting the historical value of each piece. Market prices on each item were developed based on a number of comparable items; however, since the items dated back to a time earlier than previously thought, the real value was always deemed incalculable. It was clear that any collector of Asian—in particular, Chinese antiquities—would be desperate to own some of these pieces, even if they could never be presented to the outside world. There were buyers for these kinds of articles in various parts of the world, particularly Mainland China, Hong Kong, and the US; moving them in his opinion was just a question of time.

Zhu's next meeting was limited to a smaller audience; he wanted to bounce his new strategy off others before accelerating the deal with Deng. It was a big investment, and risk, for the authorities, but at the end of the day they would recover valuable property. Closing the deal would give Deng the credibility to join the bigger fish in the bid for the new relics, plus any suspicions of Deng would be removed. Deng could insist on closing his deal based on access to the other items.

Xi considered his plan to have merit but was nervous about yet another big cash infusion; Zhu countered that now they had more information to work with. They had been lucky in snaring two big fish in Hong Kong already by wire-tapping the collectors Liu Ming and Yang had come up with; that would look good for the government in its fight against white-collar crime.

Cai Levee expressed his concern that these people were so successful they were bound to have friends in high places. What would happen if this whole operation were blown through leaks at the highest level? Zhu agreed that was his concern too, which was why he would not approach the group they had been to before for funding. He would go directly to a key official he knew, a man who was above reproach and had the authority to release funds. More importantly, he had the ear of the premier himself and knew how committed the top leader was to eradicating high-level crimes.

Zhu left the police headquarters after calling the minister, advising him the situation was becoming delicate; leaks to the criminal side were a major concern. They arranged to meet for lunch in the gardens of Beihei Park at the Jingxin (Quiet Heart Studio). Located on the eastern shore of the lake there, it featured a Ming Dynasty garden once used by royal family members to rest or study. In the garden they would be away from prying eyes and listening devices.

When Zhu walked casually into the park he headed for the area where the minister had recommended they meet. Knowing this leader Zhu got right to the details of the investigation and the most recent developments. "Minister, I have total trust in you. I apologize if I offend you for implying that other authorities dealing with me are not so trustworthy."

The minister waved Zhu's comment aside. "No offense; the problem is real. The more people involved, the chance of someone saying something at the wrong time and place only increases. We are not blind to the "guanxi" relationships that exist with unsavory people, but I assure you there are still plenty of honorable people at our highest government levels."

The leader showed his dismay when Zhu revealed the names of the two business leaders in Hong Kong who were being drawn into this affair and how they were proposing to participate. "I know them. I would never have believed them capable of something like this. Are you sure of this?"

"We have full details of their conversations and agreements. Here are the transcripts."

Zhu then outlined how he planned to proceed, and again the leader told him he would support him. "I do need to take this to the premier personally—in the greatest confidence, of course. The funding could come from our Sovereign Wealth Fund; I am a board member. We could mark the funds for 'cultural investment,' but this is a serious matter and I need to apprise the premier of what we are doing.

"It is not so much the money. It is the issue of other powerful people involved and how far the premier wants to go with this; we would be putting a number of people in the dark that have been following this matter."

Zhu assured him he understood, and appreciated his willingness to take this to the premier. Zhu gave a few more details, then the two men proceeded to revisit the "old days"; they had been close friends and Zhu had helped the minister out of a difficult personal situation. They finished the food and drink Zhu had carried with him, and they embraced briefly. The minister promised to get back to him as soon as he could.

Within twenty-four hours Zhu received a call from the minister. He had already been called to meet privately with the premier in his compound in Zhongnanhai, next to the Forbidden City, long the home of past leaders and now the current Communist government. The minister said he had spent a good hour the prior evening explaining everything as best he could. The premier appreciated the update, especially the news of the involvement of two leading businesspeople in this affair. The men were currently viewed in Hong Kong as examples to the rest of society, but had been critical of the mainland leadership in a number of areas; ironically they had often complained about corruption in the government.

The premier was adamant about guarding the treasures of China during his "watch," but he also saw an opportunity to strike a blow against illegal activities and silence the two vocal critics. He approved Zhu's plan but forcefully requested that the focus be on ensnaring the entire group of criminals and their sponsors.

By all means they should use Deng's dealings to lure the dangerous snakes from their hiding places, but they must make sure they did not slither away free. They would hold private talks with the chairman of the Sovereign Wealth Fund to establish a Cultural Relic Acquisition Fund; the police were to use that channel to complete whatever deals were needed to apprehend the participants and reclaim the lost treasures of China.

Zhu thanked the Minister profusely for his help but was warned to tread carefully; the men he was targeting had powerful allies in their court.

Deng received a new call from the as yet unidentified woman. She was friendlier this time. Wang stayed close to Deng to ensure all went well, while others listened in and tried to source the origin of the call.

"I can't speak for long, Deng. Are you ready to complete the transaction?"

"I'm ready, but what about seeing the other items?"

"Perhaps you can. A special viewing is being arranged in a few days for other buyers; you could be invited along with your appraiser. Provided you've paid the participation fee of course."

"I still don't see why I should pay when we've already done business together!'

"Not quite, Deng. Not yet. It's important for our current deal to be completed as soon as possible or the deposit you made before will be returned and the sale canceled, minus a 10 percent handling fee. Others have offered more than you're paying, you know, but we'll still honor the agreement in place if you pay right away."

Deng confirmed that funds were ready to be transferred into their account as soon as the goods were to be exchanged; furthermore, his group agreed to transfer the deposit for the additional items on the basis it would be returned if nothing was purchased.

"That's good news, Deng; we'll gladly refund the deposit. We are honorable people. We stand by our deals."

"When will we meet?" Deng asked.

"I'll call with details in twenty-four hours or less; you will be allowed to bring your appraiser but no one else. Once the funds are in our special account we'll allow you to leave with your goods."

"I still don't like your deposit, but we'll get the funding ready." Deng started to say good-bye but the phone went dead before he could finish.

Zhu and Xi were pleased to have their plan approved. They were feeling more confident now that the other side seemed to be handling things carelessly. The Triads were obviously focused on getting their money early; tracking them down would have proven more difficult if they had gone to ground and stayed quiet.

The lists of private collectors obtained from Liu Ming and the input from Yang proved crucial. The police were now successfully monitoring calls from Hong Kong and the mainland. The traces covering Xu, the buyers in Hong Kong, and two new buyers the Hong Kong contacts were bringing in were providing Zhu with more information than he had hoped for. He limited the monitoring of the calls and reports to a select few men he trusted; the last thing he wanted was the depth of these wiretaps to be revealed.

CHAPTER TWENTY-SIX

The master was confident they had enough buying capacity in place to finally move the relics. With the new commitments he was sure they could get collectors to bid higher once they saw the relics. As unhappy as Diao was with moving this quickly, he agreed they should introduce bidding once the group and the relics were together. His share was now much lower than originally expected when the collection was complete; it was in his interest to get as much from the sale as he could too.

He planned to get a fresh identity and papers to create a new life for himself, he would move from Beijing and settle in the garden city of Hangzhou, where he planned to establish his own business dealing in antiquities. The Triads had already proposed steering business his way, and to become part of the organization's money-laundering system, he would receive seed money to help him build for the future as well. He had given up his family, something he thought he could easily do but was now finding troubling, especially in respect to his only son. Leaving his family had been difficult, but Diao knew his wife would never have accepted what he had done. Giving up part of his small finger was an easier sacrifice to make, especially with a good doctor and medication to make it as painless as a bad tooth removal.

The authorities now knew almost everything. The only thing missing was the rendezvous place for the sale. Zhu was not unduly concerned; with Deng involved and the ongoing calls they would find out in time to react and make arrests.

The main concern, which even George Mathers expressed to Zhu and Xi, was how they could keep the operation secret. They had slimmed down the management involved with the operation to improve that side and were spreading misinformation whenever they could. Surveillance was kept in place covering all the areas, including Houhai, where they believed the thieves were operating from. They made sure that Yin, the informant, warned Lin Li where raids were being made but kept them away from Houhai. Xi made sure the raids were witnessed. Their goal was to make the Triads more comfortable around the Houhai lake area. When it came time to feed them critical misinformation, they needed them to be convinced it was real and react the way the police wanted.

Calls, monitored in Hong Kong between Xu and his buyers, indicated agreement had been reached for the meeting. The special showing would be within one week, provided fees were received. All visit expenses would be paid by the organization with accommodation in a first-class Beijing hotel. Private cars would pick everyone up at the airport and an opening banquet held for their first night; an expert on antiquities would give them a presentation on the items and their likely history.

There was still no indication exactly where the meeting was to be held, but everyone agreed the showing would likely be at the hotel; Liu Ming's underground gallery had been seized, as had his villa. If they could get the hotel under control early enough their task would be much easier. They now knew the names of the buyers coming, including Deng, but no details had been revealed about the false papers and specific travel plans for James Xu.

Commander Xi drew up listings of target hotels, though he didn't know if the Triads would register the buyers under false names or not. Zhu was certain they would, but expected them to travel to Beijing under their own names. He had already set plans in motion to track the key buyers from Hong Kong. Local police interacted with the buyers' company travel agents to monitor travel plans as they were made.

Soon information came back to headquarters; first-class flights had been booked and they would be staying in Beijing for a week, arriving the same day but on different flights. Zhu was pushing all his resources to get a hotel location so they could be prepared and avoid any slip-ups.

The next day monitors reported that James Xu was on the move. Zhu, through his contacts at the Chinese embassy in New York, had agents on the ground staying close to him.

———

Chinese agents trailed Xu to La Guardia Airport and watched as he checked in for an Aero Mexico flight leaving early the next morning. As soon as Xu cleared the area the ticket agent was pulled to the side and asked for information on the passenger. At first he refused to disclose any information until shown a fake FBI badge; the passenger's name was quickly printed out along with his itinerary and a ticket generated for the Chinese agent to board the plane and continue to follow him. Meanwhile word went out to others in Mexico and onward that Xu was using the passenger name of Simon Wang, Asian American, born in Boston, and traveling first class. Reservations at this stage did not show the next flight information; his name could possibly be changed again.

———

Deng received a message that the goods were ready for exchange, along with the time and general location of the area for the transaction to be completed: the Chaoyang District. He needed to ensure the funds could be transferred at that time. The exact address would be given to him early in the morning; the account transfer numbers would be supplied during the exchange itself.

Deng told her it would take a little while to complete the transfer since it was offshore, but she said that was "his problem"; only when funds were in their accounts would he and his appraiser be allowed to leave. All of this was fed to Zhu. For the time being a hands-off approach would be taken; he did not want to spook the group in any way until the main buyers showed up.

Xi decided to arrange another police sweep in an area of Beijing away from the Chaoyang and Houhai districts around the time of the exchange; Yin was to again pass the information to the woman. Hopefully this would make the woman more confident during the exchange that the police were nowhere close. The raid was set for the Russian district near Ritan Park, not far from the Alien Street Market; police would sweep through the neighborhood as visibly as they could. Reports would likely come back to the master confirming that Yi's information was good.

━━∞∞∞━━

Lin Li called Deng early the day of the exchange; the meeting was set for the Kempinski Hotel next to the Lufthansa Shopping Center at 11:30 a.m. Lunch would follow, allowing time for the funds to transfer if needed. Deng and the appraiser were to meet Lin Li and her associates in a suite rented for the day and inspect the items one last time. They were to lock them in a suitcase that Deng was to bring along; once the transaction was completed both parties could depart.

With this information, agents were urgently dispatched to be in place at the Kempinski Hotel and follow Lin Li and her associate afterwards. Taxis commandeered by the police would be parked outside the

Kempinski. If the couple left by taxi, the doorman would call one of these cars over, ensuring the woman got into one of them. If she was picked up by private car, plain-clothes police would be ready to pursue her.

In the case of a private car, the doorman was to slow the car's departure by opening the door, asking if everything was okay with her visit, and such. Others would surround the car with baggage on a cart to create a little confusion, while an agent affixed a tracking device to the car's underside.

The main effort was not to entrap the woman, but to further ingratiate Deng with the thieves and zero in on where the gang was operating. Zhu advised that no one take unnecessary risks. It was critical that the operations go unfettered and not create suspicion on the part of either the woman or whoever was with her.

The woman and her bodyguard, Han, left the villa located up from the Guang Hua Temple in a rickshaw that arrived at the gate. The case of precious stones was lodged carefully between their legs. The rickshaw driver quickly rolled down a pair of darkened shades and cycled toward the temple along a narrow alley; he headed towards the main road and on to the Drum Tower where tourists gathered around buses, taxis, and rickshaws.

One of the organization's drivers was waiting for the couple in a standard orange-and-green taxi; he had already turned away several tourists. The transfer from the rickshaw into the cab was swift and the couple was quickly on their way to meet Deng. She looked different. After the last episode she had cut her hair short and changed its color; still wearing dark glasses, she was dressed much simpler than in the past. She was recognizable, but only if someone got a good look at her.

Deng and associate Wang arrived at the Kempinski early and settled in the lobby to wait for the woman. There were enough plain-clothes operatives from Xi's department at reception and at the concierge desk to ensure that she would be recognized. As the couple walked through the rotating door they were spotted right away. The man carrying an expensive-looking metal attaché case stood out, as did the woman, despite her changed appearance.

Lin Li did not walk straight to reception as expected; someone else was waiting for her. Surveillance had thought she would check in; instead she walked directly over to the lobby area while glancing at Deng and Wang and indicating that they should follow her. All four boarded the nearest elevator as though headed for a meeting.

Xi and Zhu patiently waited for information to come in to headquarters updating them on any developments. They continued to advise everyone to stay calm; her not checking in was no cause for concern.

Lin Li and her accomplice, Han, reached the fifth floor and headed to suite 5008. A bodyguard opened the door and all four of them entered. The two bodyguards who had been waiting were asked to leave and come back later when called. Lin Li told Deng they would not be going down to lunch; she had arranged a sumptuous meal to be served in the room, with champagne to celebrate closing the deal.

She quickly got down to business unlocking her case for Wang and Deng. She was unaware of Wang's concerns about the Triads slipping in fakes he might never spot. Chen Xing had done his best to work with Wang on what to watch for ahead of the exchange. She watched as Wang and Deng inspected everything one last time before confirming their agreement.

Lin Li gave Deng transfer information for the funds. He called a private number, confirming the numbers three times with Lin Li before advising her his group estimated that within a couple of hours payment would be completed. Lin Li announced she would order lunch to be brought up, suggesting Wang transfer the items to Deng's secure case to save time; she expected no real problems in completing the transaction.

During lunch they discussed the upcoming special sale. Lin Li told them the date and time but she could not confirm the location until sometime before the meeting. There would be a banquet for the buyers and Deng was expected to stay the night with the group, assuming his deposit was received in time. The evening would be in one of the finest hotels in Beijing with five other buyers competing for the same items. They hoped he too would take advantage of the items being sold.

Diao had given Lin Li a briefing on how to describe the goods to Deng; although no expert, Deng understood these were spectacular items on offer. In some ways Deng wished the situation was different and that he was not in this with the police.

Lunch was very special, but neither Wang nor Deng drank too much champagne despite being pushed by Han. Around one thirty Lin Li received a call on her cell, following which she thanked Deng and confirmed that the funds had been received. She pushed them to have one last toast ("gambei") before leaving. While they finished their drinks and got ready to depart the two guards returned. Lin Li again thanked Deng and Wang and said they could leave. She would give them the next meeting details as soon as she could. She urged Deng and his group to pay the deposit quickly and be ready to "dig deep" at the sale. She assured him there was a lot of money to be made from these new items.

───── ∞∞∞ ─────

One of Lin Li's men watched Deng and Wang being picked up to see if anyone was following them but reported nothing suspicious going on in the lobby. Inside suite 5008 two suitcases were opened. Han and Lin Li changed into new clothes and adjusted their looks. Han was showing signs of drinking too much and was chastised by Lin Li and the two men assigned to watch over the exchange.

Han left first, no longer in a suit but in casual attire; he was not joined by Lin Li and walked shakily toward the elevator. He paid no attention to the security cameras monitoring his every step. In the lobby he took a seat to have his shoes cleaned at the hotel shoe stand, scanning the lobby to see if there were any police about; he saw nothing suspicious. Han knew he'd drunk too much, but thought not enough to make him careless.

The hotel lobby was busy with airline crews as well as a large group of German tourists assembling for tours. Han did not leave via the front entrance but turned to the back of the elevator banks, walked by the restaurant at the rear of the hotel, and headed to the You Yi Lufthansa Shopping Center. There he spent time on different floors seeming to sober up before leaving the shopping center. He then walked toward the Kowloon Hotel and called Lin Li to tell her he was clear and that no suspicious activity was apparent at the Kempinski. He was confident security had been maintained and no one had followed him.

The other two men left room 5008; each walked to opposite ends of the corridor and took the stairs down to scan the lobby area. They too gave the all-clear for Lin Li to leave. She had spent a good thirty minutes wiping surfaces clean of prints; she also cleaned the case she had brought and placed in the closet.

Agents alerted everyone as the door opened and Lin Li came out of the room in a maid's uniform. The surveillance team leader took action, calling down to the basement for improved coverage. The staff gathered and watched her on security cameras as she walked towards the service elevator with towels over her arm. Hotel security confirmed the lift was descending to the staff area of the basement, the section where the linens were managed.

Once in the laundry area, Lin Li made for a locker that she already had the key for. A female agent kept her in sight as Lin Li changed clothes yet again. The undercover agent, posing as a maid, was able to give a good description of the pant suit she was wearing, the bag she was carrying, and the scarf she had readied to put over her head upon leaving the hotel.

It was clear Lin Li was planning to exit through the staff's back door adjacent to the Paulaner Brauhaus, a German restaurant. There were no cabs on that side of the hotel, only parking spaces. They guessed she would cross the canal, head over the bridge, and pick up a car or cab on the road there. Zhu took a gamble and ordered cabs to get over to that street as quickly as possible, asking the agent posing as a maid to try to slow her down.

The agent approached Lin Li jovially and asked if she was leaving early or could stay and help with moving furniture in the staff room. Lin Li told her she had to leave right away as her mother was taken ill and in hospital. After to-ing and fro-ing as long as the agent dared, she finally told Lin Li she could manage, wished her well, and hoped her mother was okay. As Lin Li prepared to leave the agent again interrupted her departure asking which floor she had worked; instinctively she replied "the third."

Lin Li said good-bye and left via the rear of the hotel, walking briskly towards the canal footbridge. As she reached the other side and walked past Dirty Nellie's Irish bar she spotted a cab coming down the street; the driver acknowledged her raised hand. She was satisfied with herself; her getaway had been clean and the deal had gone smoothly.

The cab driver asked where she needed to go then responded to a call from his "dispatcher" for his location. He said he had a new fare and was headed for the Guan Hua Temple area. When his call was finished she told the driver she was in a hurry, that there was a good tip for him to get her there quickly.

CHAPTER TWENTY-SEVEN

Zhu and Xi breathed a sigh of relief after being frustrated by reports of losing track of Han and the other two men in the south of Beijing. They had came close to losing Lin Li too, but fortunately an officer posing as an EMS package deliverer followed her taxi as a backup. He transmitted details of the route as the taxi headed towards its destination. Xi ordered forensics to check the hotel suite from top to bottom for anything useful.

Lin Li told the driver to stop along Gulou Xi Dajie, tipped him, and walked down the alley towards the Ya'er hutong area to the street by the old temple. Suddenly she slipped into the temple and stayed for fifteen minutes or so before reappearing. She hurried along the street toward the villa, after scanning the area to be sure she had thrown off anyone following her; a side gate opened and she slipped inside. She was relieved to be back, her day having gone off without a hitch.

On Deng's arrival at police headquarters, Chen Xing inspected the stolen items he'd obtained at the meeting. George Mathers and his colleagues were there and pleased to hear the pieces could be reassembled almost perfectly. Chen guessed Diao Lijun had carried out the work and that somehow he still respected the importance of the pieces. Zhu was also pleased; he knew the investment by the government was made on the basis of getting the other items back, but least the original value of these had been maintained.

Deng was thoroughly debriefed along with Wang and allowed to leave. Zhu thanked him profusely and assured him that those at the highest levels appreciated his cooperation. As soon as Deng had left he requested that Xi's people keep Deng under careful supervision for the next few days.

Zhu was pleased with the way things had turned out. There had been a scare over the efforts to avoid detection at the Kempinski Hotel, but in the end the police succeeded in placing Deng in a trusted situation and locating where the Dragon Master and Diao were likely hiding. Zhu ordered that the owners of all the villas along that road be investigated; if there were any trouble finding out who owned them he would contact his minister friend. Xi's personal assistant was to check the ownerships quietly, cautioned that some very important people lived there; he was to report to no one other than Xi and Zhu. They could not afford anyone knowing what they were up to. If anyone asked where the investigation was focused they were to report that the two body guards were trailed to the south of Beijing, and that police were now assuming that was the gang's location.

An hour later Xi's assistant asked to see both leaders privately. He held a large folder and a roll of blueprints; he rolled out a street plan on the conference table, along with a layout of one of the villas. "Look here," he said. "I've penciled in the current owners of the villas with private courtyards along the road. This gate here, just beyond the temple, is the one Lin Li entered."

Zhu looked at the owners' names and let out a low whistle; these were important people in business and in the Party itself. Xi was not surprised. "I've known all along the kind of men who can afford those places. Not only are the villas historically important, they've been restored to a very high standard. Ownership is out of our league, Zhu."

Zhu stabbed at one villa owner's name and smirked. "He is what my friend George would call a "son of a bitch minister.' He's the one who called me asking about the time of our raids! No wonder he was so irritated when I misled him on the time for the gallery action." He paused for a moment. " I was suspicious about why he backed off from me so easily. Now I understand. He didn't want me to connect him to it!"

Xi's assistant spoke up. "The minister does indeed own the property, but it's leased out. He doesn't live there."

"This is something my team can investigate," Xi said. "If there's a connection we'll find it, Zhu."

"I know you're being careful, Xi, but I have no illusions about this character. I'm sure he's up to his neck in this. I bet we'll find his name on the Triad's lists of payoffs; he may even be directly involved in this thing."

―――∞∞∞―――

With the return of Lin Li, the Dragon Master was in a good mood; everything seemed to be going according to plan. He continued to belittle Diao's concerns about being discovered. As far as he was concerned the authorities were amateurs, whereas he himself had the skills to pull off these activities. He told Diao that mishaps were always possible, but he knew how to overcome anything that came their way.

Planning and organization of the final sale of the remaining relics was well underway. James Xu was en route from the US. The buyers were scheduled into Beijing. All that remained was to finalize the location for the meetings; they would hold that information back until the parties arrived.

―――∞∞∞―――

James Zu, posing as Simon Wang, took the 7:45 a.m. Aero Mexico flight from New York to Mexico City. He passed the seven-hour flight relaxing in his first class seat with champagne and a meal.

The agent following him secured an economy seat at the rear of the plane; his flight was to be a lot more tedious and he looked forward to its landing.

The flight arrived around 4:30 p.m. and a Mexican representative of the Hilton Airport hotel was there to greet Wang. After brief introductions the two walked to the hotel located in Terminal 1, where a suite was reserved; the Triad's man in Mexico was waiting in the room with details of the next phase of the journey.

—— ⊗⊗⊗ ——

The agent from New York was able to get a room at the same hotel; local Chinese operatives with friends in the Mexican police had their target under surveillance. The agent was to be alerted if the target left the room at all. Reports to Beijing confirmed Xu had checked in, met with one visitor, but stayed in his suite the whole time. He apparently made no attempt to make any calls; the agent assumed the visitor had directly informed Xu what his next steps would be.

The next morning, agents followed Xu as he checked out early and walked to the terminal. This time he headed to Air Canada and registered for the Shanghai flight leaving at 6:15 a.m. Again the special agent confirmed Xu was still flying as Simon Wang in a first class seat for the long flight to Shanghai. He would arrive the next day at 2:25 p.m. in Pu Dong Airport. It was not a direct flight; instead it traveled via Vancouver.

The agent tried everything he could to get a seat on the flight but it was absolutely full. The airline called for volunteers to give up seats but no one came forward. When Zhu was informed he told the agent to stand down anyway and put the word out to operatives in Canada to react if "Simon Wang" did anything strange in Vancouver.

—— ⊗⊗⊗ ——

James Xu settled in to his flight, bemoaning the circuitous route arranged for him since Shanghai had direct flights from New York, as did Beijing. He satisfied himself with the extra money he was making and hoped the route kept him safe. Once in Shanghai he would have to suffer the overnight sleeper train to Beijing, not a pleasant thought as he considered how long this simple journey was taking him. He would be relieved when it was over.

When he finally arrived in Canada he risked a brief call to China. The monitors listening in were assured that he would not be switching flights again. They would be able to pick him out easily in Pu Dong Airport and follow him to the overnight train. Everyone at police headquarters in Beijing relaxed somewhat, focusing their attention on the Houhai area and how to prepare for the Triad's planned sale.

Diao engaged fully in arrangements for the upcoming sale; he had nothing to occupy himself with until the deal was completed anyway. He was still uncomfortable with how quickly things were moving, though it seemed plans were running smoothly. Lin Li had visited all three top-class hotels along Chang'an Avenue: Raffles, the St. Regis, and the China World. He and Lin Li had agreed that the hotel of choice would be the St. Regis, one of Beijing's finest. Neither of them could see where a sale that might net over $300 million should not be in a hotel that matched the splendor of the items on offer.

The hotel was not far from Tiananmen Square and the Forbidden City. Lin Li chose the Statesman Suites and Diplomat Deluxe rooms. The Statesman rooms of the top floor of the hotel would be used for the meetings and private dinners. The actual task of making the reservations, however, was assigned to an anonymous third-party agency. The names on the reservations would not be provided until the guests arrived. All expenses were to be charged directly to the travel company.

Zhu and Xi were confident the noose was tightening around their quarry; they resisted the mounting temptation to raid the Hutong villa then and there. Zhu knew the highest level was looking to trap the Hong Kong businessmen and create a high profile success story against criminal activity; he had to hold back. They had pinpointed the location where they were certain Diao and other were working out of. They knew the three hotels that were potential hotel sites, and the names of people headed to the meetings. On top of that they had their men on the inside: Deng and Officer Wang.

Zhu was a cautious man. As confident as Xi was, Zhu knew from past experience that plans could easily go awry. He was outwardly sure of success but in a quiet moment confessed to George Mathers he was still concerned, and would only relax when it was over.

Zhu's findings on the villa ownership in Houhai were reported to his friend, the head of the Ministry of Public Security for Beijing, who alerted the premier to the situation. Both agreed with Zhu's request that no contact or investigation of the villa owner should be started until after the affair was settled; too much prying into his affairs could be dangerous. Although the minister agreed to hold off any formal investigation they both agreed the phone lines would be secretly recorded, and any suspicious transcripts provided to Zhu and Xi. Zhu reluctantly agreed but urged his friend to be extremely careful about who would monitor the Party leader.

Two plainclothes officers were sent to each of the three hotels to try to determine which hotel was being reserved. Private meetings were held with the hotels' general managers; they were advised that a police action was likely in the coming days in their hotel for routine security evaluation. They demanded their fullest cooperation, including access to all areas and security systems in the hotel. The managers were to keep this information highly confidential; they were to pass the participating officers off as auditors for a new reservation system.

Deng and Agent Wang made a call to Lin Li to ask when and where the meeting was planned, claiming that Deng might have to go out of town. She gave them a window of time but still declined giving a location. When pressed, she finally let out it would be somewhere around the Forbidden City, refusing to tell them anything more.

Diao Lijun was happy to be busy; he had equipment brought to the villa to prepare the presentation for the relics in the hotel. Lin Li confirmed that the suite would have a large plasma screen for his use. The display of the items would be set up in advance; each piece would rest on its own plinth, lit from underneath, with a description of the object and its estimated market value. He knew the Dragon Master worried this was a waste of effort and expense, but Lin Li helped Diao convince him this kind of preparation was important—and could easily add a few million dollars to the estimate expected from the buyers.

As Diao worked on the pieces he sometimes missed his old life at the Palace Museum, but shook off any regrets with thoughts about his share of the sale proceeds. He could not wait to get away from the Triad leader and regretted agreeing with Liu Ming to bring them in, but it was too late to get out now.

Xu arrived at Shanghai's International Airport in Pu Dong as scheduled and cleared customs with no problems. A large black sedan was waiting to take him to Shanghai's main railway station and the overnight train for Beijing. The ticket was already booked using a fake ID card; he would be alone in a first-class sleeper compartment.

∞∞∞

At the St. Regis Hotel a reservation had been made for five suites plus an upper floor suite with private dinner; all charges were to be billed directly to a travel company. Compared to reservations at the China World, the odds seemed higher than 90 percent that this was the targeted meeting place. This was also the only reservation where a cash deposit had been made in advance.

Surveillance plans were set in motion to cover the St. Regis for the next few days by Zhu; some officers would still be assigned to the other two hotels Lin Li had visited, but only as a precaution if a last minute switch was made. This time Zhu and Xi would travel to the St. Regis personally; the general manager there was a European so Zhu asked George Mathers to accompany them. Cai Levee and Xiao Ping were still working on the translation of the Dragon Scripts, but they were distracted by all of the police action going on. Chen Xing was back in the Palace Museum putting together a plea on behalf of the museum to display the treasures there, once they were back in the state's hands. He was even using some of the original planning materials Diao had started before joining Liu and Yi in masterminding the theft of the relics.

CHAPTER TWENTY-EIGHT

James Xu arrived at the Beijing Railway Station early in the morning. He had used a sleep aid to help get a good night's rest and had cleaned up enough to look relatively fresh on arrival. A gang member who had been on the same train keeping an eye on him rushed to grab Xu's bags as they strode to the main street. They left the station to be met by a car and driver; the car soon reached Chang'an Avenue and turned in the direction of the China World Hotel.

Xu checked into the China World and headed for a shower and to relax. He needed to check the arrangements for the meetings later in the week and where they were to be held. He had chosen to stay at the China World because Lin Li had indicated the meeting would be around the Forbidden City. He planned to rest before calling Lin Li to see if she was available to meet with him. He would also call the Dragon Master later to agree on the strategy they would use to drive the best deals from the other buyers.

When Lin Li advised the master that Xu was in Beijing and asking for a meeting he gave her approval to go to see him, but advised her to be careful. He gave her a new cell phone, which he asked her to have James use. He knew she was unaware of the special relationship between Xu and the Triads and simply told her he was going to discuss the terms of sale with Xu to get a better deal from him.

257

———— ⊶⊷ ————

Lin Li's journey from Houhai to the China World was tracked carefully. This time she was alone; while cautious at first she appeared to relax. The misinformation fed to her by Officer Yin had clearly been effective. Her visit to the China World after the arrival by James Xu was puzzling to Xi and Zhu, but their concerns eased when it was reported that Xu was only booked there for two nights and remained under tight surveillance.

Xu met Lin Li in the lobby with no effort to show any precautions as they embraced on her arrival. It was clear to observers that his greeting of her was far more intimate than expected. Agents monitoring the sixth floor watched him walk her to his room, the arm around her slim waist occasionally moving to feel her slim figure as it swayed with every step.

———— ⊶⊷ ————

It had been a passionate reunion that afternoon; Lin Li had not seen Xu for nearly eighteen months since his last visit; she had been cooped up with the master and Diao Lijun for far too long. She knew the master looked upon her as his own property but made no physical demands on her, enjoying her looks and the way other men lusted after her. She appreciated all the benefits that came with being seen as owned by the Dragon Master and part of the inner circle, except for the few that enjoyed her real attributes. She knew everyone assumed the master made the most of his beautiful concubine and used it to advantage.

Lin Li made some attempt to tidy up the bedroom after two hours of passionate love-making before talking to James about the pending events. She was confident the master had no idea there was anything between them, but suspected there was some special relationship between Xu and the master. She dressed quickly, gathering up the various pieces of clothing that were strewn from the door of the room all the way through to the bedroom. She did her best to drag the bedding from the floors that had been flung aside so readily; at least if anyone came in it would look like a business meeting was under way.

She told James the meeting would be in two days, that they would all assemble at a hotel for a banquet, followed by presentations from their expert on the relics James had seen in photos. Then everyone could handle the objects and make final offers on the pieces they really wanted. No one was allowed to offer less than they had already committed to, but they could obtain more pieces based on their bids. Although she had been told not to expose to anyone where this would take place, it took less than ten minutes for James to coax her into divulging that he would be called to move to the St. Regis Hotel on Friday.

Lin Li realized she was spending more time than planned with James; she needed to get back. The master trusted her only to a point and sometimes his challenges of what she had been up to turned violent. She tidied herself again and handed the cell phone to James, advising him to use it whenever he called the master. She importuned him not to mention that he knew where the meetings were to be held.

Zhu, Xi, two other officers, and George Mathers met with the managers of the St. Regis. Zhu was still prepared to gamble that his people had the right location picked out. The hotel people were told of an effort to break up some kind of major drug deal and the police needing full access for their officers. One or two would pose as working staff; others would monitor the closed circuit cameras throughout the building. The police would need to add sound and video to several rooms and the Statesman Suite, which was anticipated to be the main gathering location.

The managers asked if there would be any compensation in the matter, especially for the rooms officers would need. Xi took offense that the hotel would try to obtain compensation instead of performing their civic duty in assisting the state in a very important case. The German manager spoke briefly into the Chinese manager's ear; he quickly apologized, assuring Xi the hotel would cooperate fully.

They left the hotel having reserved one room in the basement as a command center. Zhu turned to George and muttered, "I hope I'm not wrong in picking this place as the target for the operation."

"We still have some time to be sure," George noted.

"Xi, make sure the officers working the reservation desks at the three hotels continue their evaluations twenty-four hours a day; in particular they should follow Xu's activities at the China World. That's already making me nervous." Zhu quickly regained his confidence. "We're going to get these some of bitches, George!"

"Sons, Zhu; it's sons of bitches."

"Exactly what I said. No?"

⊸✦⊶

The next morning Zhu held a high-level meeting. Cai Levee was at the lab feeling somewhat left out, trying to work on an area of the Dragon Scripts that was confusing them.

At the entrance to police headquarters a motorcycle approached the heavily guarded entrance only to be stopped at the gate. Dressed in full motorcycle attire and a helmet whose darkened front face shielded the person's identity, the rider handed over several food boxes. He told the officer that they were ordered by Commander Xi and a Professor Mathers. The rider offered to take them in but the officer would not allow it. Asked if there was any invoice to be paid the rider told him it was already paid for.

As the rider climbed back on to the motorcycle the officer took in the shapely figure accentuated by the tight leathers the rider was wearing. The guard had not seen the rider's face but understood it was female; he wondered if she was as pretty as her body reflected. Xi took the call from the front gate before turning to George Mathers,

"Did you order food, George?"

"No, not me, why?"

"Well, an unidentified rider has just delivered food to you and me; it's already been paid for by someone, but not me."

As Xi started to tell the officer it was not theirs and the gate officers could have it, Zhu jumped in. "Run those packages through the metal detector and get them to us right away!"

The gate officer had the packages checked and then carried up to the meeting room. Zhu was waiting at the door, a befuddled Xi watching as he grabbed the packages from the officer. Having been told that the packages were cleared, Zhu began opening the boxes and passing them around the room. The last one he passed to George. "You open it; I think it may be from your friend."

George opened the box marked differently from the others and looked inside. In the best Chinese he could muster, he shouted "Biao Zi Yang de!"

Zhu burst out laughing. "Some of the bitch, George, what does it say?"

There it was in large letters on a single sheet of paper: "Friday, St Regis, Statesman Suite, 9:30 p.m. Do not fail this time, BK."

Zhu and George smiled at each other with relief. Xi looked at them in bewilderment. They explained to him the background of the mysterious Black Knight, the unknown rider and earlier messages from this anonymous source. It was strange that they had not heard from him for so long, yet suddenly he popped up again. Who he or she was remained a mystery. Zhu was delighted with the information. Xi continued to be puzzled but Zhu told him they were thankful for this opportune intelligence. The source had to be in contact with someone close by. But who was it? Zhu wondered. Could it be Xiao Ping despite her denials? Was there a connection there?

CHAPTER TWENTY-NINE

Xi received an urgent call later in the day from officer Wang. Deng was getting cold feet, convinced now that if everyone was arrested and he was not part of the arrest the Triads would know he had been the informant. He was sure he would be hunted down and killed. Wang was worried that Deng might even turn on them; he had blurted out that he could make a lot of money simply by telling the woman when she called what was really going on.

Xi brought everyone into the discussion. Zhu was as concerned as Xi that Deng would either crack or be too nervous to carry this through. Zhu wandered away from the table for a few minutes to stare out the window. He returned to the table and asked if Wang was still on the line.

"Officer Wang, you know Deng well. Do you think he will go through with this if we push him?"

"General, I've never seen Deng this bad. If it were up to me I would pull him out. We'd need a good story, though, not to cause any alarm or cancellation of the meeting."

Zhu turned to Xi. "I think canceling at this stage is impossible. If we pull Deng out now we have to control him one hundred percent for the next few days."

"I agree; we'll work up a story for Deng to give but bring him into headquarters under Wang's supervision until it's over."

" Wang, Deng is not to have phone access to the outside world unless the woman calls. The phone must be controlled by you."

"Can't someone else babysit Deng, sir?"

"No, Wang, it needs to be you. Bring him in right away while we work up the story. Don't alarm him either with some prison cell; there are a couple of decent guest areas he can be put in. Get moving right away!"

Once off the phone Xi and Zhu acknowledged they would need to be even more careful in the few remaining days. The Black Knight's note had definitely helped ease Zhu's concerns enough to risk allowing Deng to avoid the meetings. Everyone agreed in the end that Deng was right to worry; there would be a real risk for him if everyone else was arrested and only he walked away a free man.

When James called the master that evening after meeting Lin Li he was in a good mood; he had no doubt the sale was going to generate more money for him personally, as well as for the master and the Triads. After the usual welcoming banter they began to go over the details of the meeting, the master never indicating where it would be held. James didn't ask as he already knew.

"Look, James, all the buyers are arriving on the same day. We'll meet at 6 p.m. in the evening for cocktails followed by a banquet, presentations, and finally the auction. I expect you to be at your best."

James could sense the master's confidence. "That's all fine," James said, "but who is going to make the presentations? Surely not you? And what does Lin Li know about such things? She's no expert."

"Don't worry about that; I have the expert on hand."

"And who have you found to risk handling a deal like this?"

"How about someone called Diao Lijun from the Palace Museum?"

"You're joking?"

"No. Didn't you hear he was missing?"

"Yes . . . but . . . that's incredible! And he's agreed to this?"

"Agreed? He's involved in this up to his neck."

"I never would have believed it. You're a genius," James said.

"We need him only to complete the sale; after that he's of no use to us. His share will sit well in my account."

The master told James to stay out of sight at the hotel for another day. On Friday morning, a limo would pick him up and move him over to the St. Regis Hotel. They talked briefly about how James could appear to be independent while helping drive the prices up. He was being well compensated to make a convincing show of it. The next day would be spent ensuring plans were fine-tuned to the point where there was nothing to do but wait.

The call to Deng came as expected and Wang was there to talk him through the call. Deng told Lin Li he was deeply embarrassed that his group's key financial investor had decided to back out; without him Deng would only be able to invest another five million or so. Lin Li told him how disappointed she was to hear it, especially this late in the day. She tried to convince him to change his mind but Deng told her he was not in a position to act alone.

"Can you let me know if any items are unsold at my level?" Deng asked.

"Sure, but I doubt there will be any unsold items; interest is high."

"I feel badly about having to withdraw this way."

"Let's see what happens, Deng, maybe there are other ways we can do business in the future. We still appreciate you being one of the early buyers and for settling your account. I'll have to discuss the refund of the deposit; there will be a deduction from the deposit for backing out so late."

"I understand, but if in the future such items became available please call me. Our main patron's problems I think are temporary. His conglomerate's current losses will not continue for long, assuming the economy in his business returns to normal."

Deng expected a response but the phone clicked dead. He was sweating profusely but to Wang's surprise he had remained relatively calm.

Wang was satisfied with the way the call went and reported everything to Xi. The woman had not discussed the meeting location; Zhu was happy to hear that. If Deng had pressed for the time and location after backing out it may have raised suspicion.

The Dragon Master was in a rage hearing that Deng's group was backing out at such a late stage; he immediately called James Xu on his direct line and told him, but Xu was as buoyant as ever and told the master not to worry. He had the entire sale covered and more with the buyers in attendance. With some relief the master apologized to Lin Li for his rough handling of her news of Deng's cancellation, but only to a point. He asked pointedly if she had given out any details of where and when the meeting was to be. She swore on her family's grave that she had not. The only thing Deng knew, she said, was the day itself, Friday.

She told the master he had not even asked when or where the meeting was to be held, something she would have never given it to him anyway. She pointed out that if anything were left over she could tag Deng for a further five to ten million dollars but after James's comments he told her nothing would be left over after Friday night. He told her to continue putting the finishing touches on the arrangements for the evening and weekend.

Two people sat in police headquarters feeling uncomfortable: Deng in decent quarters, a guest for the next few days; Yin in a bleak cell, still being held as an informant but trying to redeem himself by providing the Triads with misinformation.

Xi was busily planning a Friday "sweep" of an area far away from the St. Regis Hotel that would be leaked the day of the real operation. It would involve a large number of officers for maximum exposure. A local TV reporter, one of the nightly news readers, was invited to be imbedded in the operation and report the news. It would be purported to be a major raid on organized crime with a view to recovering stolen goods. Not only would Yin be transmitting the information, but also internally this activity would be more "loosely" controlled. The raid on the St. Regis Hotel was an entirely different affair.

Two centers of operation were set up, one at headquarters and one in the St. Regis. Zhu took the hotel responsibility while Xi reluctantly agreed to be the very visible leader of the diversion effort; around 8 p.m., however, he would rush to the hotel for the final take-down, assuming all went well.

On Friday morning a van arrived outside the villa near the Guan Hua temple. The gates were opened and the van backed in; a sign on the van said Bright Opportunities Presentations Company. Agents reported items being loaded into the van, as well as two men and a woman climbing into the rear before it left. Long-range cameras identified the three passengers as the so-called "Lin Li," the Triad's muscle man Han, and Diao Lijun.

The van was escorted front and rear by two SUVs with blackened side windows and other men inside. As the entourage left the area orders were given to leave the vehicles a wide berth, to stay well clear of the villa while continuing to monitor any activity there. Based on this information and the phone calls that still emanated from the villa it was clear the master, whoever he was, had not left. The police contingent arrived in the hotel very early on Friday morning to get positioned ahead of any arrivals, but also to be sure all the monitoring equipment and personnel were in place.

When Lin Li arrived with her "production company" they were welcomed by the general manager and led up to the Statesman Suite. Lin Li and Diao would stay in two of the bedrooms in the largest suite, where the master expected to sleep with Lin Li if he stayed the night. Han would remain in the room during the proceedings as a guard, while other Triads would mingle among the crowd in the hotel lobby.

Everyone was to dress well and present themselves in an orderly fashion. Late morning Lin Li received a call from James Xu that he had checked in to the Diplomatic Suite one floor below the top (nineteenth) floor. She excused herself from the activities to welcome him and provide details of the evening's activities. She descended one floor by the emergency stairs and knocked on his door. Xu came out to greet her; she glanced up and down the hall, and seeing no one kissed him as he pulled her into the room.

She told him if she stayed too long Han was likely to come looking for her. Forty-five minutes later the door opened and she left the room, straightening her chi pao dress that was split to the thigh. She appeared flustered, arranging her hair as she headed back to the stairs, unaware that her every move was being watched. She left Xu naked in bed watching the latest financial news on the TV, keeping abreast of the stock market situation in the U.S., concerned as always how it might affect his personal and company holdings.

James Xu had enjoyed Lin Li a second time since his arrival; she was beautiful and experienced in bed, much more so than Sally. If she were not tied to the master he would consider a change in bed companions.

He decided to get dressed and be ready to receive the other buyers as requested by the master. They were to arrive by midday and he was to organize a buyer group luncheon, while Lin Li and Diao prepared the evenings events.

James had made reservations for the buyers at an outside spa for an afternoon of relaxation and special treatments. Not knowing their personal desires he would handle those arrangements with care so as not to offend anyone. He need not have worried; the visitors were more than ready and in effect demanded he organize so-called "special services" for them. The girls working in the massage area of the selected club were not only spectacular but also experienced in the pleasures of men. They were probably the highest paid female spa attendants in Beijing, something of no surprise to anyone serviced by them.

At lunchtime Yin received a call from Lin Li to ask if there was anything happening that day or over the weekend. With officers standing over him Yin had no choice but to follow their instructions. He had worried earlier about his future once the affairs were over and the Triads were looking to settle scores. Commander Xi had agreed he would work toward a very short sentence for him, then help him to relocate his family away from Beijing. Yin acted nervous and replied, "There is something you need to know about."

"What is it, Yin? Tell me quickly!"

"There's a sweep of an area near the 798 warehouse district looking for hideouts and stolen goods; even the press is involved."

"The press? What for?"

"Our leaders are trying to put on a demonstration of police capability. It starts Friday morning, should last all day, maybe into Saturday too."

"Thanks, Yin. If it's true you'll see some more of our appreciation."

"Just watch the evening news at six p.m."

Again the phone clicked dead before he could say more.

———— ᴏᴚᴂᴑ ————

Lin Li called the master and passed along the information; he was pleased that the police were still sniffing around far from where they were operating. There were Triads in the area Yin referenced, and word would go out to move to safer locations.

Once the Statesman Suite was laid out and ready for Diao's presentations the hotel was advised it could begin preparations for the in-room banquet. Lin Li and Diao had selected the dishes for the evening as well as the finest French champagnes and most expensive baijiu the hotel had. They would work to have the buyers as well lubricated as possible, part of the effort to pry as much money out of them as they could.

The room where the actual presentations were to be held was off to the side in an area, usually used for playing cards or mahjong. All the items were displayed beautifully on illuminated plinths; the effect was spectacular when the lights were dimmed. This was the setting that Diao intended for the buyers to walk into after dinner and cigars; until then the items would be covered in purple velvet to avoid prying eyes. The room was locked with Han remaining there while hotel staff prepared the main room for the banquet.

———— ᴏᴚᴂᴑ ————

Around 3:30 p.m. Zhu called the Minister of Public Security and brought him up to speed on the events of the day. He assured him that everything was in place. Surveillance of all the participants was under way; the Dragon Master was still in the villa and had not yet left for the meeting.

The minister thanked him and said he would pass the update along to the premier. It took a half hour for the minister to track down the premier, who was in his office with staff preparing his speech for a state banquet in the Great Hall in Tiananmen Square that night. The premier listened intently, asking to be called on his private cell when the operation was successfully completed. He said he had every confidence in the people handling it and looked forward to a positive outcome.

As soon as the call disconnected a secretary two offices away took an ear piece out, closed her phone line, and told her colleagues she needed to go to the restroom. As soon as she arrived she closed and locked the door behind her. Nervously she entered a special number and waited several minutes before a voice answered. She repeated as closely as she could all the details in her notes and hurriedly concluded the call; she could not be away for too long. The man thanked her profusely for the information, assured her it was quite safe and that she would be well compensated for the information.

Lin Li soon received a call from the master; he was clearly bothered about something and indicated to her that he was being called away to an organization meeting on urgent matters. He assured her that they did not really need him anyway at the sale; the people that could make things happen were herself and Han. He could be contacted by phone but if not she should understand he was tied up. He thanked her for all that she had done and said he would call later to see how everything went. He ended the call by remarking that if she needed help she could trust James Xu, as he was a close friend.

Diao was surprised to hear the news, especially since the guests would soon arrive at the Statesman Suite for drinks. He was confident in his abilities to manage the sale and felt the master would have brought nothing to the meeting anyway. Han, on the other hand, expressed surprise and wondered aloud if there was anything amiss.

At the villa the master packed a suitcase. He had a reputation and capacity for quick thinking in difficult situations; this was one to really test him. He said nothing to the two men with him, other than asking them to prepare the car for him. He walked out of the villa wearing the suit he planned to wear to the banquet and sale while carrying a suitcase for the evening. He made no attempt to disguise his appearance other than dark glasses and moved as swiftly as he could into the rear seat of a black SUV.

Expecting to drive to the St. Regis the two men were surprised to be told to head straight to the Beijing Airport, Terminal 2, one of the domestic airline departure areas. When the car was clearly not heading to the hotel, agents trailing them called in for instructions on whether to let them continue wherever they were headed or block them right away. Zhu told them to simply follow them, not to let the master out of their sight; if they interfered before the sale time an alert would go out. The gang members were likely armed in the hotel and he was fearful a blood bath could ensue with many innocent bystanders being killed.

Xi's sweep of the 798 district was under way and word of it had spread through the Triad organization; members had melted away from the area. The raid itself revealed nothing, but reports of the raid went out on the news as planned.

Zhu called Xi after the recent turn of events and told him he might as well get over to the St. Regis whenever he could; he declined to tell Xi over the phone what was going on, concerned about who might be listening.

———— ⚬⚭⚬ ————

The meeting at the hotel had started well, as the cocktails and champagne were poured. Lin Li surprised everyone when she walked into the room fully made up, her hair bound tightly at the back. She wore an exquisitely embroidered chi pau dress, which fit her every curve tightly, the back sculpted to reveal her smooth back down to below her waist.

Her jewelry was exquisite; indeed, one of the diamond-studded armlets she wore was one of the relics.

The guests were awed, both by her and the armlet she wore. The biggest stir was the introduction of Diao Lijun to the group. A number of them knew him by reputation; when comments about his apparent disappearance were brought up he simply told them not to believe everything they read in the news.

James, who had met Diao in the past, noticed the bandage on Diao's hand and asked if he had a problem to which Diao responded with a smile, "It's nothing; a minor accident."

After a half hour of cocktails Lin Li announced dinner. The seating had been carefully arranged such that she sat opposite James, where she could look directly into his eyes, but between the two main buyers from Hong Kong. During the dinner her legs gently caressed the legs of her guests in a seductive manner, much to the consternation of James, who saw what was going on. Han stood back from the table watching; he knew exactly what she was up to.

During dinner bottles of the finest Mao Tai baijiu were brought to the table. After a mild start to the toasting the drinking became quite heavy. Lin Li moved around the table with ease as she gambei'd ("bottoms-upped") with everyone. As the dinner continued the air was filled with smoke from expensive cigars smoke; hands under the table made moves along both sides of Lin Li's thighs. She did nothing to stop them and moved to accommodate them. Soon Lin Li had offers for the evening, but told each of them that she would only entertain the highest bidder. Standing off to the side Han read her lips and smiled, understanding what was being proposed.

CHAPTER THIRTY

Agents watched as the master walked into the airport and joined the long check-in line for tickets to Guangzhou on China Southern Airlines. He was carrying a suitcase and large attaché case. Two men, clearly bodyguards, stood close by. After about ten minutes he motioned the men to hold his place and he strode off with the attaché case to the bathroom. Two plain-clothed officers walked casually to the bathroom to wait for him to reappear.

The master had made his move after surveying the check-in area; he said nothing to his men to avoid any suspicion on their part. He left the line and headed to the busiest men's room he could see off to the side and was fortunate not to have to wait for a stall to open up. He knew he needed to be quick as he laid the attaché case on the toilet seat and took out the things he needed. He checked the door lock and was pleased to find the device could be manipulated with a magnet on the opposite side. After he was finished he closed up the case and set it on the floor along with the shoes he had worn on entry. He exited the end stall, carefully turning his body against the door to hide the magnetic handle he used to move the lock over. To a surprised onlooker he joked that his friend was still inside as he shuffled out lazily, carrying a smaller knapsack.

Slightly stooped over he left the bathroom calmly, making sure he was not drawing too much attention other than sympathy for an old man. He exited the terminal and climbed into the nearest cab heading for the Beijing South railway station. His last change of clothes was in his knapsack along with a fake ID that would get him out of the country.

He wondered about the decision he had made but told himself he had no choice; he would have been a dead man anyway. Better to use the cover of the relics to get away rather than raise the alarm. He had more than enough hidden from the organization and knew how to disappear better than most. He regretted feeding his colleagues to the wolves but others would fill their places in the future. Lin Li was easily replaced in that regard. His assets were already being moved further into the shadows as he made his escape.

———⁂———

Agents could see the master's two men look at their watches. One of the men left the line and walked over to the bathroom and joined the throng of men going in and out. An agent followed him in. The man called out for his boss over an occupied stall. There was no reply and he quickly left the bathroom. He grabbed the other man's arm and said something to him. Both men looked alarmed; then glanced around, then picked up the suitcase and headed for the door.

Agents raised the alarm with the command center right away. There were a few expletives around the room as Zhu screamed down the phone to take the two men down. He added to his bellowed order "shoot if you have to!"

The two men were detained before they made it through the exit. Xi directed his men to find out what happened to the Dragon Master as fast as they could. They reported waiting outside the bathroom watching him and other passengers entering and leaving the bathroom but had not gone in. It was only later when the team viewed surveillance tapes they understood what had happened. One figure had come out who never went in, distinctively dressed in a very old style of Chinese garment, a gray outer robe that flowed to the floor with white collar and cuffs. The stooped man had a graying mustache and wore Chinese slippers, round glasses, and a large-brimmed black fedora.

After dinner Diao and Lin Li assemble the evening's presentation while the banquet table was cleared. The buyers had sat with her sharing stories of their wealth and acquisitions, all light-headed and confident after copious toasting with fiery liquor. She was a professional drinker, but Diao had limited himself to a few drinks; he knew that Lin Li could drink everyone there under the table.

At the right moment Diao announced that presentation of the items would begin. He drew back the sliding doors to reveal a darkened room on which sat the relics. Balanced on their illuminated plinths, the staggering array of precious stones evoked gasps from the buyers. They moved from each display in amazement at what was in front of them. The remaining items dwarfed the armlet that Lin Li had impressed them earlier with. Diao smiled at her as if to say this was going to be a very easy sale.

Sitting in comfortable seats Diao proceeded to outline the historical significance of the items using his experience and knowledge as director of the Palace Museum. He had brochures available on the pieces covering not only their design, but also the estimated values of the finished pieces and the individual jewels and precious stones used in their construction. In the end he emphasized that it was, of course, difficult to put a final price on them; they were truly priceless. One of the buyers from Hong Kong asked if these were the items rumored stolen from the Palace; Diao confirmed that they were. "These are not items for public display," he said. "What you choose to do with them is your decision once you've acquired them."

The listening devices installed earlier in the room worked perfectly. Following Diao's remark Zhu muttered the Chinese equivalent of "Gotcha!" There was now no denying that the buyers knew the goods were stolen. Following the presentations the buyers were given time to handle the items. They were also told that very expensive and accurate copies were available; although they were not on display they were included in the pricing.

Zhu asked everyone to be on full alert and ready for the word to go. He wanted no casualties unless someone needed to defend his life. He particularly wanted Diao taken alive.

Xi had arrived at the hotel and was led down to the room where everyone was monitoring the progress. After getting an update on the events of the last few hours, he settled in to see how things would now evolve. He voiced concern about the master's escape, but said he felt confident that this phase of the plan was under control. He was ready for a fight, if needed, but agreed with Zhu that the hotel was not the right place. Any violence and bloodshed should be avoided.

The bidding for the pieces moved rapidly; offers already stood at $500 million, yet the two Hong Kong buyers were trying to outdo each other on certain pieces. Zhu decided that he had more than enough on tape and was ready to head to the nineteenth floor. Why the Dragon Master had sent no warning mystified him. Perhaps he knew it was too late and was more concerned about his own escape than supporting his own people. Zhu would worry about who had alerted the master later. He told Xi to give the word to everyone to complete the operation. George Mathers was to stay behind until the all-clear; then he and Chen Xing could come check the articles and secure them with his team.

There was trouble with two of the gang members in the lobby as officers grabbed them. Both were injured but not fatally, and only one of Xi's officers suffered an injury. The area was rapidly secured and guests were escorted to one of the large hotel rooms until the operation was over. On the nineteenth floor quick work was made of the one Triad guarding the suite. The officers posing as servers had lured him down the hall for a few moments, then quickly silenced him and dragged him to the fire exit stairway.

Zhu was one of the first to enter the Statesman Suite. He and other officers had entered in silence while the heady bidding was reaching a close. Everyone in the room was shocked when the team rushed in. Han was the only one to make a move; pulling a gun from his jacket he put a bullet straight through one officer's throat, but with four guns pointed at him he could do no more. He did try to fire again but was taken down quickly with bullets to his legs and arms. The team was under orders to keep the suspects alive if possible.

Lin Li screamed at the sight of blood spilling from the dead officer and from Han's lower extremes. The buyers were in complete panic. While officers moved around the room arresting each of the attendees, Zhu walked directly to Diao and glared into his eyes. "We are going to have a very long and private meeting," he said. "It is going to be very painful for you!"

When George Mathers and Chen Xing arrived at the room those arrested were being led. Lin Li was sobbing uncontrollably. The Hong Kong business leaders were pleading for lawyers; James Xu showed little emotion and stayed silent. Zhu was leading Diao Lijun out. Chen and George looked at Diao directly, both with the same questioning look that said, How could you be so stupid? George pondered how such a learned man could ruin his life and career, plus have the deaths of other people on his hands.

Diao hung his head, but Zhu grabbed his face roughly and forced him to show his shame. Zhu looked at George and smiled. "I told you I would get the son of a bitch, didn't I?" He said it perfectly for the first time.

George couldn't help but laugh. "I never doubted it, General!" he said. "Never! "

Events moved quickly. Chen and George supervised the packing of the relics to safeguard them from any further mishap. Chen was pleased to see that the copies were all there in a large suitcase; he was relieved that none would ever appear in the marketplace. They recovered all the notes covering the work that Diao had done on the articles. Chen kept muttering "What a shame." He considered the brilliant work that Diao had done on the pieces, which would be of tremendous help in the future.

Xiao Ping and Cai Levee, both at the university awaiting news of the operation, were delighted to hear that the relics were secure and George was safe. It was very late that night when George made it back home and crawled into bed alongside Xiao Ping. If she had thoughts of anything other than sleep, she was sorely disappointed. His head hit the pillow and he snored the whole night through.

George told Xiao Ping the next morning that he thought they should have a celebration dinner with their little team on Saturday evening. George would bring them up to date on everything that had happened; they could return to the dragon scripts with renewed enthusiasm on Monday. For some reason George was suddenly feeling a resurgence of interest in the scripts. If the latest translations were accurate, there was even more treasure out there for them to find.

CHAPTER THIRTY-ONE

The premier was delighted with the outcome of the operations led by Zhu and Xi. He used the entrapment of the Hong Kong businessmen to great political advantage, although lawyers on the Mainland and in Hong Kong would fight to keep them from long periods in jail. In the end they would receive shorter sentences than everyone expected; however, they were ordered to forfeit the equivalent monies and more, which they had been prepared to bid for the relics, as an additional penalty. The funds would go towards the exhibiting costs envisaged for the relics. They would also pay the Sovereign Wealth Fund back for its investment.

Xi took most of the glory for recovering the stolen treasures; Zhu insisted he remain in the background, not that his military superiors would have allowed otherwise. He was not one to revel in any kind of publicity; he had his man and was amused that he had solved his first civilian case.

Xi continued to press for Zhu to be transferred to his arm of Public Security; he felt the two working together could do great things. The military, on the other hand, wanted him in their intelligence and anti-terrorism group; nonetheless, Zhu was pleased that he had made a favorable impression with the civilian branches and the premier.

Zhu stayed in contact with George's group from time to time as they worked on the scripts. There was still much discussion about who the

Black Knight might be. Some suspected Xiao Ping was the woman on the motorcycle, something she always denied with a twinkle in her eye.

Zhu wondered where his own man Commander Yi was in the U.S., but counted the fact that the Dragon Master had slipped through their fingers as his biggest mistake.

Chen Xing's standing with the Party's cultural leadership grew immensely due to his involvement in the recovery of the relics. He tried to do what he could for Diao but to little avail. He continued to work towards Diao's original blueprint for display of the relics at the Palace Museum, but a final decision on the location remained pending.

The following Monday George Mathers and Xiao Ping walked into the university, George still tired from the events of the past week. As they passed Professor Ding's office the old man jumped up and shouted to George, "Dragons, I said. Dragons. Ding knew. Ding always knew!"

George yelled out to him in his passable Chinese, "Absolutely right, Ding. You were right. It's dragons; always has been. You're brilliant!"

After seeing Ding they went into their offices, where Cai Levee sat in his chair, cowboy boots on the desk, a leather jacket draped on his shoulders. He wore a broad-brimmed hat and was holding a new bull whip in his right hand. He jumped up as both of them walked in.

Xiao Ping was speechless. George stopped in his tracks. "What the hell is going on here, Cai?" he asked.

"Well?" Cai said to them, grinning.

George shook his head. "Well what?"

"What do you think?"

"What on earth are you talking about, Cai?" George asked as Cai's face dropped and smile faded.

Xiao Ping suddenly burst out laughing and gave George a shove in the side. "Don't you get it, George? He's trying to be like that Indian Jones character!"

Cai brightened and turned to George. "You don't go to the movies? Have you spent your entire life with your head in the sand? At least you married someone with intelligence!" he said, and hugged Xiao Ping.

George still looked puzzled, and for once he was without words. Cai finally smiled. "Well," he said, "I'm dressed and ready for our next adventure. What about you guys? Are you ready to take off for Changbaishan?"

George finally got it. He had been so wrapped up with the relics he'd lost sight of the fact that the Dragon Scripts promised more treasure. He hung his head sheepishly, and Cai and Xiao Ping each put a comforting arm around him. "Don't worry, old friend," Cai said. "While you've been playing around with the bad guys Xiao Ping and I finished the second batch of scripts. And we worked further on the supporting maps."

Then Cai turned quite serious. "You may think what we just went through was wild, but what we're about to get into will blow your minds!"

George raised his hands and shook his head as if to say enough already. Cai was clearly excited about their recent translations, as was Xiao Ping. While George felt a surge of enthusiasm he was as skeptical as ever. Then he thought back to his pessimism when Cai claimed to have figured out where the second coffin was—and turned out to be right. He wasn't ready to bet against Cai again.

"I'm not saying no, Cai," George said, "but convincing me to look for more treasure will take a lot more evidence from the scripts."

Cai smiled. "Oh, I'll convince you, George, I really will!"

"We really will, George," Xiao Ping whispered as she kissed his cheek.